This

Magnificent

Dappled Sea

ALSO BY DAVID BIRO

One Hundred Days: My Unexpected Journey from Doctor to Patient

The Language of Pain: Finding Words, Compassion, and Relief

This Magnificent Dappled Sea

A Novel

David Biro

LAKE UNION
PUBLISHING

Text copyright © 2020 by David Biro
All rights reserved.

Published by Lake Union Publishing, Seattle

www.apub.com

Amazon, the Amazon logo, and Lake Union Publishing are trademarks of Amazon.com, Inc., or its affiliates.

ISBN-13: 9781542019811
ISBN-10: 1542019818

Cover design by Rex Bonomelli

Printed in the United States of America

First edition

To my home: Daniel, Luca, Daniella

I celebrate myself, and sing myself,
And what I assume you shall assume,
For every atom belonging to me as good
belongs to you.

—Walt Whitman

It was near midnight, almost twenty-five years ago, when I heard the boy murmuring. The ward at the Ospedale Santa Cristina was dark and still, all the children fast asleep. There, in bed 6, lay Luca Taviano, lips moving, eyes trained on the window, as if he were talking to someone outside—the moon perhaps, or the tall oak tree whose twisted branches brushed up against the windowpane.

He comes from a faraway land and crosses mountains and valleys, seas and oceans.

My first impulse was to cover the little mischief-maker's mouth, so he wouldn't wake any of the other children on the ward. But I checked myself, remembering what had happened the last time I tried to subdue him. I remained in the shadows by the medicine cart and listened.

Orlando is a big man, very strong and very true. He has a long, furry beard, where he hides his precious jewels and gold. He wears a black cowboy hat and rides a big horse, the fastest horse in the world, a Maremmano.

The boy's voice rose as he added on detail, paused for a second, added on more. Though I couldn't see his face, I imagined him smiling beneath his mop of unruly red hair, that naughty smile punctuated by an army of freckles waging battle across his nose.

We meet after dark at the Castle outside Favola. Orlando always asks if there's anyone in trouble. He likes to help people.

Did the boy realize how much trouble he was in at that moment, how much help he needed? The doctors believed only a miracle could save his life. Maybe that's exactly what all the whispering was about. Luca wasn't telling himself stories. He was, in his own way, praying for a miracle.

Now, many years later, as I look back on that night and write down these words, so, too, perhaps was I.

PART I: THE BOY

Spring 1992

Italy

1

The arrival of spring is a happy time in Italy as the rains wash away the winter frost, the land grows green and lush, and the first crop of wild strawberries makes its way to the open markets. This year was different. A line of dark clouds swept northward from Sicily, casting a pall over the country. On May 23, Giovanni Falcone, the courageous prosecutor in the war against the Mafia, was brutally assassinated. A bomb under the motorway outside the Palermo airport took out a chunk of road along with Falcone, his wife, and three police officers. It was all over the news and in the papers. Even in Favola, a tiny, out-of-the-way town in the hills of Piedmont—a town of fewer than three hundred people, whose center consisted of a sixteenth-century town hall, a small baroque church, a tobacco shop, and a bar that doubled as a restaurant—even here, everyone talked about the disgrace of a government that stood helplessly by while a gang of lawless Sicilian thugs wreaked havoc.

Everyone except nine-year-old Luca Taviano. He was far too absorbed in his own misfortune. Mario Severese had infected most of his third-grade class with a runny nose and hacking cough. While the cold typically lasted a few days, it was taking longer to pass through Luca's system. His grandmother was worried. "I'm fine, Nonna," he tried to assure her. She called Dr. Ruggiero anyway.

This, Luca feared most. Dr. Ruggiero was the only doctor in town, an ancient man in his nineties. Unless there was a serious emergency, everyone still knocked on his door. His age, Nonna said, was an asset; he clearly knew what he was doing, keeping himself alive and well all those years. Luca disagreed. He remembered only the doctor's wayward hairs and speckled skin. His house was scary too—always dark no matter what time of day, cobwebs everywhere, and cats teeming over counters and furniture. Franco Morelli was convinced he saw a wild boar his last time there. Mario Severese swore there were bats, possibly even vampires.

So while all Italy mourned the loss of their brave prosecutor, Luca schemed of ways to avoid a trip to Dr. Ruggiero's haunted house. After intense discussions with Franco and Mario during recess at school, he came up with a plan.

The following morning, Luca pretended to be asleep when his grandmother entered the room. From the corner of his eye, he saw Nonna rubbing her hands together, heard the faint crackle of her breathing. As she placed her right hand on his forehead, Luca held his breath and waited.

Normally, he'd be praying for fever since that meant a day off from school. Not today. Today, his body had to be cold, as cold as possible. The night before, when everyone was asleep, he snuck downstairs and hid a pair of socks at the bottom of the icebox. By the time he retrieved them, right after he heard Nonna's footsteps in the bathroom at dawn, they were frozen solid. He kept them on his forehead until his skin burned so badly he couldn't take it anymore, then stashed the socks beneath his pillow.

Warm as the rest of his body may have been, his forehead was now ice-cold. He could feel it under Nonna's hand and was so sure of victory he couldn't wait to share the good news with Franco and Mario. But Nonna did something unexpected that morning. She slid her hand down Luca's cheek, then to his neck, and finally under the covers to the left side of his chest, where his heart beat so fast he was afraid it might break through the skin and explode in her hand.

"Fever" came the verdict.

"But, Nonna." Luca bolted upright. "That's not possible."

She looked at him sideways. "I thought you were sleeping."

Luca shrugged, wishing he had listened to Mario when he'd suggested sticking not only his socks but his entire body in the icebox. Then he wouldn't be in this situation.

"Get dressed. We leave for Dr. Ruggiero's after breakfast."

2

Luca Taviano wasn't the only person having a bad day as the sun cleared the horizon and began to shine down on the neighboring town of Rondello. Rondello was a larger town of some ten thousand people, with an official soccer stadium, a small museum that housed Roman antiquities, and a hospital that served most of the province. In an apartment on a narrow street that climbed the steep slope leading to the central piazza, Nina Vocelli awoke with a sharp headache. She had consumed almost two bottles of wine the night before, after receiving that despicable letter from Matteo Crespi—the bastard didn't even have the nerve to tell her in person.

He regretted to say, read the letter as if it were written by a lawyer, that their relationship could no longer continue. His daughter had discovered the affair and told her best friend, the daughter of Santa Cristina's chief of medicine. Once the chief found out, he made it clear the affair would not be tolerated, and threatened to fire one or both of them if it didn't end immediately. For the sake of his only child's well-being and his own career, Matteo had to make peace with his wife for the time being. He was terribly sorry and hoped that Nina would understand.

Understand?

For the last ten years—*ten years!*—Matteo had been telling her that his marriage was in shambles, that his wife had taken a lover of her own.

When his daughter left for university, they would get divorced and he and his Ninetta could live together. He promised this, over and over again.

Except it was all a lie, all this time.

How could she have been so stupid? Her friend Carla had repeatedly warned her not to trust the oncologist, who had a reputation for womanizing. But she couldn't help it. She was drawn to him—his dark height; the silver streaks in his hair; his swift, confident walk; the leather-and-lemon smell of his aftershave.

And it wasn't only his looks—she was also drawn by his way with patients and their families. Matteo saw the hardest cases, patients with incurable cancers, yet he always managed to find the right kind word and reassuring gesture. She'd never forget how he'd sit with Signore Boninno, the owner of the salumeria that made the best arancini in town. Boninno was a large, red-cheeked, bubbly man who fell apart after learning he had advanced liver cancer. He became so depressed and terrified that he refused all treatment, insisting he be left alone to die. Somehow Matteo managed to talk sense into him and give him hope. In the end, Boninno lived another five years, long enough to see his teenage son join him at the shop and teach him the secret rice-ball recipe.

Yes, Matteo was handsome and a compassionate doctor. But perhaps what humbled Nina most of all was the way he could look directly at her face, her terrible face, and tell her how beautiful she was.

She didn't know whether to laugh or cry or scream as she fumbled for aspirin in the medicine cabinet. She cringed at the sight of her reflection in the mirror. Her thirty-nine-year-old eyes were bloodshot, with dark circles starting to form underneath. The birthmark covering the right side of her face smoldered like the embers of a dying fire. It used to be bright red when she was a child, but over the years, the color had darkened into a deep purple. A large eggplant covering half her face. *Melanzana,* her classmates used to call her in school. Beautiful? Who in their right mind would possibly think that?

The only thing remotely beautiful was her body. From the time she'd filled out in eighth grade, everything from the neck down turned out well, as if to compensate for the blight above.

Matteo Crespi might have been looking at her face, Nina was beginning to realize, but the only thing he saw was a place to put his cock. She laughed again, this time with tears in her eyes, recalling that long-ago day when her father went berserk in the kitchen, screaming and hurling dishes against the wall. But it wasn't her fault, Nina had wanted to tell him; she was barely sixteen when the high school history teacher took advantage of her. *"Puttana!"* her father had yelled, grabbing her arm when there were no more dishes in the cabinet left to break. "The only thing she'll ever amount to," he announced to her mother, "is a whore."

Her parents were ashamed of their daughter, even before the disaster with the teacher, from the very beginning, in fact, when she entered the world with her ugly red mark—*"Il segno del diavolo,"* her mother whispered to the priest after Mass one Sunday. They were simple, uneducated people—her father worked on the docks and ran errands for one of the local Mafia bosses; her mother cleaned houses and prayed to the Blessed Virgin every day. They believed the mark was a sign of sin, their daughter's and their own, and could never see past it.

Alone, she visited the secret clinic in the basement of an abandoned building on Via Cavour, where women went to pay for their sins. So scared she could barely speak, Nina somehow managed to confide in a nurse, a young, smart, political type from a well-to-do family, who bristled as she heard Nina's story. The nurse urged Nina to leave Naples and go north, where more forward-thinking Italians, who didn't break their children's arms when they made a mistake, lived. She should consider a career in nursing, helping people who needed help, like herself at the moment. There was a small nursing school outside Turin, the nurse told her; she gave Nina the contact information and made her promise to call. And two days after high school ended, Nina left home with a rucksack and her good-luck-charm bracelet, hoping to find those forward-thinking Italians who would accept her for who she was. The teachers were sympathetic when she arrived and helped her get settled. Nina proved to be a natural at nursing. Instinctively, she understood the language of the vulnerable.

After graduation, Nina took a job at the Ospedale Santa Cristina in Rondello, where she'd remained for over fifteen years. She was now a senior nurse, in line to become head nurse.

Yet just as her father had predicted that morning in the kitchen, she'd turned out to be a whore after all—Matteo Crespi's whore.

"Puttana!" she yelled at her reflection in the mirror.

3

Dr. Ruggiero lived on the northern edge of Favola, a few meters off the main road that ran through town. His house had two floors and a red-tiled roof like everyone else's, but that's where the similarities ended. Ruggiero's house looked like no one had lived there for years. The burnt-orange paint had faded and was peeling, the windows were cracked, shutters hung at odd angles, and weeds and wildflowers sprouted from every crevice. The house appeared so rickety that a strong wind might topple it over at any moment.

Luca tugged at his grandmother's coat when the doctor didn't answer the bell, begging her to leave. Only after the third ring did the door open. Ruggiero stood gaunt and frail like his house, hunched over to one side, his skin mottled and wrinkly. Yet he dressed as if he were going to the opera: a white collared shirt under a red V-neck sweater and tweed jacket. His brown suede shoes matched his jacket.

"Ah, what do we have here?" He smiled, taking the fruit tart Letizia Taviano had baked for him. This was how most Favolans paid their doctor, a basket of fresh fruit from the garden or a prepared dish. "Just in time for breakfast. Come."

They followed him as he shuffled toward the kitchen, Nonna practically dragging Luca through the narrow hallway—dark, dank, and creepy, just as Luca remembered.

"So," he asked, not turning around, "the boy is still sick?"

"No," snapped Luca. "The boy is fine."

Nonna gasped. "Luca!"

"It's okay, signora. The saltiness is a good sign. Please, sit." He gestured toward the small farm table in the kitchen. "I was just having my morning coffee and craved something sweet."

Ruggiero withdrew a small pocketknife from his pants and began carving up the tart with the meticulous strokes of a surgeon, despite the tremor in his hand. He offered them a piece, but Nonna insisted they'd already had breakfast. They waited while he sipped his coffee and ate one piece of tart after another.

"So how is Giovanni?" he asked, crumbs falling from his lips and catching on the snags in his sweater.

"He's good," Nonna replied unconvincingly.

Ruggiero's eyes narrowed. "You'd better tell him to come around. He's due for a checkup."

Nonna nodded. As much as she worried about her husband, she didn't believe the doctor could help. At seventy-seven, Giovanni was still strong as an ox, working the farm from dawn to dusk, weekdays and weekends. His problems had more to do with the mind than the body. He was so hard on himself whenever something went wrong—with his family, with the farm, with just about everything. If only he could relax more and see the good in life.

"That was delicious," said Ruggiero, wiping his mouth and making room on the kitchen table. "Time for business. Up you go, boy."

Expecting a wild boar to round the corner at any moment, Luca shook his head and clung to his grandmother's arm. Nonna, too, was surprised by the doctor's odd request.

"The lights in my office are out," explained Ruggiero. "So don't keep me waiting, boy—hop up here on the table."

"Luca," Luca said defiantly. "My name is Luca."

"Of course it is. Who could forget Luca Taviano and his beautiful red hair?" the doctor said with a smile. "We don't see many boys with hair like that in our country, isn't that right, signora?"

It was true, and it made Nonna proud, just like the red hair of his father, Paolo, before him. Giovanni had gone all the way to Genoa in the middle of the war to adopt the baby from an orphanage run by the Sisters of the Sacred Heart. He had told Letizia that the nuns had no knowledge of the baby's background, but it hardly mattered—the Blessed Virgin had answered her prayers and given her the child she always longed for but couldn't produce on her own.

"Come, Luca, take off your clothes, and let's have a look."

After some goading from Nonna, Luca reluctantly complied. As Ruggiero rose and moved closer, his old-man smell became overpowering. He had just a few teeth left, the color of rotten bananas. While Luca closed his eyes and held his breath, Ruggiero inspected his patient's legs and arms, felt for lymph nodes, peered into his mouth and ears, and finally listened to his chest.

Ruggiero stepped back, thumbed his chin several times, then issued his verdict. "Santa Cristina."

"Santa Cristina?" Nonna repeated weakly. The mere mention of the place made her shudder. It brought back a terrible memory, the worst night of her life, a night she had tried hard to erase from her mind for the past ten years.

"The cold seems to have moved into his chest."

While his grandmother dreaded the idea of having to return to the hospital in Rondello, Luca couldn't have been happier. The examination over, he would soon be out of the clutches of the disgusting old man and his wild animals.

"There's nothing to be alarmed about, signora. The boy will get some antibiotics and a few blood tests."

"Blood tests?"

"Just to make sure, signora, just to make sure." Ruggiero watched his patient leap off the kitchen table.

Luca was already in the street, bouncing and running, when Nonna emerged from the house. It was a beautiful spring day, and he was outside, no longer cooped up in that awful house with that awful man. In fact, he was so excited that he almost forgot to ask Nonna about Santa Cristina.

"It's a place where people go when they don't feel well," Nonna explained, looking off to the side.

"Oh," Luca said, lapping up as much fresh air as he could. "But not like Dr. Ruggiero's house, right, Nonna?"

"Right, my child."

"That's good."

"There will be other children there. And big rooms with nice, clean beds."

"Beds?"

"Sometimes people have to stay there for a while."

"Oh," he said, still unclear. "You mean it's like a hospital?"

"Santa Cristina *is* a hospital, Luca."

Suddenly, all his good feelings evaporated. Luca's eyes went wide with fright. Santa Cristina was the hospital in Rondello where they took Mario when he broke his leg. It was also where Franco's sister went when she had the infection in her brain. Santa Cristina was a bad place. A terrible place. Far worse than Dr. Ruggiero's. According to Mario, his sister had spent a week there without sleeping a wink, because everybody cried all night long.

"I don't want to go, Nonna."

They passed Favola's central piazza, where carts and tables were lined up in rows, as they were every Tuesday and Thursday morning, filled with fruits and vegetables, meats and cheeses, from Favola and the surrounding towns. "Look, Luca, the *fragoline di bosco* are in season. Your favorite. Why don't we buy some?"

"I hate wild strawberries!" he shouted.

"Don't be upset," urged Nonna, hugging him. "It won't be so bad, I promise, and Nonna will stay there with you."

Luca didn't believe her. Images of screaming, crying children flooded his mind. Soon, he would be one of them. He threw himself down on the cobblestone street, covered his face with his hands, and refused to budge.

4

"Are you okay?" Carla asked when Nina picked up the receiver.

No, she wasn't okay. She was far from okay.

"I was worried when you didn't show for coffee."

They met every morning before work at the coffee bar across from Carla's apartment, 7:00 a.m. sharp. As soon as Lorenzo, the barista, saw them, he'd make a cappuccino for Carla and an espresso for Nina. They would split a chocolate-glazed cornetto and a biscuit. But Nina hadn't made it to the bar this morning.

"I can't believe how stupid . . ."

"It's not your fault. Guys like Crespi don't give a shit about anyone but themselves. You'll get over him. Meanwhile, you can't lose your job—it's past nine, and Giulia is looking for you. We just got a new admission, a kid with fever who's making a big scene. She figured if anyone could handle him, it would be you."

"All right, I'm coming," she said, hanging up the phone.

Nina hadn't realized how late it was, and this only upset her more. She had always prided herself for being on time. Even when she didn't feel a hundred percent, she'd put on a good face and do everything expected of her without complaint. Yet this morning, she continued to procrastinate, brushing her teeth until her gums bled, then making a mess of her makeup. The thought of people seeing her in this state, people who knew about her and Matteo and would know about the split. She'd be a laughingstock.

By the time she got on the bus at Piazza Goldoni and found herself wedged between an overweight ticket collector and a group of rowdy students, her dread and shame had given way to a growing anger.

Santa Cristina was two blocks away from the train station. The ugly, modern four-story brick hospital stood next to a seventeenth-century baroque church believed to house an important relic, a piece of wood from Christ's cross, where patients and families went to pray during stressful times. As Nina walked through the hospital doors, she decided to go straight to the doctors' lounge and confront him. *That bastard, making peace with his wife. Hah!* Maybe she'd grab a scalpel on the way up and slit his throat. That's what he deserved.

But Carla spotted her at the elevator bank first. "Thank God I found you," she said. "The kid I was telling you about, he just bit an orderly. They need you now. He caused such a scene in urgent care they brought him straight up to the ward. We'll take the stairs."

Nina felt as if her head were about to explode, from the letter and the wine and the idea of Matteo slinking away with his cowardly excuses like a thief in the night. She could hardly think straight. If only there were time for a quick coffee.

Carla wouldn't hear of it and charged ahead until they reached the pediatric ward. Bed 6 was in the far corner, the curtains drawn. Entering, they found a young boy with red curly hair, sitting on a chair by the bed and shaking his head defiantly at an orderly. An old woman knelt beside him, pleading with the boy: "They're only trying to help, my love. You have to stay still. Nonna is right here next to you. Please, Luca."

Despite the throbbing in her head, Nina sized up the situation immediately: With certain children, you only had a small window to carry out a simple procedure like a blood draw or IV placement. If you didn't act quickly, the window closed, and no matter how much you explained or pleaded, you would only ratchet up the child's anxiety until the task became impossible. The best thing to do now was to leave and come back later.

But as she turned to go, Nina was seized by an overwhelming surge of anger. The old lady in her floral dress, her soft, doughy face and whiny voice, was especially annoying as she begged the boy to hold out his arm one minute, then positioned herself between the boy and the orderly the next minute so he couldn't get close to Luca. "Don't leave," said the old woman, now begging Nina.

The indecisiveness infuriated Nina, and for reasons she didn't understand at the time and would likely never fully understand, she took the old woman's pleading as a challenge. "Fine," she said. "Step away, signora."

When the old woman didn't move, Nina shoved her aside. "Let's go, kid." She grabbed the boy by the wrist. "I don't have all day."

"Nina," Carla gasped, "what are you—"

"I'm getting blood from this patient, isn't that what you wanted?" she snapped. Her head was pounding, the right side of her face turned a deep maroon. Rage welled up inside, toward anyone who stood in her way: the waffling old lady, the obdurate boy, Matteo Crespi—especially Matteo Crespi—the entire world. "We're doing this now, you understand? Whether you want to or not," she said from a cold distance.

"No!" screamed Luca, trying to free his hand. When he realized that Nina wasn't going to let go, he spat in her face.

"Brat," hissed Nina. "Get over here, Carla. Take his arms—sit on them if you have to. And you," she directed the orderly, who looked like he was about to run for the hills, "grab hold of his legs."

Luca squirmed and screamed, then bared his teeth and began to lunge at the nurse, but Nina stuffed a wad of gauze in his mouth just in time. "You're not going to bite anyone else on my watch, kid," she fumed. "Hold tight, everyone." And with the boy subdued, she tied a rubber band below his shoulder, slapped the vein in the crease of his arm, and plunged the needle into his skin as if she meant to punish him. After filling one tube of blood, she reached for another. When the job was finished, she released the rubber tourniquet. "Done," she said, scowling at him. "And you're still breathing."

The room went silent. Nina had completely obliterated every ounce of fight left in Luca. Shaking, he ran to his grandmother and burst into tears. The old lady was equally distraught. Wrapping her arms around the boy, she, too, looked like she might cry.

Only then, as Nina surveyed the mess of gloves and gauze strewn around the bed and the shocked expression on the faces of Carla and the others, did she realize what had transpired. The room was suddenly stifling. Without a word, she threw open the curtain and rushed out of the ward, down the stairs, and through the front doors of Santa Cristina.

Her hands shook as she removed a cigarette from the pack in her front pocket. My God, what had she done? She'd been a nurse for almost twenty years, known for her compassion and patience when everyone thought the sky was falling. And yet just a few minutes ago, the sky fell. She had become completely unhinged, ruthless, like her father in the kitchen on that terrible day. Pulling back the curtains around bed 6, she hadn't seen a frightened child that needed calming, but a wild animal to be tamed. Somehow, she, too, had become a wild animal, pouring out her frustration and rage on him. She inhaled so deeply on the cigarette that her throat burned. *Shame on you,* she told herself. How would she be able to face her colleagues after this? How would she be able to face the boy or the old woman? She closed her eyes and shook her head and wished she could take it all back.

5

Giovanni Taviano had always been quiet. As a child, he had a slight lisp and was the last in his class to read. He met Letizia Moretti in high school. Gregarious as he was shy, Letizia couldn't stop talking and making jokes. Maybe that was why they got along so well; they balanced each other out.

When Luca was admitted to Santa Cristina, Giovanni became even more withdrawn. He couldn't sleep, ate little, and began to neglect work on the farm. The one thing running normally—running overtime, in fact—was his mind, playing and replaying events in the past and present until he grew dizzy and sick to his stomach.

Walking was the only thing that distracted him, so he walked. He walked in the morning, up one side of the wheat field and back along the other, around and around the cattle pen. He walked at night, from one end of town to the other. He passed through the main square; the church with its cemetery, where Paolo was buried; Ruggiero's tilted house; the crumbling, ancient stone wall that Luca and his friends called the Castle. He talked to no one, and no one talked to him.

Giovanni returned to the house just before 8:00 a.m., the time they'd arranged for Letizia to call from the hospital. He waited in the empty kitchen, trying to stop the thoughts flooding through his mind, until the phone rang. "No news yet," his wife announced. "But come, Giovan. Luca wants to see you."

There was no way he could go, not after what had happened yesterday. Thankfully he'd missed Luca's first day at Santa Cristina, which Letizia recounted in only the broadest strokes, afraid at how he might react if he heard what happened with the nurse. But Giovanni was present on the second day. He'd watched in horror as the doctor produced the biggest needle he'd ever seen and plunged it straight into Luca's spine. He stood helplessly by, listening to his grandson scream while the doctor withdrew a vial of spinal fluid. It felt like the needle was being plunged into *his* spine, and he wished it were. No, he would not go back today.

I'm sorry, he wanted to tell Letizia on the phone, but all that came out of his mouth was a grunt.

Besides, he already knew what would happen. The tests were bound to come back bad.

He knew this as surely as he'd known it ten years ago, when he was standing in the very same kitchen—the one they'd lived in for half a century, with its washed-out wooden countertops and white-tiled floors, the stained pots and pans hanging on hooks above the sink, a picture of the Virgin Mary above the table—standing and holding the same phone in his hand, through which the news had come then and would come again today, bringing disaster anew to their home.

He'd known even before the doctor from the emergency room uttered a word that night ten years ago. Something had happened to their son, Paolo, and his wife on their way back to Milan. Something bad. Giovanni and Letizia had gone to bed a few hours after Paolo and his wife visited with their new baby, Luca. He was their first grandchild, and Letizia had made osso buco, Paolo's favorite, to celebrate the occasion. The couple lived in an apartment near the University of Milan, where Paolo taught economics. They seemed happy, full of hope with their newborn son.

Giovanni's legs were burning. He collapsed onto one of the chairs at the kitchen table. The phone, still pressed against his ear, the line long dead, slipped out of his hand and hit the ground with a thud. He didn't bother to pick it up.

No, the truth was he'd known even before the call ten years ago that disaster would strike their family. As far back as the war, that night in 1943, the last days of December, bitterly cold even for that time of year, when the man in the tattered coat came out of the forest with his bundle to meet him. He spoke in a language Giovanni didn't understand, German maybe or Polish. Still, Giovanni understood what was being asked of him when he accepted the bundle and the folded piece of paper the man pressed into his hand before running back into the forest. It wasn't long after that the shots came, echoing in the frigid air—pop, pop, pop. He'd hurried away, pulling his hat down over his ears to muffle the sound. Giovanni had known then, even if only dimly, that someday every ounce of hope and joy rising from the swaddled infant he held in his hands would be destroyed.

As the images zigzagged in his head, Giovanni eyed the dark patch on his pants above the left thigh. It was warm and wet to the touch. He pushed against it until a jolt of pain shot up his leg and into his groin. It made him smile. He'd never been religious like Letizia with her pictures of the Virgin and the Crucifixion all over the house. Yet there was no way of missing the similarities: Jesus on the cross with his open wounds, atoning for the sins of the world.

The seeds had been planted on that cold winter night in the forest, or perhaps generations before. He was aware of them as he built his life with Letizia; as they raised their new son, whom they called Paolo after Giovanni's father; as they expanded the farm and flourished. The Tavianos had one of the biggest, best-producing farms in the area: corn, wheat, livestock. People respected them. But Giovanni couldn't care less about the opinion of others; what mattered was providing for his family and leaving Paolo with something to be proud of.

Nourished by the hearty Favola soil, the bad seeds took root and sprouted alongside the good ones. Fleeting images—of the warm bundle and the man in the tattered overcoat, the note slipping from his hands and swallowed by the snow, the pop, pop, pop of gunfire—gnawed at him, forcing him to gnaw back. It started as a sore on his upper thigh that he couldn't resist scratching. He realized if he kept breaking off the scab and removing the newly formed skin, it wouldn't heal. And so it grew, gradually spreading outward. He would pick at the edges until they bled. He would probe the center until he touched a nerve and saw stars. It was his stigma.

Now in the kitchen, under the gaze of the Virgin Mother, he watched the dark-red stain on his pants spread. Blood seeped into the fabric and dripped down onto the white-tiled floor.

After Paolo died, the wound became an obsession. Now there could be no doubt: he was cursed. His son had always been a good, careful driver. No possibility the accident was his fault, despite what the driver of the truck had told the police, that Paolo must have been drunk the way he swerved on the road. Oh no, it was the workings of a vengeful power. Giovanni was paying for his sins.

The wound became a sort of friend, someone he could talk to and confide in. At times, he tended it with the same care and concern that he tended the wheat in his field. Other times, he would argue and grow angry at it. He'd yank away the scabs, jab at the wound, until one day, he hit an artery that wouldn't stop bleeding. Letizia rushed him to old Ruggiero, where the doctor, after many starts and stops, was finally able to tie off the injured vessel. Letizia knew her husband was a worrier, a man who blamed himself when the rains flooded his fields or when winter lasted longer than expected or when Paolo and his family set out for Milan after a big meal with lots of wine—but she never imagined he would harm himself intentionally. She believed him when he told her the wound was an accident, that he had struck himself in the field with his scythe. She knew nothing about his new friend. It was a secret he was determined to keep from her.

Dr. Ruggiero wasn't so easily fooled. "The boy's got a fine head of red hair," Ruggiero whispered to him on the side when they brought Paolo to him as a baby fifty years ago. "From a convent in Genoa, huh? I can't imagine there were many like him over there."

Giovanni shrugged, as he would with similar questions and innuendos over the years.

The day Ruggiero repaired the blood vessel, he asked his patient, "When was the last time you went for confession, Giovanni? Go before you kill yourself one of these days."

Over time, Giovanni learned to avoid the bigger vessels as he nourished his stigma. Slowly, painfully, the darkness lifted. Though they had to bury Paolo in the San Stefano cemetery, there was a grandson to care for in his place. Luca was the spitting image of his father, red haired and freckled. He was just as smart too, speaking and reading before most of the boys his age, making up stories with complicated twists and turns.

Giovanni was thrilled when Luca began taking an interest in the farm, telling him he wanted to be a *buttero*, a cowboy. He dared to think that maybe the worst was over, that the curse had been lifted and he was being given another chance. "You'll be my right-hand man," Giovanni told Luca. Of course, he would get him a horse for his tenth birthday.

He laughed at his own stupidity. He knew now there would be no second chance. The curse would never be lifted until he and his entire family were crushed. Giovanni grabbed the knife he always kept in his pocket and started cutting around the red, warm patch on his pants to expose the wound, then attacked it, clawing and digging until the blood came more heavily and a searing pain tore through his body. Today he would show no mercy, just as the doctor at the hospital had showed no mercy when he drove the needle into Luca's spine.

6

Santa Cristina was worse than Luca had imagined. The ward was the size of the gym at school, packed with beds and sick children of all ages. It stunk of ammonia and other nasty chemicals. The nurses and orderlies were stricter than his teachers, and the food was disgusting, especially the minestrone soup that tasted like mud. All he could think about was how to escape. If only he could get word to his friends, they would help him figure a way out. And if all else failed, he could always count on Orlando. He would know something was wrong when Luca didn't show up at the Castle. Thank God Nonna stayed with him at night, keeping guard on the chair next to his bed, though he wished she wouldn't go to the cafeteria for coffee so often.

What he feared most was the return of the horrible witch. His arms were still black and blue from her squeezing. Dr. Ruggiero was disgusting, with his flaking skin and banana teeth, but the witch was evil, with her purple face that sizzled when she got angry. Maybe she was a devil witch that needed to be exorcised. Mario would know what to do; he was an altar boy at San Stefano. Luca would call him later in the afternoon, after school. In the meantime, he'd find a cross and keep it under his mattress.

Just as he was about to ask the older boy in the bed next to him, Luca caught sight of the witch entering the ward. Panicking, he looked for a place to hide, but there was nowhere to go. He lay down and threw the blanket over his head, praying she wouldn't see him.

"You still sleeping?" The voice came from above him. It wasn't as harsh as he remembered.

"I brought you something," she said, "something I think you'll like. I don't blame you if you're mad. I'd be mad too. All I can say is that I'm sorry. I was having a really bad day. Do you think you can forgive me? You may not believe it, but the only thing I want right now is for you to get better so you can return home as soon as possible. You do want to go back home, don't you?"

Luca tried to keep still, holding his breath so the blanket wouldn't move and she'd assume he was asleep.

"Of course, you could stay here as long as you want." Nina smiled as the blanket shifted ever so slightly. "The fact is we can use a strong boy like you at Santa Cristina, to help out with the other children—"

"Are you crazy?" he blurted out.

"You could say that." She laughed. "I'm glad you're not sleeping. I have something for you. A book with pictures of horses from all over the world. Unless, of course, you're not interested in horses."

He pulled the blanket back a crack so he could see what she was talking about. The witch had moved the chair closer to his bed; she was holding a large book in her hands.

"There's some good stuff about the Tolfretano, the Maremmano, and the Haflinger horses. There's even a section on the cowboys of Lazio. Hey, you know what?" she said, leaning forward to inspect his face. "You could pass for one of those cowboys yourself."

He quickly slid back under the covers. It must be a trick. The minute he relaxed his guard, she would pounce on him, maybe even kill him. No way would he give her the chance.

"I see you'd rather rest now. That's fine. I'll leave the book by your bed. Maybe later we could take a look at it together."

Never, he thought, remaining as still as he could.

The next day, he found a bag of gummy bears by his bed. He thanked Nonna, but she explained that it was the nurse who brought them, not her. "She feels bad for what happened," Nonna said, "and wants to make it up to you."

"She's a witch."

"No, Luca, she just lost her composure. It happens, even to me and Nonno sometimes."

Luca didn't believe her. Whenever he saw the nurse coming, he turned the other way. When she tried to talk to him, he ignored her. On his fourth day at the hospital, however, she surprised him while he was leafing through the book on horses.

"How about a truce?" she asked.

He didn't answer.

"There must be something I can do to make amends. Anything. Please."

Not lifting his eyes from the book, he twisted his mouth as if he were chewing on something. He chewed like this for a while, then finally stopped and pointed to the horse on the front cover. "This one with the thick, long neck," he said. "That's a Maremmano."

"It's beautiful."

Luca thought so too. "And very strong. The best horse for herding cattle. Nonno promised he'd get me one when I turn ten. I'm going to be a cowboy when I grow up."

"Wow, I had no idea."

Nina wasn't telling the truth. She had had a long talk with the boy's grandmother before she left the hospital the day of the now-infamous blood-drawing incident. After calming down, she sought out Letizia

Taviano, desperate to apologize, having learned who the old woman was, and promised to do everything she could to make her and her grandson's lives easier in the coming days.

"Yes, I remember her," Nina had admitted to the charge nurse after being reprimanded for the incident. "I was here at the hospital that night ten years ago when they brought in the bodies," she said. The old woman's son and his wife had been so mangled after the accident on the highway they were practically unrecognizable. A head-on collision with a truck, the police told her. It flattened the entire front half of the car, but somehow the baby, secured in a car seat in the back, managed to survive. She still had nightmares about it.

Yet instead of comforting Letizia when she showed up at Santa Cristina again, the baby having grown to become nine-year-old Luca, Nina had behaved despicably. She wanted to kick herself, a lot harder than the charge nurse had just done.

"All you need now," Nina said to Luca, "is a cowboy hat. Maybe that's what I could get for you."

He shook his head. "I already have three."

Tentatively, Luca raised his eyes from the book. He noticed that the witch was sitting with her head turned to the right. That way, he could only see the left side of her face, where the skin was smooth and normal looking. He craned his neck for a glimpse of the other side.

"You're looking for my beauty mark. Hah, now there's a silly name for a port-wine stain," she said, laughing. "A *beauty* mark. But if you want," she said, shifting around in the chair, "be my guest. Pretty ugly, don't you think?"

Yesterday, perhaps even a few minutes ago, he would have said yes and made a mean face, to hurt her like she'd hurt him. Then he remembered what Nonna had told him, about the nurse feeling bad about what had happened. "Well." He hesitated. "No . . . not really. It's not so bad."

"It's okay, I'm used to it. They used to call me *melanzana* in school. Lots of other names too. Like *faccia bruta* and *rossa*."

"Hey, they call me *rosso* at school, too, because of my red hair."

"No kidding. Then I guess we have something in common. I don't know about you, but the names don't bother me anymore."

Luca was unable to take his eyes off the strange mark on the nurse's face. The only other person he could think of with a mark like that was the young knight in the comic book series he and his friends followed. But Teobaldo's mark was small and barely noticeable compared to the nurse's.

"You want to touch it?" asked Nina. "It won't bite."

She moved closer and placed his hand on the right side of her face.

"It feels warm," said Luca, "and wait . . . is there something moving around under there?"

"That's a vessel close to the surface where you can feel the blood flowing by."

"Cool!" Luca didn't want to withdraw his hand. "Did you ever try to remove it?"

She shook her head. "Nowadays they have a special laser, but it only works when you're a kid. They didn't have it when I was young—at least not in Naples."

Luca suddenly had a thought. "Hey, I have a friend who might be able to help."

"Is your friend a doctor?" The last thing she needed, Nina thought, was help from a doctor.

"Oh no, he's a lot better than a doctor. His name is Orlando."

"Is that so? What does he do, this Orlando?" Nina cringed when she saw the bruises on Luca's arms. She knew she'd manhandled the poor boy, but she never expected the bruises to be so extensive—his entire left arm was black and blue. The charge nurse was right to make her stay home the next day. She would have been right to suspend her for a week. People were fired for lesser things.

"He's a cowboy with special powers who likes to help people. Like my friend Mario when he rode his bicycle into the ditch and nobody knew where he was. He would have stayed there all night in the cold and rain if Orlando hadn't been watching out for him."

"I see."

"He told me where to look, led me to the exact spot where Mario crashed. And it's a good thing, too, because Mario had broken his leg and was in a lot of pain. They had to take him to the hospital and put on a cast."

"Poor Mario. But it sounds like Orlando is a good person to know. Come, I'm going down to the cafeteria for a coffee. I'll get you a hot chocolate if you'd like, and you can tell me more about this cowboy with special powers."

"Sure," he said, jumping out of bed to join her.

7

Nina saw them talking in low voices at the nursing station, Carla and Giulia. Six days had passed since she received the letter, five days since the blood-drawing incident, and four since her twenty-four-hour suspension. She knew they were talking about her, because they stopped as soon as they spotted her. "What?" she asked Carla when Giulia left.

"Bad news," she answered. "Crespi is being called in on the Taviano case."

Nina winced. She'd been seesawing from one emotion to the other these past few days: the shock of Matteo suddenly ditching her; anger at the cowardly way he avoided her; and, lately, a terrifying despair that she had been waiting around all this time for nothing and now her life was ruined. But forgetting her own problems for the moment, she didn't understand why Matteo would be called in to see Luca Taviano. He was a cancer specialist.

"Have you been listening to anything I've said?" Carla had a hand on her hip and, with the other, was flipping through Luca's labs. "The blood tests are all out of whack. His white counts are high, and he barely has any platelets."

Nina was surprised. Despite the low-grade fever, Luca didn't look very sick. On the other hand, it made sense when you considered those horrendous black and blues. Maybe it wasn't her fault then, she thought. Well, at least not entirely her fault—the boy had a platelet problem; of course he was going to bruise. Did the charge nurse know? Did Signora Taviano?

"Do you want me to switch shifts with you?" asked Carla. "I don't think you should be around that asshole right now."

God knows the last thing Nina wanted was to be near him. But she'd made a promise to Signora Taviano. She'd sworn that she would always be around to look out for Luca. She wasn't going to renege now. Sooner or later, she'd have to deal with Matteo anyway. "I'll be okay, thanks."

"Let me know if you change your mind," Carla said. "And don't forget about tomorrow night. Eight p.m. at Da Lucia's. Look sharp. Giacomo's friend is a catch—mark my word."

Nina shook her head. They'd been friends for almost twenty years now, ever since nursing school in Turin. Nina had already been there two years when Carla entered the program, pushed into it by her parents, her father a doctor, her mother a schoolteacher. The first time they'd met in the library, Carla was in tears. She'd made a big mistake. Besides not being good in science, Carla confessed that she grew queasy at the sight of blood. Nina lied, told her it was the same for her when she started, and convinced her to stick it out a bit longer. She took Carla under her wing, showed her the trick of closing her nose and breathing through her mouth to avoid queasiness. Before long, her new friend began to like nursing. When Carla finished school, Nina helped get her a job at Santa Cristina and made room for Carla to live in her apartment. Now the roles were completely reversed. Carla was married, had three children, and was looking after Nina. How in the world did that happen?

"Look, I'm just not ready to meet someone right now."

"Sorry, the table's booked. You're coming if I have to drag you." Carla wagged her finger at Nina, then left before she could object.

Nina took down Luca's chart and read the latest entry. The blood tests must have come back late yesterday after she'd left the hospital. Carla was right; this was no simple viral infection. She saw the request for the consult, but there were no notes from Matteo yet. She checked her watch: 10:00 a.m.

As she steeled herself for his arrival, she heard his voice—deep and strong with a slight rasp that always reminded her of Claudio Baglioni, the Roman singer all the girls in high school went crazy over. Matteo was standing behind the nursing station, in the hallway by the elevators. He seemed to be talking to a patient's family.

Closing her eyes, she strained to listen. Despite everything that had happened, she still wanted to hear his voice. It took her back to when everything was still good and she was happy. He would talk to her when they made love, whisper in her ear. Yes, this is how it was when they made love, her eyes closed, the sound of his voice behind her. She couldn't help it—despite everything, she still wanted him.

"Nurse," she heard him call out.

What?

"Nurse Vocelli," he called again.

The tone of his voice had sharpened, losing all its warmth and obliterating everything she'd felt a moment ago. She stood up and walked over to Matteo. He was with Letizia and Giovanni Taviano.

"Nurse, I was just explaining the test results to the Tavianos."

Nurse?

"Dr. Ruggiero was right to send Luca here," Matteo continued, nodding sympathetically. "He may have had a cold, which is certainly going around now—in fact, I have a bit of a cough myself—but I believe there's something more serious going on."

Letizia fell backward. Had there not been a wall for her to lean against, she might have collapsed onto the floor.

"Don't be upset, signora," said Crespi, putting his hand reassuringly on her shoulder. "Whatever we find, there will be treatment, good treatment, and Luca is a strong boy, a healthy boy. I'm confident he'll respond to the treatment. You'll see."

Letizia Taviano was a stocky woman with thick arms and legs, but her soft, doughy face and the cotton floral dress she wore made her appear fragile. Her husband, on the other hand, looked sturdier. Lanky and tall, he had angular features and deep lines etched across his forehead and around his eyes. He stood fixed and silent like a tree rooted in the ground.

"Signore Taviano, are you okay?"

Matteo was right to ask, Nina thought. The men she encountered over the years might appear strong with their stoic expressions, but they rarely held up well in these situations, and almost always less well than the women.

Giovanni answered with a grunt.

"We'll be fine," said Letizia, recovering her composure. She took hold of her husband's arm. "Please take care of our Luca. He's all we have."

"I promise," said Crespi. "We'll talk again later after the bone marrow test and come up with a plan."

As they turned to go, Nina followed. She wanted to reassure Letizia and also get away from Matteo as fast as she could. But a tug at the back of her shirt held her back.

"Nina, wait."

The voice was behind her again, low and tender.

She turned. "So now it's Nina and not Nurse Vocelli."

"I'm sorry," he said, reaching out to her.

"Don't touch me."

Matteo looked around to make sure no one was watching. "I had no choice, Nina," he explained. "I've never seen the chief of medicine so mad. 'That's why we have rules,' he shouted at me, 'and you know what happens when the rules are broken.' He was referring to the time when Roberto and Franca were caught screwing in the on-call room while their patient was coding."

Nina knew exactly what the chief was referring to.

"He said if we didn't end the affair immediately, he'd have no choice but to let you go."

"Let *me* go?" That's not what the bastard had said in his letter. Then again, why should she be surprised? She was just a nurse, a woman in a world ruled by men. If one of them had to be fired, it wouldn't be Matteo.

"Naturally, I smoothed things over with the chief. I told him it was a mistake and assured him that our relationship would be strictly professional from here on in. As long as we stick to our roles at the hospital, make a good show of it, we should be safe."

"We?"

"Yes, we. It hasn't been a week, and I'm already going out of my mind. Screw the chief, he can't keep us apart," he said with pleading eyes. "We were meant for each other. You know that in your heart. In two years, when Francesca goes to university, Maria and I will get divorced. I promise."

"Liar," she whispered harshly.

8

In a cordoned-off area at the back of the blood lab was a small desk, on top of which lay an old, basic microscope, and a cabinet filled with slides. A shelf above the desk housed a row of hematology textbooks. Matteo Crespi placed the slide he held in his hand on the microscope platform. He peered through the lens and adjusted the focus until the blood cells began to materialize, red and blue and shades in between, different shapes and sizes, representing distinct lineages and stages of development. In all these years, it never failed to amaze him, this magnificent dappled sea of bone marrow, ever regenerating and replenishing itself in an ongoing cycle that made life possible—red cells that carried oxygen to the tissues, white cells that fought off infection, and platelets that made the blood clot.

Magnificent. Yet within this surging sea of marrow, Matteo knew he would find an interloper, an enemy of life—the answer to Luca Taviano's lingering fever and cold that wasn't going away, the extensive bruising. Somehow, it had eluded him on the normal blood smear a few days ago, but it would be there now on the marrow smear.

Sure enough, the abnormally large purple cell appeared before his eyes. With a pale-blue rim and a dense, dividing nucleus, it, too, was magnificent. But the lymphoblast was deadly. Created by a mutation in the genes that halted the maturation process and caused it to keep replicating, the malignant clone would grow and grow until it crowded out the normal cells in the marrow and they were no longer able to carry out their duties. The body would be deprived of oxygen, unable to protect itself from bacteria and other pathogens, and powerless to stop itself from bleeding. The body would become incompatible with life.

The Taviano boy had leukemia, just as Matteo had suspected.

Yet the revelation didn't depress him. Despite the devastation childhood leukemia had caused in the past, there was good treatment for it now. What had been a death sentence when he started medical school in the 1960s was now mostly curable. Indeed, it was the most impressive advancement in cancer treatment in the twentieth century, perhaps in all of medicine. Luca Taviano may be harboring a deadly disease, but Matteo Crespi was armed with weapons that would wipe it out.

Matteo sprang from the desk and exited the lab like a sprinter who had just won a big race. The entire hospital was rooting for Luca. It wouldn't be fair for the Tavianos to suffer another tragedy. They were good people. The grandfather was a bit odd perhaps, but who wouldn't be under these circumstances? And his wife couldn't be nicer, bringing cakes and fruit for him and the nurses every day, sometimes twice a day. He'd grown fond of Luca, too, with his red hair and freckles, the future cowboy of Favola. Not that Matteo wasn't aware of Luca's little tricks, patting down the sides of his hair and tapping the side of his nose with his finger. The little mischief-maker was imitating *him*, laughing behind his back, and giving his best performances when Nina was around. It was hard not to smile.

Matteo would fight for this boy and for his family. He had all the weapons he needed in his armory. He'd eradicate every last one of those malignant lymphoblasts, be the hero of Santa Cristina, and endear himself to Nina in the process.

It was obvious she was bending over backward for the boy. No doubt she felt guilty after the blood-drawing incident. But there was something more going on. The other day, he watched them from the nursing station for almost half an hour, Luca sitting forward on his bed, Nina on a chair inches away, utterly captivated by each other's presence. Luca turned his head this way and that, studying Nina's birthmark. "You want to touch it?" she asked. "It won't bite." Tentatively, he reached out his hand, then carefully ran his fingers over the purple-colored patch of skin. "It feels warm," he observed, his eyes wide with delight. "Is there something moving around under there?" Nina laughed and explained that a port-wine stain is composed of blood vessels. They talked about horses, Luca's best friends Mario and Franco, Nina's apartment in Rondello, the arancini at Signore Boninno's salumeria. Soon, Luca was rubbing his hands together and launching into a story about how Orlando saved Mario's life when he fell into a ditch, Nina listening intently all the while. Matteo couldn't help feeling jealous at the intimacy developing between the two.

Shaking the memory from his mind, Matteo nodded to the nurses in the nursing station and retrieved Luca's chart from the rack. He entered the findings of the marrow smear and wrote a detailed plan of action, the sequential combination of chemotherapy drugs that would attack the cancer.

Glancing up, he saw Nina open the curtain around Luca's bed. If only he could go over and take her in his arms, apologize for sending that rash letter, convince her of how much he loved her. But it wasn't possible now. They had to be discreet until things settled down. It was the only way they could both continue working at Santa Cristina and have a chance at a future together.

"Nurse Vocelli," he said, trying to remain cool, "let's start treatment for the Taviano boy as soon as possible."

"Yes, Doctor," she said, avoiding his gaze.

9

Letizia brought Luca's friends to the hospital on Saturday for a visit. It had been almost four weeks, and her grandson was restive. He was also due for his second chemotherapy infusion. The first one had not gone well; he needed some cheering up.

"I want to prepare you boys," she told Mario and Franco when they climbed into the car. "Luca looks different than when you last saw him. He's lost a good deal of weight. His hair too. Try not to make a big deal about it."

As she said this, she couldn't help noticing in the rearview mirror that the two boys in the back seat had an abundance of what Luca now lacked. Chubby Mario probably didn't weigh much less than she did, and Franco had thick, curly black hair that reached down to his shoulders.

They both nodded hesitantly.

"I didn't mean to scare you. He's still the same Luca you knew at school, and he'll be so excited to see you."

When they arrived on the ward, Letizia poked her head through the curtain around Luca's bed and announced that she had a surprise for him. Luca had been staring down at a muddy bowl of minestrone soup that had just been placed on his tray. His eyes lit up when he spotted Mario and Franco.

"I'm going down for a coffee and will leave you boys alone for a while. Promise me there'll be no trouble while I'm gone," she said, shaking her index finger.

"Sure," said Luca, ditching the soup and motioning for his friends to come closer. "I hope you guys brought me something good to eat. I'm starving."

Mario slowly removed the paper bag he had concealed under his shirt, tipping it in Luca's direction so he could see the candy inside. But he didn't budge from his spot by the curtains. Nor did Franco.

"What's with you guys? Bring it over here."

Mario stared at his friend's head in horror. "I didn't realize it was that bad."

"You mean my hair?" asked Luca, tapping the few strands of hair remaining on his head.

"You were right about what you told us on the phone—she's evil," said Franco. "More evil than we imagined."

"Who?"

"The witch. I hope we have enough of this brew," said Franco, withdrawing a small container from his pocket. "We found the recipe in the library. It's a mixture of lizard legs and different spices. You need to get her to eat some. Then she'll lose her powers."

"Nurse Vocelli?" asked Luca. "No, no, I was wrong about her. We're friends now."

"The witch that beat you? The one with the purple mark that smokes and sizzles? It's a sure sign, believe me. All she has to do is look at you and your hair falls out. We need to get rid of her."

"Relax, guys. Like I told you, I was wrong. She'll be here soon, and you'll see for yourselves."

Both boys took a step backward, prepared to run for their lives if necessary.

"I promise. Now get over here with that candy."

Mario and Franco gradually approached Luca's bed. Mario dumped out the candy, and each boy grabbed the things he liked best. Luca asked about their gym teacher—was she still bending over so everyone could see her boobs? Was Bernardo still being mean to them in the schoolyard? What movies were playing at the Nazionale in Rondello? Nonna promised to take him when he got better, and they could come too. Had they been to the Castle and heard from Orlando? Did he have any new missions for them?

They were talking and stuffing their mouths with candy when Nurse Vocelli entered the room. As soon as they saw her, Mario and Franco jumped off the bed and backed up against the curtain.

"Don't worry, *ragazzi*, I don't bite, provided I can have one of those gummy bears," she said, winking at Luca. "I'm going to have to steal your friend for a while so he can get his treatment. He won't be too long."

As the nurse led Luca out, Franco kept nodding in the direction of the container of witch's brew on the bed, trying to get Luca's attention. Now that he saw the purple mark on her face for himself, Franco was more convinced than ever that the nurse was evil, even if she'd fooled Luca into trusting her. She needed to be eliminated before she made all their hair fall out.

"They're afraid of you," said Luca as they arrived at the infusion center on the second floor, a small room with four reclining chairs and a TV on the wall.

"They'd better be," Nurse Vocelli said, baring her teeth.

Luca laughed.

"But because they're your friends"—she patted him on the shoulder—"I promise to show mercy."

One of the nurses waved them over to a chair by the window where she'd already set up Luca's treatment bag. "Have a seat here, young man," she said.

Luca shook his head no. He had nothing against the nurse—in fact, she had a kind, old face that reminded him of his grandmother—but ever since they'd become friends, Nurse Vocelli was the only person he trusted.

"I'll take care of this," Nina said to the nurse. "Lie down and put your arm on the sidebar, Signore Taviano," she told Luca with a smile. Nina rolled up his sleeve and placed a light tourniquet above his elbow. She patted the skin on his hand and, as gently as possible, slid the needle through the skin and into the vein. "How's that?"

"Didn't feel a thing," he said nonchalantly, looking at the TV on the wall. The news was on, broadcasting the latest from Sicily. The police had made several arrests in the Falcone case. All were tied to organized crime. There was hope that the head of the Sicilian Mafia, Totò Riina, would soon be brought to justice.

"Do you know anything about this?" asked Nina.

Luca felt a tingling under his skin as Nina turned on the IV and yellowish fluid started flowing through the tubing into his arm. Not pain exactly, but it didn't feel good either. He tried focusing on the TV, the photo of the elusive mafioso boss, a short, stocky man with a square face and beady eyes. "He looks pretty scary."

"He's a bad man," agreed Nina. "He killed two very brave judges, and I hope he pays for it. I'm sure your friend Orlando would agree."

Luca nodded. "Orlando always punishes bad people. Like Bernardo, the bully at school who picks on the smaller kids. Orlando made him trip one day in gym while he was showing off in front of the girls. Served him right."

"Is that so?" Dr. Crespi entered the room with a wide smile on his face. His white coat was newly pressed, his hair slicked back, tie perfectly done. "*Buongiorno, ragazzo.* How is my favorite patient doing?"

Luca gave him the thumbs-up sign.

"Glad to hear. This is the strong stuff you're getting today, isn't that right, Nurse Vocelli?"

Nina adjusted the IV, pretending she didn't hear him.

"You remember what I told you about this medicine?" Though he was talking to Luca, Crespi kept looking over at Nina.

"Yeah, I remember. It kills the bad blood cells, which are bad because they grow too fast and make it difficult for the other cells to do their jobs. That's why I was getting the fever and bruising. But the medicine can also kill the good cells in my body and make me feel sick, especially my stomach."

"That's exactly right." Crespi applauded him. "Our patient is a smart one, don't you agree, Nurse Vocelli?"

Luca smelled a strong, lemony scent in the air. It seemed to be coming from Dr. Crespi. "Are you wearing perfume?" he asked the doctor. The smell reminded him of Nonna when they went out to eat at a restaurant.

"Men don't wear perfume, Luca, they wear cologne. They wear it to impress the girls." He winked. "I'll bring you some the next time I come."

The minute Crespi left, Nina stopped fidgeting with the IV pole and sat down next to Luca. He could tell she was relieved. He smiled naughtily, then tapped the side of his nose with his finger.

"You're very funny, you know that?"

"Dr. Crespi is too, and he doesn't even try."

Nina laughed. "He's right about you being one smart kid, though," she said, patting him on the back. "How do you feel?"

"Fine," he answered, though he was starting to feel queasy. The first time he had the treatment, he felt so sick he vomited. Nonna had been with him and gotten scared. She tried to pretend otherwise, but Luca knew better. He hated seeing Nonna so upset and vowed that the next time, he'd be stronger.

"I'm fine," he repeated. "Tell Nonna it was much better today."

10

As May turned into June and June into July, what used to be Matteo Crespi's favorite time of the year—when he would ride his bike through the countryside, drive with the top of his convertible down, take his coffee outside at the café in the central piazza—was becoming an uphill slog. Until now, Matteo had sailed through life with neither hitch nor adversity. He was an only child to upper-middle-class parents from Turin, and his mother and father had doted on him. He'd been handsome and athletic and well liked since grade school, a good student at university who graduated with high honors from medical school. Although Santa Cristina was a small, rural hospital, he was the chairman of his department.

Lately, though, it seemed his luck had changed for the worse. Maria had been a thoughtful, beautiful girl when they first met, with deepblack eyes that he'd wanted to dive into and never resurface from. But over the years, his wife had transformed into a cold, self-absorbed prima donna he hardly recognized. Nothing was good enough—the backwater town they lived in, the too-small house, the vacations that doubled as medical conferences. *He* was not good enough.

Matteo never imagined falling for a woman with a port-wine stain. Yet Nina's birthmark intrigued him, the way its color shifted with her mood and pulsed with life, hiding the right side of her face, her gently sloping nose and full, rounded lips. He'd come to think of the mark as a mask that she allowed only him, and no one else, to peer beneath—a secret of sorts, their secret. Nina was young, fun, and passionate; he could do things with her that he could never do with his wife. Only now, after he'd caved in to the chief's demands without a fight and then rushed off that foolish letter, Nina no longer seemed to notice him, no matter what he did to get her attention.

Work, too, was beginning to unravel. In the past, Matteo was always able to find solace in medicine. He'd been fascinated by the body and disease ever since his father started showing him X-rays of his patients' lungs—a new world under the skin he never knew existed. In medical school, he traveled even deeper into the body, to the cellular level, and deeper still, to the genes that were responsible for the growth of cells and tissues and organs, the same genes that when damaged would cause cancers capable of destroying everything they once built up.

But science was only part of the allure. Matteo was a social creature drawn to the art of medicine, being able to explain the science to patients in layman's terms, sympathizing with their predicaments, motivating them, and instilling hope. This was where he really excelled. The staff at Santa Cristina were convinced that his patients did well in large part because they believed in him.

Yet as he reviewed the charts for the weekly oncology conference on Tuesday morning, Matteo was starting to have doubts: after all these years, maybe his luck and his skills were running out. The Taviano case particularly rankled him, a textbook case of leukemia. As he had told the boy's grandparents, there was excellent treatment for it. Nine out of ten children were cured—*cured*—by a well-proven cocktail of chemotherapeutic drugs. Somehow, Luca wasn't one of them. After six weeks of the regimen, there was no response.

Matteo read and reread the notes and orders in Luca's chart, the boy's weight and dosing of medication. It all seemed accurate. He returned to his microscope at the back of the blood lab and reviewed the smears, wondering if he had missed anything. But that checked out too. Where had he gone wrong?

"I'm surprised," Matteo confessed to his colleagues as the oncology meeting for the second week in July got underway. "Usually, we can achieve at least a temporary remission, and everything was pointing in that direction, but in Taviano's case, the cancer hasn't budged."

They met in the conference room on the fourth floor, a long oval table around which everyone involved in the care of cancer patients at Santa Cristina gathered, doctors, nurses, social workers, and clergy.

"Is there any rationale for switching to another regimen?" asked Leonardo Franconi, a colleague in the oncology department. "Or changing the dosing of the current one?"

"That's what I plan to do," Matteo replied. "Although from experience, I doubt it will make a difference." He could see the disappointment on their faces, especially after he'd been so confident that things would turn out differently. He was disappointed too. "The prognosis, I'm afraid, is not good."

An uncomfortable silence permeated the room. People looked down at the floor, up at the ceiling, out the window, at the old baroque church next door, anything to distract them from Matteo's grim report.

"Any other thoughts?" asked Giancarlo Romano, the chief of medicine. "It's almost eight, and there are a number of patients still left to discuss. Shall we move on?"

A tapping noise could be heard at the far end of the room. Nina Vocelli was tapping the wooden surface of the table with her pen.

"Nurse Vocelli, is there a problem?" asked the chief.

Nina was staring at him, her face reddening, her birthmark turning a deep purple. It was obvious she didn't want them to move on, hoping someone might have another thought, yet holding back at the same time.

Romano frowned, glancing over at Crespi as if to say this was his fault and something they would need to address once again as soon as the meeting was over. "Who's the next patient?"

"Wait!" Nina Vocelli finally blurted out. "There has to be something else we can try."

The room went still. The charge nurse reached over and placed her hand firmly on Nina's arm. It was not proper etiquette for anyone to interrupt the chief during rounds, especially a nurse.

After clearing his throat several times, Matteo turned to Nina. "As I said, from my experience—"

"Then maybe it's time to get someone else's experience."

Matteo's mouth fell to the floor. Nina had questioned his competence in front of the entire oncology department. How humiliating and hurtful, coming from someone he loved, and whom he thought loved him back.

"You must remember Antonio Tosti," said Nina, addressing Matteo's colleagues at the table. "He worked at Santa Cristina several years ago before moving to the cancer institute in Genoa. He'd be the perfect person to consult—"

"That's enough, Nurse Vocelli," said Romano brusquely, recognizing that Crespi was too unnerved to shut her down himself. "You and I will continue this in my office after the meeting."

Matteo felt his hand trembling. From the corner of his eye, he could see Nina fuming in her seat, with not a smidgeon of remorse for what just happened. Maybe she was right: he wasn't the hero he imagined himself to be, certainly not in Luca Taviano's case. Maybe there was someone better out there.

11

It was near midnight when Nina heard the boy murmuring. The ward was dark and still, all the children fast asleep. There, in bed 6, lay Luca Taviano, lips moving, eyes trained on the window, as if he were talking to someone outside—the moon perhaps, or the tall oak tree whose twisted branches brushed up against the windowpane.

He comes from a faraway land and crosses mountains and valleys, seas and oceans.

She stood in the shadows by the medicine cart, listening, vacillating. If she went over now, she realized, there would be no turning back. But she couldn't help it; she felt drawn to the boy.

"Aren't you supposed to be sleeping, signore?" she said, tapping him on the shoulder.

He turned and smiled.

"I promised your grandmother I'd look in on you."

"Nonno's leg is acting up again," he explained. "So Nonna had to stay with him."

"Then it's a good thing I'm here."

Normally Nina wouldn't be at the hospital this late, but it was part of her punishment. The chief was furious after her outburst at the oncology meeting the week before. It was the second time he'd called her into his office in less than two months. He'd placed her on probation, given her a month of night-shift duty, and warned that if she pulled another stunt like that again, she'd be relieved of her duties permanently.

"You're a brave man, Luca Taviano." She used to like weaving her hand through his mop of curly red hair. Tonight, she would have to be content with stroking his bare scalp. The skin was soft and smooth, though some areas were tender, and Nina watched him wince.

"I told you about my friend Orlando, Nurse Vocelli?"

"Nina," she chided. "You're supposed to call me Nina, now that we're friends. And yes, you've told me quite a bit."

"He's from far away and has to cross mountains and valleys and seas and oceans to get here."

"That's some trip."

"He has a long, furry beard where he hides his precious jewels and gold. He wears a black cowboy hat and rides a big horse, the fastest horse in the world, a Maremmano."

"Your favorite, right?"

"Yeah. We meet at the Castle just before it gets dark."

The Castle, Nina learned from Luca and his grandmother, was what remained of an old Roman wall on the outskirts of Favola, now mostly just a few uneven rows of crumbling, washed-out stone blocks. Clearly the boy had an active imagination.

"Orlando lets me and the boys know when someone's in trouble and needs our help. Signora Perelli for example. They were going to take her cow away because she couldn't pay a debt."

"Is that right?"

"She's an odd one, that Signora Perelli, always muttering to herself and spitting at the ground. But we felt bad for her because she's poor. So we moved the cow the night before they were coming to take it, hid it behind Dr. Ruggiero's house, where no one would ever look."

"Good thinking."

"A few days after we brought the cow back, Signora Perelli found enough money under her doormat to pay her debt. Nonna thinks it was a gift from one of her neighbors. But I don't believe that."

"No?"

"Orlando was behind it, I'm sure. I told you how rich he was."

"You did."

"When they let me go home, you'll come visit and I'll take you to the Castle."

"I'd like that."

Luca shifted in his bed. "I'll be able to go home soon, won't I?"

"Soon," she said, biting the underside of her lip. *If only that were true.*

Her mind flashed back to the day Luca was admitted to Santa Cristina when she lost her temper. "Jesus, Nina, what the hell do you have against that poor kid?" the charge nurse had grilled her afterward. A week later, Carla noticed the little presents Nina brought Luca each morning and asked whether they helped ease her conscience.

True, guilt had been a big factor at the beginning. But that wasn't the case anymore. She had grown fond of Luca, of his defiance and fieriness, the very qualities she had tried to quash that first day and that continued to rile the nerves of the house staff. He made her laugh, the way he mimicked Matteo, massaging his hair to make sure everything was in perfect order.

Gradually, a bond had formed between them, one she thought about a lot but couldn't entirely explain. The boy had no parents, just like her. And just like her, he was *rosso*, different from others and made fun of for it, he with his red hair and she with her port-wine stain. Matteo's betrayal must have also played a part. Suddenly, she was alone, a sea of roiling emotions that no longer made sense. They whirled around her without respite until they encountered Luca and began to settle by his bed on the far side of the ward.

It scared Nina, the intensity of her feelings for this boy she'd known only two months. It was like nothing she'd experienced before—with other patients; with her best friend, Carla; even with her mother when she was a child. Almost like falling in love, yet that wasn't it either. She wasn't physically attracted to Luca, of course. It was the desire to act on his behalf, the fierce and unthinking desire to do for him, even sacrifice herself if necessary. Wasn't that at the heart of love?

"Try to sleep," she whispered, covering Luca with the blanket. "You're going to need your strength."

"Okay," he said. "You're not worried about me, are you?"

"Of course not. A brave cowboy like yourself, with a friend like Orlando. Not in the least."

Nina watched him close his eyes and waited until his breathing slowed and she was sure he was asleep. She was worried all right. And it killed her seeing how innocently unworried and unknowing Luca was.

The next morning, defying the orders of the chief, Nina went ahead and contacted the oncologist in Genoa. The prognosis was indeed grim, Dr. Tosti said after hearing the details of Luca's case. This was an aggressive leukemia that failed to respond to standard chemotherapy and would most certainly prove fatal if they didn't find a better alternative quickly. But the cancer institute was a major academic research center, constantly developing new protocols and experimental treatments. There would be options at the institute unavailable at Santa Cristina. "Have Dr. Crespi send the patient's chart and blood sample," he suggested, "and we'll see what we can do."

Nina agreed and thanked him, realizing there was no time to waste trying to convince Matteo to act. She would have to do this on her own and in secret. She'd make a copy of the chart notes when no one was looking, draw a tube of blood on the sly, then drive them up to Genoa herself—consequences be damned.

PART II: THE RABBI

Summer 1992

Brooklyn, New York

1

Far away from the tall oak tree outside Luca Taviano's hospital window, across mountains and valleys, seas and oceans, Rabbi Joseph Neiman and his wife, Sarah, entered the Poly Prep auditorium in Brooklyn, New York. Yet despite the distance, in kilometers or miles, things were not so different on the other side of the Atlantic. For there were sick children in America just as in Italy, and just as in Italy, the Americans were fighting a war against the Mafia. In fact, on June 23, their own *capo di tutti capi*, John Gotti, was finally sentenced to life in prison. But the big victory for justice wasn't on the minds of the parents streaming into the auditorium that night. They were there to watch their children perform in the middle school play.

The couple eventually found seats in the third row. Sarah sat upright, her hands folded stiffly on her lap, with little desire to engage in conversation with the other parents. She never felt comfortable at the private, supposedly nondenominational school in Bay Ridge. "It's a chapel, Joseph, not an auditorium," she'd chide him whenever they attended a school function, "with pews and an organ, where they sing hymns and pray to Jesus Christ."

It was a source of contention between them. Sarah wanted to remain with the religious community in Flatbush, where she'd grown up and met her husband. She wanted their son to continue at the yeshiva, the same one they attended, where everyone was like them. Rabbi Joseph, on the other hand, had begun to see things differently over the years. He was convinced that many of the problems in the world stemmed from a tribal, us-versus-them mentality that pitted one group against another: Jews against Christians, Israelis against Arabs, white against black, and countless other divisions. The Orthodox Jewish community was particularly insular, and slowly but surely, he veered away from its rigid, claustrophobic ways, while never losing any of the passion he felt for Torah. At rabbinical school, he opted for a conservative track, the most relaxed version he could find. Afterward, he found a job in the mixed community of Bay Ridge, participated in interfaith services with Father Lazzaro at the church across the street and Imam Hussein at the mosque two blocks down, and would end up sending his son to a secular school.

"The Nussbaums are going to be late," said Sarah, craning her head in search of the only other Jewish family in Samuel's class.

Sarah had only agreed to Poly Prep because it was close to their new house, and because Samuel wasn't doing well at yeshiva. He neglected his homework, was disruptive in class, and had developed a reputation as a troublemaker. "I don't want to go to a Jewish school anymore," he told his parents after receiving a detention for fighting with a classmate. "I'd rather be in Bay Ridge with my new friends." Though Joseph was as upset as Sarah by his son's pronouncement, he convinced her that at least it would give Samuel a chance to start over again with a clean slate.

"We'd better save seats for them," said Sarah.

It was too late. A well-dressed couple sat down next to Joseph before he could say anything. The woman wore bracelets stacked the entire length of her arm and reeked of perfume. Sarah pinched him on the side.

Nothing had changed for Samuel at Poly. Just a few weeks ago, Rabbi Joseph was summoned to the headmaster's office. "Did Samuel tell you what happened?" the headmaster had asked. Joseph shook his head and braced himself. "We believe your son stole money from the charity box in the front office. He was the last person in the room before the money went missing—although no one actually saw him take it. We can't tolerate that kind of behavior at Poly, and if anything like this happens again, he cannot continue here."

The perfume from the woman next to Joseph made him queasy. It was the same feeling he had when he left the headmaster's office, mortified and bewildered. Maybe he had been wrong; maybe expanding Samuel's horizons only fueled his rebellious spirit. How were they going to deal with him? He knew what *his* father would do: a severe beating, followed by a prolonged grounding. But that wasn't the way anymore—and Samuel knew it: "I can do whatever I want," he'd shout at Joseph. God forbid Joseph ever said that to his father.

As these thoughts needled and gnawed at him, the drama teacher stepped onstage. He motioned to the back of the room, and the lights dimmed one after another. Joseph saw Sarah finally relax in her seat as the curtain went up. He took her hand in his. In the silence and darkness of the chapel, nothing mattered but their son acting in the school play. There was no need to worry about him getting into trouble and disappointing them. They could simply watch him shine for a change.

Emily Nussbaum walked onstage first. She wore a blue dress with a starched white shirt underneath, her curly brown hair pulled back in a ribbon. "How adorable," Sarah whispered to Joseph.

They both liked Emily, and not just because they liked her parents and prayed together in the same synagogue. The twelve-year-old was a straitlaced, hardworking, and serious girl. For reasons they couldn't quite fathom, she had befriended Samuel, who was very much the opposite, taking almost nothing seriously. They hoped the two would remain close, and that her good example would eventually help steer their son onto a better path.

"Does Emily look a little pale to you?" asked Sarah. "Her mother said she hasn't been feeling well lately."

Joseph squinted so he could see better. Emily had a thick layer of white makeup covering her face. Maybe that's why Sarah thought she looked pale. He shook his head no.

Just then Samuel appeared onstage. They were surprised at how composed and smartly dressed he was, with his red paisley bowtie and hair parted to the side. Now it was Sarah's turn to squeeze Joseph's hand. "So handsome," she whispered. "Just like his father."

Joseph's eyebrows shot up: *Just like his father?* He wasn't sure about that. Still, Sarah was right about the physical resemblance. Samuel was tall like him, almost six feet already, and had the same round baby face and big brown eyes, minus the bushy beard sprouting from his father's chin. He also had the same ambling gait, adding a sideways dimension to his forward movement.

"It would have been better if he looked more like you," Joseph whispered back.

"Shush." The woman on his left had swung around and glared at him, the stacked bracelets on his wrists clanking as she turned.

Joseph put up his hand apologetically.

If Samuel inherited his father's looks, he possessed his mother's energy and confidence. He exhibited no trace of fear as he performed. That was all Sarah, who, despite her petite size, had a commanding presence that she used to great effect, whether she was heading the local chapter of B'nai B'rith or managing her household with a firm hand. "My little general," Joseph called her. He, on the other hand, had always been on the more reserved side and would never have volunteered for the school play.

Joseph was happy that Samuel had tried out and then followed through with the rigorous rehearsal schedule. Maybe theater was where his talent lay. Maybe it would give him the confidence to be more productive at school. He wanted to say this to Sarah, but was afraid of angering the woman on his left.

Samuel's character was named George in the play, and Emily was Emily. Rabbi Joseph watched George and Emily go to school together. He watched them become friends, then fall in love. If only that happened in real life.

"Something's wrong," Sarah whispered into his ear. "She's not herself."

"Who?" he said, trying not to make too much noise.

"Emily—can't you see?"

Joseph had painted such a pretty picture in his head—Emily Nussbaum pairing off with his son, Samuel—that he didn't want to mar it by introducing any flaws. But now that she mentioned it, there was something odd in the way Emily's head kept falling to one side.

"She's perspiring too."

Joseph leaned forward in his seat. There were droplets tracking down Emily's brow, causing her makeup to smudge. Black streaks appeared on her cheeks, and her eyes had a dazed look. If he could see this from the third row, shouldn't the actors onstage see too? And yet they all went on as if nothing were wrong. He turned to his left, wondering whether the angry woman with the clanking bracelets had noticed.

Just then, Sarah gasped. She was standing up, her hand pointing to the stage. The lights in the chapel had gone on. Other people were standing, too, watching the commotion. There was more gasping and shouting. In the din, someone called for a doctor. All the while, Emily lay motionless. Samuel knelt beside her, cradling her head.

2

A month later, Rabbi Joseph Neiman stood before his congregation at the synagogue in Bay Ridge. With his eyes closed, he listened to the cantor singing as a wave of heat rose from the base of his neck to his face. He tried to shrug it off and return to the lovely melody of the cantor's voice. This morning's Torah portion was on the wanderings of the Jewish people in the wilderness, the great promise awaiting them at the journey's end. Yet the heat continued to distract him until he finally opened his eyes.

The synagogue was practically empty, with only twenty or so worshippers scattered in the first few pews. The carpets were faded and torn in spots, the paint chipping from the walls, and one of the beautiful stained-glass windows had been boarded up. He listened for the sound of the aging air-conditioning unit but couldn't hear its familiar rattle. No wonder he was hot.

Most jolting of all was the sight of Zev Saferstein seated in the front row, praying intently, his head bobbing as he chewed on his thumb. It made Joseph angry. The moment of calm, even exultation, that the passage from Leviticus had brought was obliterated, gloom and doubts rushing back at him again. Not that he hadn't harbored doubts in the past, but lately they had grown fierce and oppressive: How does one go on believing in a God-made world that is so deeply flawed? He was having trouble coming up with acceptable answers. At home, away from home, in every home, it seemed the divine light was dimming.

He reached back to adjust his tallit. The soft linen cloth moved easily beneath his fingers, yet at the same time, it freighted his shoulders.

Samuel was in trouble again, most recently for stealing money from the tzedakah box at school. How could a boy preparing for his bar mitzvah do such a thing? "Why, Samuel?" he had asked him after his meeting with the headmaster.

"I didn't do it," his son swore.

How could Joseph believe him when there were so many of these incidents? "What about the fighting?" Samuel just shrugged his shoulders. He never had any answers—or if he did, he showed no interest in sharing them with his father.

Joseph didn't tell Sarah about the meeting at school. He was afraid of how she might react, afraid that she would blame him for taking Samuel out of yeshiva, for raising a boy that kept disappointing them. But it wasn't right to keep her in the dark.

Then there was the poor Nussbaum girl in the hospital after collapsing onstage. A child only twelve years old with such promise, her life now hanging in the balance.

The cantor continued to sing the blessings, that God may grant wisdom, forgive our sins, help those living in exile . . .

So many terrible events weighing on his mind. Last week, the front doors to the synagogue were defaced with swastikas. Two months before, there was a bombing at the Jewish embassy in Argentina, with nearly thirty innocent people dead at the hands of terrorists. The threat of more hatred and extremism loomed on the horizon. How was it possible, after all that had taken place in this cursed century? Was there no end to the suffering?

As Rabbi Joseph stood on the podium, shaking his head, the cantor and the small group of congregants collectively asked God to heal the sick, rebuild Jerusalem, have mercy . . .

Even in their very midst lurked evil: pious Saferstein bobbing his head and chewing on his thumb. The synagogue had been struggling, despite the recent influx of immigrants, who hardly gave and, when they did, only in tiny increments. So they counted on wealthy Saferstein, the owner of a chain of successful grocery stores, to keep them afloat and help rebuild their deteriorating synagogue.

"You don't know how sorry I am, Rabbi," Saferstein had confessed to him after services last month. "So much stress on every side," he explained, cradling his raw, reddened thumb. "Managing the business, my mother dying, the kids causing all sorts of *mishigas*. I just lost my temper with Judith. But it's not the way I am."

Rabbi Joseph rested his elbows on the bimah for support. The air was stifling. Watching Benny Levin, the synagogue beadle, walk up the left-hand aisle, he tried to get his attention. *Can't you get that AC running?*

Judith Saferstein came to him a week after his talk with her husband. She whispered, even though it was only the two of them in his office. "He hits me," she'd told him. *No,* Rabbi Joseph wanted to say, *it's not possible, not after the man swore on his dying mother.* "What, you don't believe me?" she'd asked, her eyes flickering nervously. She rolled up her sleeves to show him the bruises. Joseph saw, yet said nothing, because he didn't know what to say. Clearly, this was no aberration, as Saferstein claimed, but precisely the way he was. How could the man be so cruel?

It didn't matter. He was urged by the head of the synagogue's board to make sense of it, for the good of the congregation. So instead of telling Judith to leave her husband at once, he promised he would talk to him again, that they could still figure out a way to repair their relationship. Shame on him!

We acknowledge you, O Lord, that you are our God, the rock of our life, shield of our help, immutable from age to age. We thank you and utter your praise . . .

Joseph's knees buckled under the heat, the tallit driving into his shoulders and back. He had to tighten his grip on the bimah to prevent himself from falling. So much evil and suffering in the world, and what was God doing about it? What was *he* doing about it? A rabbi already at the midpoint of his career, at the midpoint of his life, having turned fifty-three in March—wasn't he supposed to make things better? He was starting to think that his personal mission to be more inclusive and understanding had been misguided. Once that mission had given him purpose and strength. Now he was unsure about everything.

Thou art good, thy mercies endless . . .

The words echoed across the synagogue walls and into his ears. He longed to believe those good words, longed for the words to fill him with purpose again.

For thy kindnesses never are complete: from everlasting we have hoped in you. And for all these things, may thy name be blessed and exalted always and forevermore . . .

The cantor finished the prayer and returned to his seat. He adjusted his robes and looked over at the bimah. The congregants said their amens. All waited on Rabbi Joseph.

He was having trouble standing, trouble seeing, too, as a heavy mist had materialized before his eyes. Only a small section of the service was left for him to conduct. He mustn't forget his plea for the young Nussbaum girl. But the worries kept piling up, assailing him, sapping all his strength. No, he motioned to the cantor, he could not finish the service today.

3

Bay Ridge is among the most diverse communities in Brooklyn. It sits on the western tip of Long Island, greeting ships from faraway lands as they enter New York Harbor. While a fair number of Italians live there—the Verrazzano-Narrows Bridge was named after a Tuscan adventurer with a large castle near Florence—there are also Norwegians and Irish, Arabs and Turks, Greeks and Albanians, Russians and Chinese, representatives from just about every place on the globe. You see them fishing, side by side, for striped bass on the pier across from Owl's Head Park, jogging and cycling along Shore Road and the Belt Parkway, haggling over prices at the discount stores on Eighty-Sixth Street.

Bay Ridge also hosts a dwindling pocket of Jews, who worship at the run-down Jewish center on the corner of Eighty-First and Fourth Avenue. The temple occupies the main floor of the building; its basement is set up for social functions, bar mitzvahs, honorary dinners, lectures, and committee meetings. On this Sunday afternoon, the basement was being used for a bone marrow drive organized on behalf of Emily Nussbaum.

A team of technicians from the blood bank had set up a staging area in the middle of the room for blood drawing and vial labeling. A few feet away, there was a table filled with snacks and fruit. Rabbi Joseph sat next to the table in an oversized chair with a pillow behind his back.

Sarah and members of his congregation fussed over him; he wished they would leave him alone.

"I'm not an invalid," he said to his wife.

"You stay right where you are," she said. "You've been sick the entire week and shouldn't even be here today."

There was no point in arguing. Sarah had been the boss since they started dating in high school. She chose his food at the school cafeteria, shopped with him for clothes, orchestrated their social schedule. He never minded; in fact, he admired her resolve, since he was often so indecisive about navigating the day-to-day.

Nonetheless, this afternoon, as he hankered to participate in the drive for Emily, he wished things were more balanced. Not that he wasn't worried by how he had been feeling lately, the gloom and anxiety, the annoying mist before his eyes. He had gone to see Dr. Sokel the Monday after he was unable to finish services at the synagogue. Dr. Sokel did a thorough exam but couldn't find anything wrong. "Maybe you're coming down with something," he had suggested. "Why don't you take a rest and call me if you develop any other symptoms?" Joseph knew he wasn't coming down with anything, although the flu was as good an excuse as any. Better to blame it on something definite and physical, rather than vague, undiagnosable symptoms that made him look and feel weak.

As such, Joseph had contracted a bad case of the flu and was now sidelined to a chair.

"I'm happy you're feeling a little better, Rabbi," said Penny Burstein, his wife's best friend. "You know how much we worry about you. Thank God Sarah is here to pick up the slack. The drive is a big success."

They watched Sarah coax a teenage boy, who had been spooked when the technician unsheathed the needle, back to his chair. "Come, Peter," she said, gently nudging him along. "In less than a minute, you'll have a mitzvah under your belt." She continued to distract him with questions about school and summer camp until the procedure was over, then patted him on the head.

Sarah, as usual, had risen to the occasion, not only rallying their congregation but coordinating with congregations all over Brooklyn. Now, two hours into the drive, they had over one hundred samples, and Sarah was in her element, for this was where the benefits of being part of a close-knit community really paid off—Jews helping other Jews. "We have to take care of our own," she would remind Joseph, "because no one else ever will."

It made him wonder: Would he be able to convince his congregants to turn out in the same numbers for someone of a different faith, a member of Father Lazzaro's church, for example? Not likely. And it would be even worse, he hated to admit, if the sick person were from Imam Hussein's mosque.

Still, Joseph was pleased. Everyone at the synagogue liked Emily Nussbaum and was shocked by the dramatic turn of events. Six months ago, they had celebrated her bat mitzvah in this very room; now she was lying in a hospital bed, fighting for her life. The night she collapsed onstage, they assumed she fainted because the auditorium was hot and she hadn't eaten anything all day. But her blood tests were all abnormal, the white count high, the red cells low, and the platelets at particularly dangerous levels. Mrs. Nussbaum had noticed that Emily had been tired the past few weeks, but until the night of the play, there were no signs to indicate anything serious.

That changed with the results of the bone marrow biopsy. Emily was diagnosed with leukemia, an aggressive type that doctors said was often resistant to chemotherapy. Most likely she would need a bone marrow transplant. Since none of her siblings were a match, they would have to search for an unrelated donor. Unlike a blood transfusion, Joseph learned, a marrow transplant depended on genetic testing far more complicated than simple blood typing. Thus far, they had been unable to find a match for Emily on any of the bone marrow registries in this country or abroad.

Joseph shook his head. How could such a thing happen? It made him think of William Blake's poem where a worm finds its way into a bed of luminous, red roses—*O world thou art sick.*

He tried to divert himself by focusing on the drive. People were lining up to get tested. He watched them offer their arms to the technician; the dark-red fluid flowing from syringes into glass vials; the vials placed into plastic crates; the crates stacked one on top of another. The blood would be screened in a laboratory for the specific genetic markers on white blood cells and then compared to Emily's. Hopefully, a match would be found.

As Joseph watched, he began to feel less gloomy. Despite the worms in the rose bed, most people were good. There would always be sickness and suffering; there would always be a few who lied and cheated and struck their wives. *But most people care, don't they?* He watched as his congregants gave of themselves and their bodies to ease the suffering of another and thought, *Yes.*

4

Like everything else at the Bay Ridge Jewish Center, the rabbi's office was in need of repair, with its shabby dark wainscoting, peeling paint on the walls, and prints yellowing in their frames. Still, it belonged to him, and he felt comfortable there, surrounded by his books, with a big cushioned chair to read in. It was quiet enough so he could think, particularly on this weekday afternoon with morning services and his meetings for the day over.

Joseph had been reading Ecclesiastes, an outlier in the Hebrew canon. He couldn't stop reading it. Like many of his colleagues, he had always considered it a vexing text, preferring to keep it at a distance, so full of doubt it was, some would even say bordering on blasphemy. Now with so many ugly things happening, King Solomon's words called to him. The ancient patriarch had himself been at the midpoint of life, equally worried that God's promise of meaning might not be fulfilled:

> Futilities of Futilities! All is futile! What profit does man
> have for all his labor which he toils beneath the sun? A
> generation goes and a generation comes . . . the sun rises
> and the sun sets . . . all words are wearying, one becomes
> speechless . . .

Could it be that all was futile? The Hebrew word *hevel* was translated by one commentator not as futile but as "a mist" before the eyes. That was exactly what Joseph had been experiencing lately—a gauzy, white mist separating him from the outside world. When it started several months ago, he was sure something was wrong with his eyes and went to see an ophthalmologist. The doctor assured him his vision was perfect.

The mist would eventually be accompanied by the feeling of a heavy weight bearing down on him, from the top of his head to his neck and shoulders, squeezing his lungs so that it became difficult to breathe. Dr. Sokel assured him it wasn't his heart. At times, and not always because something bad happened, he would suddenly burst into tears. He realized that while many of his symptoms were physical, their origins might be more in mind than body. Was he having a midlife crisis? Worse, was it depression? Should he go see a psychiatrist? What would Sarah say—Sarah who was never sick a day in her life? Or his deceased father, the conscientious, hardworking owner of a shoe store on Nostrand Avenue who went about his life without a hiccup of self-doubt? "Get up, Joseph," he would bark at the crack of dawn. "No time for dawdling when there's school and work to be done."

That was exactly what he lacked at the moment: the energy and conviction that propelled his father and Sarah forward. Surely, he'd possessed them at one point—where had they gone?

His chair, upholstered in soft red velvet, suddenly didn't feel so comfortable. His throat was bone dry. "Get up, Joseph," his father barked from the grave. There was a water fountain in the hallway. He dragged himself out of the room and splashed water on his face.

Joseph tried to talk himself out of the funk by listing all the positive things in his life. Apart from being slightly overweight and having a few minor medical problems—a heart murmur and high cholesterol—he was in good health. He jogged and biked along Shore Road at least three times a week. He was married to a fine, strong woman. After twenty-five years of marriage, he was still smitten with her, with the way she pinched her eyes, making her look stern and alluring at the same time.

He loved his son, Samuel, despite all the pain he caused. The boy was immature, reckless. He did stupid things. "As do many kids his age," the guidance counselor at school explained. "They experiment and test their boundaries, trying to figure out who they are, and in the process, they make mistakes, some more than others."

Samuel would eventually grow up. Just look at how he showed up at the marrow drive with eight classmates from Poly. "Eight, Sarah," he'd quietly exulted before his wife, "and I bet none of the boys were even Jewish." There was no way he would steal as an adult, or beat his wife. It wasn't possible.

And he was happy at the temple, in his shabby office, reclining and reading in his chair. It might not have been the most prestigious or lucrative posting, like those netted by colleagues in the fancy Westchester and Long Island towns, but it suited him—there were fewer personalities and know-it-alls to deal with, allowing him the time to peruse texts like Ecclesiastes. No, there was nothing wrong with his life, nothing whatsoever.

Just as he arrived at this positive conclusion, the tears would start anew, as if it weren't enough that nothing was wrong and that despite such abundance, there was something still missing. Maybe too much thinking was the problem. "One foot in front of the other," he could hear his father shouting at a customer. "You don't have to think about it."

"Joseph?"

He jumped at the sound of his name. His wife stood at the door, pinching her eyes, this time more sternly than alluringly. He quickly brushed the tears from his cheeks so she wouldn't notice.

"Is that what you do here all day, sleep?" There was a bite to her voice.

"I was reading," he replied, picking up his book from the floor where it had fallen.

She shook her head. "Why didn't you tell me what happened with Samuel?"

He blushed. They had vowed long ago not to keep anything from each other, after the time he suspected Penny's husband was having an affair with another woman and didn't tell Sarah. She had been so angry she didn't talk to him for a week.

"I went to pick him up at school today," she said. "He was in detention."

"I'm sorry, Sarah."

She charged into the room and stood over his chair. "Do you know why he took the money?"

Joseph had no idea. "I was hoping he didn't take it."

"Oh, I'm sure he did," she shot back. "They had a plan, him and those troublemakers he hangs around with."

Joseph closed his eyes, afraid of what was coming next.

"They used the money at a massage parlor in Brooklyn Heights."

A massage parlor?

"I found the card in his room. But I don't think that's what it really was. I think they went there to have sex with prostitutes—our son, Joseph, twelve years old, about to be a bar mitzvah."

It isn't possible.

Sarah paced back and forth, shaking her head. "Always worrying about everyone but your own son, and now we find he might be sleeping with prostitutes. It's disgusting. What next?"

Joseph was at a loss. "I can't believe that Samuel—"

"Believe it. And I blame you—for choosing this neighborhood, sending him to that *goyishe* school, all of it." Sarah stopped pacing and pulled up a chair next to him. She took a deep breath, trying to compose herself. "I know you thought you were doing the right thing," she said, now in a softer tone, "when you turned your back on the way we were brought up, that whole modern attitude you latched on to at college, preaching about pluralism and tolerance between the different religions and races. I knew how much it meant to you, and I wanted to be supportive. But can't you see it doesn't lead anywhere? When anything and everything goes, there are no real values, no definite right and wrong. Our son has lost his way."

Joseph could feel tears welling up behind his eyes.

Sarah leaned forward and cupped his face in her hands. "Don't tell me you're not having doubts. I can see it's upsetting you too. You haven't been yourself. It's time to stop all this nonsense."

Joseph didn't want to believe that.

"Otherwise, I'm afraid something bad will happen to Samuel."

Joseph summoned what little strength he had left in his bones. "I'll talk to him."

"Talk? He doesn't need any more talking. He needs to be punished. You need to lay down the law. Promise me, Joseph."

Just then, the beadle, Benny Levin, appeared at the door. "Hello, Mrs. Neiman," he said. "Sorry to break in like this, but it's urgent."

"That's all right," said Rabbi Joseph, thankful for the interruption. "What's going on?"

"Well, I'm not sure I should—"

"Please, I don't keep anything from my wife."

Joseph could feel Sarah glaring at him.

"It's Judith Saferstein."

"Yes?"

"She's in the emergency room at Maimonides hospital," Benny said. "She was beaten up, I'm afraid. She said some young kids from the neighborhood assaulted her."

"That's terrible," said Sarah. "Will she be okay?"

"They think so."

"Did they catch the kids?" she asked.

"From what I heard, no one saw anything."

Joseph had to hold on to the side of his desk. He felt like he couldn't breathe. The ceiling and walls of the room were bearing down on him, crushing him.

5

Rabbi Joseph had always looked forward to Tuesday afternoons at the Bridge Diner with his friends Father Lazzaro and Imam Hussein. It made him feel better knowing that he was not sitting idly by while ugliness and hate dictated affairs of the world. At least he was doing his part to promote a measure of goodwill. He had always been fascinated by periods in history where people of different races and religions got along peacefully, even flourished as a result of tolerance and intercourse: Spain in the fifteenth century, Holland in the seventeenth, and more recently the city of Sarajevo until the Serbian nationalists went crazy a few months ago. Why shouldn't Bay Ridge follow in this impressive tradition, since it, too, was a melting pot of race and religion?

The leaders of Saint Peter's Church and the Masjid Al-Farooq Mosque had expressed similar thoughts, and the three had committed to building bridges between the three great religions of the Book. They held discussions and debates, sponsored joint ventures at the schools and service projects in the community. They all believed their work together was paying off, as did local politicians and newspapers. At the diner, they were greeted like celebrities, escorted to their special table in the back by the window—one man in his robes, another wearing his clerical collar, the third a yarmulke.

On this particular Tuesday, however, Rabbi Joseph could hardly summon a smile.

"What's wrong?" asked Imam Hussein. "I hope you're not going to lecture me on the status of Palestine again, or the right of return? The last time that happened, we had to forego lunch."

He shook his head.

"Still sick from the flu then?" asked the priest.

"No," he answered. "Just feeling a little down."

"Good," said the imam. "Because I can't help you with the afflictions of the body, but up here," he said, pointing to his head, "that is something we can definitely work on."

Joseph wasn't so sure. More and more, he felt like he was drowning in his head problems.

"We start with the small pleasures in life," said Imam Hussein, raising his index finger. "Do you smell that wonderful smell?"

As if on cue, the waitress appeared with a pot of steaming coffee. "I followed your instructions to the letter," she assured him.

"Excellent." The imam smiled. "I ordered these coffee beans from Yemen, the best grower in the entire country, a small farm in the Haraz mountains in the North. A nice, dark arabica. Can you smell that rich chocolate smell?" He inhaled deeply. "And the bitterness—also part of life, unfortunately. Drink up, Rabbi. It is the cure for all your ills."

"*Salute,*" said the priest.

Rabbi Joseph drank the coffee's dark chocolate along with its bitterness, a bitterness that burned the back of his throat. They were usually frank with each other when they met, but he couldn't possibly share what was weighing on his mind today. Judith Saferstein had ended up in the emergency room, in large part because of him, because he did nothing to protect her. What a hypocrite! He was a complete and utter failure—as a rabbi, in his mission at building bridges, even his faith in God was starting to fail. It was all so shameful and embarrassing, especially as he looked across the table at his friends, who radiated the very strength and conviction he now lacked.

"And once we finish with the small delights," the imam went on, "we can tackle more difficult subjects—like Gaza and the West Bank and, yes, if you insist, Rabbi, the role of women in the clergy. Here, have a fig, my friend. These are from Egypt," he said, laying a box of figs wrapped in plastic on the table. "The sweet goes well with the bitter of the coffee."

Joseph took one of the figs. "There's a sick girl," he said after a while. "Emily Nussbaum, a friend of my son, Samuel. She needs a bone marrow transplant. We organized a drive to test our members and several other congregations in Brooklyn. I was just informed that nothing came of it. They didn't find a donor."

Father Lazzaro put down his coffee. "I'm sorry."

"If only there were something we could do," said the imam.

"I have an idea," said Father Lazzaro, raising his index finger. "Why don't we increase the probabilities? We can organize another drive, a bigger one, more diverse. I will call upon my members and speak to priests from other churches. Imam—"

"But of course, what an excellent idea! I will do the same in the Muslim community."

"That's very kind of you," said Rabbi Joseph, "but I'm afraid it won't help. As I've learned, finding a match is almost impossible outside one's ethnic group. Emily, like most of our congregation, is an Ashkenazi Jew."

"That may be, but it doesn't mean we shouldn't try," said the imam. "Isn't that the point of our getting together? Solidarity between the different religions. Our Tuesday bridge-building sessions at the Bridge Diner, am I right?" he said with a smile. "It's a perfect opportunity. Who would refuse the chance to help a sick child?"

"Yes, you're right," answered Rabbi Joseph. He took a sip of coffee, then a bite of fig, as the imam had just done. That was right, too, a balancing of the bitter with the sweet. He let the sweet linger on his tongue. He tried to be hopeful as he thought of the long list of bitter in the world. He tried hard, and as he tried, he realized that a second bone marrow drive would provide him with an opportunity, an opportunity he had missed the first time around. Now he could get tested like everyone else in the congregation. He bit into the fig and let the sweetness pass down his throat.

PART III: THE NURSE

Summer and Fall 1992

Italy and New York

1

Three days after being reprimanded by the chief of medicine, Nina was in Carla's car, speeding toward Genoa. The Cinquecento rattled and wheezed like an old asthmatic as she pressed down on the gas pedal. It felt good to be on the open road, the window down, the wind rushing at her face. It felt good to be moving toward a goal with clarity and purpose, Luca's hospital chart and blood sample on the passenger seat next to her.

By then, she'd forgiven herself for giving in to Matteo when he called last Thursday. It was inevitable, considering how bereft she'd felt. Suddenly, there was nothing to look forward to, no silly banter in the hospital hallways, no dinner at their special place outside Rondello, no warm body next to hers, just a chilling emptiness. So when he said he desperately needed to talk, she agreed—despite all that had happened, despite the anger she'd harbored, despite the vow she'd made not to fall for his nonsense again.

He was waiting at the railway station, two blocks from the hospital so no one would see them. From the moment she entered the car, he didn't stop talking, going on and on about how he couldn't live without her any longer, that it was killing him. He didn't care if the chief found out, if he was fired and could never get another job again, he simply had to be with her. There were tears in his eyes as he pulled over to the side of the road when they were outside town and took her in his arms.

Of course she saw right through him, sincere as he sounded and probably believed himself to be. She wasn't stupid. Still, after years of fierce desire for this man with his dark eyes and gravelly voice, bonds had formed. It wasn't a matter of resisting in the car that evening. She wanted what he did.

They moved to the back seat. He kissed her beauty mark, her lips, chin, chest, navel. He pressed the length of his body against hers, holding both her wrists in one hand above her head, moving slowly at first, then a little faster, then faster still.

She wished she could close her eyes and experience it again, right now on the Autostrada. It felt good having him inside her, even when he started getting rough, grabbing and squeezing a little too hard, even when it began to hurt.

"*Basta!*" Nina screamed, pulling the car over to the side of the road before she lost control and had an accident. She threw her hands over her face and started to cry.

In all this time, she had never questioned the roughness, never questioned much of anything really and just followed his lead. As an oncologist, Matteo dealt with sick and dying patients day in and day out; he needed a release. She did too. Maybe a little pain was part of it—a kind of punishment for the times he missed a diagnosis or didn't continue the chemo long enough. Punishment for the times she messed up, too, leaving in an IV for too long or forgetting a dose of antibiotics. Why shouldn't they feel a fraction of the pain their patients felt?

When he'd finished, Matteo collapsed onto the seat next to her. "Don't ever leave me, Nina."

She was strangely calm. "Take me home," she told him.

"What about dinner?" he asked. "I booked a table at I Rampicanti."

"Take someone else."

Cars and trucks whizzed by as she idled on the shoulder of the Autostrada. To her right were vineyards and a large, open field with cows grazing. One of the cows had lifted its head, its mouth full of grass, and was staring at her.

Life was simple and complicated at the same time, she thought with a bitter taste in her mouth. There were reasons why people did what they did, not always in agreement. There were also reasons, less good, why people did nothing and simply accepted their fate. Her father was right when he said Nina wasn't meant for a normal life. She was a whore—Matteo Crespi's whore.

"*Basta,*" she said again, gripping the steering wheel. It was time to change things, to take control. She reached over and tapped Luca's medical chart on the passenger seat. That was where she would focus her attention.

Luca had lost so much weight these past few weeks. While his eyes still flashed when he talked about the latest exploits of Orlando, the rest of his body had slowed. What a change from two months ago, the fiery redhead ready to fend off the entire hospital staff. If only she had possessed a fraction of his defiant spirit when she was a kid, faced with the taunts and nicknames of her classmates, or more recently, in her lopsided relationship with Matteo Crespi.

"There's a lot more to go," he'd told her last night on the ward.

She didn't understand at first.

"In Orlando's story," he explained. "A lot I haven't told you about."

She smiled weakly.

"You *are* worried," he said. "I can see it in your eyes. But the medicine they're giving me is strong. Dr. Crespi said the bad cells don't stand a chance against it. And Orlando will help."

"Of course," she answered, with as much conviction as she could muster.

Yet now there *was* hope that someone might come to Luca's rescue—maybe not the fabled Orlando, but Dr. Antonio Tosti from the cancer institute in Genoa. And Nina Vocelli too.

She took one last look at the cow, shifted into first gear, and steered back onto the highway. In under an hour, she'd be in Genoa.

2

A week later, Nina stopped by the Taviano farm after work. She had information to share with Luca's grandparents in person. She also wanted to see Luca. Crespi thought the boy needed a break from the hospital after being there for two months straight and let him go home for a few days in between treatments.

She found Letizia in front of the house, pacing. Alarmed, she hurried out of the car. "Is everything okay?"

"Yes," Letizia answered while staring in the direction of the fields. "Luca is fast asleep. We went to see Signore Fabbio's new ponies this afternoon. By the time dinner came, he was so tired he dozed off in his chair. I had to carry him to his room."

"Then what's wrong?"

"Giovanni. He went for a walk hours ago and is still not back. He can't bear seeing Luca sick," she explained. "Without the hair, always tired. So he walks. But I don't like him out this late."

"Should we go and look for him?" asked Nina.

Letizia shook her head. "He'll be back soon. In the meantime, come—I'll get you something to eat, and we can talk."

Nina sat down at the kitchen table, a long, thick slab of rutted oak, its heavy trestle legs resting on the white-tiled floor. The room smelled of freshly baked bread. On the wall across from her hung a painting of the Blessed Virgin.

"She gives me strength," explained Letizia as she filled the coffee-maker with water at the sink.

Nina nodded. Her mother had also been a religious woman who regularly conversed with images of the Blessed Virgin. Despite the differences in their speech and homes—the farmhouse was a lot more spacious than the cramped third-floor apartment on Via Goldoni in Naples, and no one from these parts would understand her mother's dialect—Letizia Taviano and Maria Vocelli could have been sisters. Both were short and stout, running around the kitchen with their aprons and hearts on their sleeves. As much as she liked Letizia, though, Nina had almost no feeling left for her mother and would never be able to forgive her. Maria Vocelli might not have physically thrown her daughter out of the house, but in Nina's mind, she'd abandoned her nonetheless. Nothing was ever mentioned about the visit to the secret clinic on Via Cavour, but her mother knew and looked at Nina coldly afterward, as if she were a stranger in her home.

"I met with Dr. Tosti at the cancer institute," said Nina as Letizia laid a plate of ciabatta rolls and Taleggio cheese on the table.

Just then, the front door opened and Giovanni walked in. He had a noticeable limp and looked exhausted. Letizia rushed over to take his jacket. She pulled out a chair for him to sit on. "Finally, Giovan, I've been so worried. Come, Nina has news from Genoa."

He muttered something and looked at Nina suspiciously, without a hint of warmth or gratitude. *What a bizarre man*, Nina thought. One minute he could be talking to his grandson in the sweetest voice, the next muttering and glaring at her like a crazy person.

Embarrassed by her husband's behavior, Letizia began absently stroking his hair, hoping it might calm him.

"Yes," said Nina. "I have some good news."

"Thank God," said Letizia, drawing the sign of the cross over her chest.

Nina explained that Dr. Tosti was used to dealing with the most difficult cases, ones that didn't respond to the conventional treatment they had tried with Luca. "And because there are usually options in Genoa that they don't have in Rondello, he's had more success."

Nina saw a flicker of hope in Giovanni's eyes.

"He believes Luca's best chance is something new, a bone marrow transplant. They destroy the bad bone marrow where the cancer cells live and replace it with good marrow from a healthy donor. It's a risky procedure that was developed in the United States only twenty or so years ago, but they've gradually been getting better at it ever since, especially in Seattle, Washington. Tosti spent a year there, learning the procedure. He's now doing the transplants in Genoa and has had excellent results."

Letizia clasped her hands as if in prayer. "You see, Giovanni? There is hope after all. When can we start?"

"I understand your eagerness, signora, but here's where it gets tricky. The ideal marrow donor is a sibling, a brother or sister who shares many of the same genes with the patient. You see, when the genes don't match up well, the transplant doesn't usually take."

The Tavianos looked at her blankly.

"Unfortunately," said Nina, "Luca has no brothers or sisters."

"Oh Santa Maria," sighed Letizia.

"No, no, don't be upset, signora. There are other possibilities. Successful transplants have been done with other family members—"

"Let it be me," Giovanni blurted out, rising to his feet. "I'd give him my heart if I could. Anything for the boy."

"Of course, Signore Taviano, we will certainly test you and your wife," she said, realizing they hadn't fully understood her; since the Tavianos weren't actually related to Luca, they likely wouldn't have many genes in common. "But even if that doesn't pan out," she went on, trying to remain upbeat, "there is still another option. We can look outside the family for an unrelated match. Just three years ago, they started a registry in Italy for people willing to donate marrow to patients like Luca."

"So tell us what to do," said Letizia.

"Of course," Nina said, though for a while she couldn't summon the nerve to continue. She knew full well the next part of the conversation would be the most difficult. She took a deep breath. "There is something else I should mention. It came as a surprise. Luca's genetic markers. They don't fit with the usual Italian profile."

"I don't understand," said Letizia, growing more and more frustrated.

"Luca's genes are typically found in people of Eastern European descent. Specifically, they show a Jewish ethnicity. Ashkenazi Jewish."

Giovanni began to fidget in his seat.

"Jewish?" said Letizia. "How can that be? We don't know any Jewish people, isn't that right, Giovan? It must be a mistake."

"The test was repeated and confirmed. Luca could have inherited the genes from either his mother or his father."

Letizia shook her head. "Like I told you, Nina, we adopted Paolo from the Sisters of the Sacred Heart. All the babies there come from good Italian mothers. Tell her, Giovan."

Giovanni said nothing.

"It's true," said Letizia, "that he didn't look like other—"

"Shut up!" shouted Giovanni. "Not another word."

Nina quickly stepped in front of Letizia to shield her from her husband, so shocked she was by the violence in Giovanni's voice and afraid that he might strike her. Clearly, the man was crazy.

Meanwhile, Letizia slumped into a chair. Nina could see how confused and upset she was. Where was the good news I had promised her? she must have been thinking.

"I realize this is hard to digest," Nina said to Letizia while glancing warily at Giovanni. "But these are the facts, and if we want to help Luca, we can't ignore them. What about Luca's mother? Is it possible she had some Jewish ancestry?"

"Oh no, she came from a wealthy, old Milanese family," answered Letizia. "They were married at the cathedral in Milan. The bishop was a close friend of the family. Her parents are no longer alive, but I'm almost sure her brother is still around. He never wanted anything to do with his relatives from the country, but I could try to track him down."

Giovanni clutched his leg.

"Good. It's important to have everyone related to Luca tested. And of course both of you too."

"We could do it right this minute," said Letizia, offering up her arm.

"In due time, signora. Remember, if we don't find a match, we can look for an unrelated one on the registry. There are also registries in other countries, though they've only just started to coordinate with each other. The good news is that Dr. Tosti has contacts all over the world. He promised to send Luca's genetic profile to colleagues in the United States and Israel, the countries most likely to have a match for him."

"Please, Nina, promise us you'll—"

Nina put her arm around Letizia. "You don't have to ask, signora. You know how fond I am of your grandson. I will do everything I can for him."

"How will we ever thank you? Giovan, please say something to Nina."

But Giovanni remained silent and stern, his eyes fixed on the leg he held in his hands.

3

Rabbi Joseph lay on the red lounge chair in his office, reading about life's futility in Ecclesiastes and feeling disconsolate, when Benny Levin appeared in the doorway.

"Someone from the marrow registry is on the phone," he said. "She sounds excited."

Joseph looked up from the chair. The marrow registry? Were they calling about the drive? True to their word, Father Lazzaro and Imam Hussein had spoken to their flocks about Emily Nussbaum, and a bone marrow drive had been organized in the gym at Fort Hamilton High School two weeks ago. It was a big success, with over five hundred people getting their blood tested. Naturally, the rabbi was touched and appreciative of the efforts of his friends. It was a victory for their bridge-building efforts and would expand the number of Muslims and Catholics on the national bone marrow registry. But given the odds, there was no way a donor for Emily would be found.

"Rabbi, don't you want to take the call?"

"Sure, Benny. Put it through." He picked himself up from the chair and walked over to his desk.

"Am I speaking to Joseph Neiman?" The woman sounded excited, just as Benny had said.

"Yes, this is he."

"Well then, I have some very good news for you."

Was it possible?

"I can't tell you how happy these calls make me," said the woman. "It is so difficult to find a bone marrow match, given all the variables and different ethnic backgrounds. The odds are less than—"

"Yes, miss, I'm aware of all that. But please tell me, have they found a match?"

"I'm delighted to say the answer is yes indeed, we found a match. A perfect match. A three-out-of-three allele match."

Joseph could hardly believe his ears. A month ago, he'd sat glumly at the Bridge Diner with his friends, explaining the complex genetics of bone marrow testing as best as he understood, openly expressing his doubts about their very generous but likely futile proposal. Now it seemed he was wrong, and they were right. He wished the imam and priest were in the room so he could thank them.

"It really is quite remarkable, Mr. Neiman. There's someone out there with the exact same markers on their blood cells. Someone out there who can be saved by your marrow."

Joseph's head jerked backward. "I'm sorry—did you just say *my marrow?*"

"You sound surprised. Are you not Joseph Neiman, born on May 22, 1940, in Brooklyn, New York?"

"Yes."

"And you were tested at Fort Hamilton High School on August 10, 1992?"

Yes, he was. So focused on the 499 Muslims and Catholics that showed up that day, he'd completely forgotten that he, too, had a blood sample taken.

"Then let me be the first to congratulate you, Mr. Neiman."

Slowly, fantastically, it began to sink in. Joseph himself would be Emily's donor. He would give life to thin, wan Emily, propped up by pillows in her hospital bed. He remembered how her mother tried to make small talk while she cleaned the room over and over again, her father standing silently by, staring at his child as she kept shrinking with each passing day.

Rabbi Joseph felt equally helpless on his visits, offering only the faintest comfort. But that would soon change. With a relatively simple operation—the extraction of a pint or so of marrow from his pelvic bone—Joseph would be able to make this child well again. Not with words, not with counseling, but with direct, bodily action.

"This is the best news I've heard in a long time," he told the woman from the marrow registry.

"I'm glad to hear that, Mr. Neiman."

The best news in years, thought Joseph as his gaze swept around the office, taking in the peeling paint on the walls, the papers piled atop his desk, his red reading chair, the tattered copy of Ecclesiastes. It dawned on him that what bothered him most about the path he'd chosen for himself was its powerlessness, his inability to make a real difference. A rabbi's work was more conceptual than dynamic; it involved more reading, listening, counseling than making, building, doing. He envied the doers of the world.

That sense of impotence was precisely what led him to Father Lazzaro and Imam Hussein and their bridge-building efforts in the community. But the prospect of becoming a marrow donor—being able to give a part of his body to save the life of young Emily Nussbaum— was in a different league altogether.

"Mr. Neiman, are you still there?"

His mind had been so consumed by the news and its ramifications that he'd completely forgotten he still had the phone in his hand. "Yes, yes, I'm here," he told the woman. "I can't tell you how happy—"

"Mr. Neiman, I'm so sorry, but I have to put you on hold. Someone just walked into my office."

"Of course," he said. "I've known Emily Nussbaum her whole life. My son is in the same class at Poly—"

But the woman was already off the line.

No matter. With news like this, Joseph had all the time in the world. He sat back in his chair, his head held high, a tingling sensation at the tips of his fingers.

Benny Levin popped his head in the door. "Was I right?"

Joseph smiled. *More than you can imagine,* he thought to himself. The mist in front of his eyes was beginning to lift, the weight bearing down on him lightening. Life was about to turn a corner.

4

Letizia woke in the middle of the night. When she switched on the light, Giovanni was missing, a puddle of blood in his place. She rushed downstairs and found her husband sitting at the kitchen table with a bloodied dish towel pressed against his left leg.

"Santa Maria," she cried. "What happened?"

Giovanni didn't answer.

"There's blood everywhere!" She pointed to the red trail leading down the steps, through the foyer, and into the kitchen.

"It's nothing," he replied brusquely.

"You're pale as a ghost, Giovanni. Let me take you to the hospital."

"Stop screaming, or you'll wake—"

It was too late. Luca had heard the commotion and now stood in the kitchen doorway in his pajamas, still half-asleep, but alarmed at the sight of the bloody towel.

"Now see what you've done!" yelled Giovanni. "Woken the boy. I told you—"

"Nonno, are you all right?" asked Luca.

"I'm fine, my child," he answered. Giovanni's tone changed when he spoke to his grandson, lowering, gentling. "The leg is acting up again, the one I injured in the fields. But it feels better now. You and me, we're cowboys. We can fight off anything—am I right?"

Luca looked cautiously over to his grandmother, who did her best to smile, then turned back to his grandfather. "Yes, you're right."

"Now go back to bed. Growing cowboys need rest. I'll be up soon myself. Go," he said, nudging him toward the stairs.

The second she heard the creaking of Luca's bed overhead, Letizia picked up the phone. "If you won't go to the hospital, I'm calling Dr. Ruggiero. I won't be able to sleep until I know you're not in danger."

"It's after midnight," he said. "You can't disturb the man at this hour."

Letizia wouldn't listen. Only after the doctor finally answered and agreed to come over could she breathe easier. "I don't understand, Giovanni," she said, setting down the phone. "With all that's happening, you refuse help. There's already one sick member of this household. I can't handle another."

"I told you, I'm fine."

"No, you're not. You haven't been fine for a while. You take every bad thing that's happened and blame yourself. For God's sake, you have to stop."

Giovanni looked like he was about to say something but could only shake his head.

"It's true we've had our share of bad luck," she said, taking his hand. "But we've also had good luck. Just when we thought we'd never have a child," she said, staring at the picture on the wall, "the Blessed Mother sent us Paolo. Remember when he started taking out the tractor by himself, waving as he drove by? Playing football at school, always one of the best on the team? We'd stand on the sideline and cheer when he made a goal. Graduating from the university in Milan. Marrying that beautiful girl. Come, Giovan, you can't say he didn't make you proud."

"For how long?" asked Giovanni in a harsh whisper.

"He died too young, it's true, and it killed a part of me too. But he gave us our Luca, beautiful just like his father, with his red hair and lively spirit, making up all those stories about Orlando, the hero he meets at the Castle, who rescues people in trouble."

A fierce pain ripped through Giovanni's leg, causing him to shudder. "It's my fault."

"No, it's not, Giovan. You're a good man. I knew it from the very beginning, the way you were with your parents, always helping your mother around the house and your father on the farm. My mother took me aside before she died and told me that I couldn't have made a better choice. She was right."

"No."

"You have to be strong," she said. "There's always hope. Just listen to your grandson's stories. And believe in the Blessed Virgin—just when things seem most bleak, a light suddenly appears. Like the nurse who takes care of Luca, running all over the country to consult with doctors. Nina will help us, you'll see."

The bell rang as she kissed her husband on the forehead. Dr. Ruggiero stood in the doorway, holding his medical bag. As he walked in, a breeze rustled the fabric of her nightgown. She felt naked standing next to the doctor, who despite his age and the time of night, was dressed in his usual, tie and jacket and V-neck sweater.

"I'm so sorry you had—"

"No need. I always take care of my patients, signora."

Ruggiero entered the kitchen and saw Giovanni with the bloody towel wrapped around his leg. "You might want to leave us alone, signora. Just get me a bowl of hot water and something to put on the floor so I don't make a mess."

"What have you done now, Giovanni?" asked Ruggiero as soon as Letizia left. There was no door to close for privacy, so the doctor spoke in a low voice. He spread the towel on the white-tiled floor and lined up his supplies on the kitchen table—gauze, scissors, forceps, clamp, sutures, and styptics. He pulled over a chair and laid Giovanni's foot on top of it, then positioned himself to face the open wound.

"Like I've said before, one day you're going to kill yourself, whether from the bleeding or an infection that develops afterward. You realize that, don't you?"

Giovanni shrugged.

Ruggiero poured some iodine in the hot water, dipped the gauze into the mix, then placed it over the wound. He tried to stop the bleeding with the styptic, but that didn't work. Ruggiero shook his head. "We'll have to tie off the vessel." He removed his jacket, loosened his tie, pushed the sleeves of his sweater up to his elbows. Despite the tremor in his right hand, he worked patiently and methodically. After stitching the severed vessel, he cleaned and dressed the wound. "Do you need something for the pain?"

"Pain," Giovanni scoffed, "doesn't bother me at all."

"I can see that, and it's precisely what I want to talk to you about," whispered the doctor. "Nurse Vocelli called me yesterday. She is a most persistent woman, causing quite a riot at Santa Cristina. All for a good cause, though. I think she's on to something. I knew Antonio Tosti when he worked at Santa Cristina and can assure you, he's one of the smartest men I've ever come across. You're very fortunate that he's offered to help."

Giovanni grunted.

"On the other hand," he said more grimly, "it will come to naught if you don't help him. I'm talking about the genetic tests that the nurse told you about."

Giovanni looked away.

"I can't say I'm surprised. Remember, I took care of Paolo when you supposedly brought him back from the orphanage in Genoa. Paolo with his red hair and pale skin looked nothing like the babies I'd seen over the years. Naturally, I was curious and made sure to check his genitals. I wanted to see if the boy was circumcised; he wasn't. Still, I knew something wasn't right, so I wrote to the Sisters of the Sacred Heart. Sure enough, they confirmed my suspicions."

Giovanni flinched.

"But after doing some more digging and finding nothing, I stopped. I never mentioned your fabrication to anyone. The war was a crazy time in this country—people turning on one another, going hungry, getting shot because they were Fascists or anti-Fascists, communists or anarchists, leaving behind a trail of broken men and widows and orphans. *Che disastro questa guerra!* When I saw how happy you and Letizia were, what a good home you provided for the baby, I decided it didn't matter how you got Paolo."

Giovanni remained silent.

"But over the years, while I kept your secret, I saw it was eating you up, even before Paolo's accident and this wound of yours. You were always a quiet man, but it was different after Paolo. Behind the happiness that came with your new family, I could sense there was a great guilt building in you."

Giovanni cursed under his breath.

"Now is the time to come clean, Giovanni. Not just to ease your conscience—you have an obligation to your grandson. The poor nurse will go on a wild-goose chase, trying to track down the relatives of Paolo's wife. I'm sure the Jewish genes are on Paolo's side. Where did you get the child, my friend?"

Still, he made no answer.

"Are you listening to me? Your grandson is dying. You don't have much time."

5

"Are you still there, Mr. Neiman?"

Rabbi Joseph wasn't sure how long he'd held the silent receiver in his hand, a few minutes, an hour maybe, during which time he danced and turned cartwheels on the rooftops of his mind like Tevye in *Fiddler on the Roof.*

"I'm definitely here," he answered. "I wondered if you've notified the parents. If not, I'd like to do so myself. I've known the family for years, and my son, Samuel, is close friends with Emily. They were just in the school play—"

"Emily?"

"Yes, Emily Nussbaum. Father Lazzaro and Imam Hussein organized the drive for Emily—"

"Let me stop you there, Mr. Neiman. I'm afraid you don't understand how this process works. Unless you're a family member, marrow donation is an anonymous process. We cannot divulge any information about the recipient, and that most certainly includes their name. The only thing I can tell you is that the match was not found on the registry here in the United States. It came up on an international search."

"International?"

"Yes, the patient resides outside the United States."

The words sucked the wind right out of him. All along, he thought the call was about Emily, that he of all the people tested would be the one to save her, to save her entire family. How could this be? Every time something good happened, it was taken away, snatched right up.

"I don't understand," he said, a note of hysteria creeping into his voice. "What about Emily?"

"I can't say, Mr. Neiman. Hopefully, this woman you speak of will find a match at some point. What I can say for sure is that marrow drives like the one you and your friends organized are beautiful gestures that produce potential donors for many sick people all over the world."

"I see," he said in practically a whisper.

"Mr. Neiman, I can tell you're upset, but try to see this another way. There is someone in the world that is just as sick as the woman you know, who has family just as distraught. You will be able to help that person, that family, with your marrow. *You*, Mr. Neiman, do you understand?"

Yes, he wanted to say, but his mouth was so dry he could barely get the word out.

"Why don't you take some time to digest the news. I'm going to send you more information about the process, a checklist of what you need to do, including consent and medical release forms. If you decide to go ahead with the donation, as I hope you will, you'll have to be cleared by your doctor. Naturally, we wouldn't want to put you at any risk. Have a good day, Mr. Neiman, and I will get back to you soon."

6

Rabbi Joseph left his office after hanging up the phone. He needed air, a walk to clear his head. He would go to his favorite spot by the Narrows, underneath the Verrazzano Bridge.

As he passed Saint Peter's, he thought of visiting Father Lazzaro. But that wasn't necessary. He knew exactly what the priest would say. Just as he knew what Imam Hussein would say. The act of giving, and giving outside your tribe, was precisely what their work was about.

Yet that wasn't his first reaction. Joseph felt his stomach tighten. He had been selfish. No, it wasn't just the world conspiring to bring him down—he continually let himself down.

He walked up Fourth Avenue with his eyes cast downward, faster than usual, almost as if he were running, running away from himself. The noise of the cars and buses on the street washed over him, along with the smell of exhaust fumes in the close summer air, the glare of the sun. None of it bothered him. All he could hear were the words of the woman at the registry. "Try to see this another way, Mr. Neiman. There is someone in the world that is just as sick as the woman you know. You will be able to help that person."

Why didn't he see that straightaway? Granted, he was caught off guard, disappointed. Still, the woman had presented him with a great opportunity, one he should have embraced, not balked at—to help someone by giving of himself, by actually doing something rather than just talking and preaching. It was what he had wanted for so long.

"Hello," a voice called out. He looked up and saw the Chinese man at the gas station waving at him. He waved back. *Such a nice man.* Even though Joseph didn't bring his car there very often, the man always remembered him. On the next block was a hookah bar, dimly lit by fluorescent purple bulbs placed at odd angles on the walls, and the Norwegian bakery, with its travel posters of stunning fjords and quaint fishing villages. Farther on, he passed Il Bucatino, the restaurant Father Lazzaro had introduced him to and that had since become one of Joseph's favorite places in the neighborhood. The front door was open, and he peeked inside, hoping to get a whiff of the eggplant parmesan. If only he could convince Sarah to come one day. But no matter how hard he tried, she refused to eat at an Italian restaurant. "Never," she would say with a defiant look in her eyes, not after what happened to her father in Italy during the war.

By the time he arrived at the Verrazzano, Joseph was starting to feel better. There weren't many people on the walking path—a few joggers and a fisherman leaning lazily over the black metal railing. He watched the birds circle in the sky, followed the currents moving steadily along the Narrows and out into the Atlantic, a large freighter filled with brightly colored containers heading toward him.

Joseph breathed deeply of the salty sea breeze and exhaled slowly. He watched tiny particles of air moving upward into the blue summer sky and down into the glittering water below. Of course he would share his marrow with the stranger from another country. He pictured himself at the Bridge Diner on Tuesday afternoon, sitting with Father Lazzaro and Imam Hussein at their special table in the back, drinking coffee from Yemen and eating figs from Egypt. Of course he would share his marrow. He had never been more certain.

Sarah was in the backyard, pulling out weeds in her garden, when Joseph reached the house. "You're home early," she observed, looking up from the ground. "Is everything all right?"

He explained his hurry, the phone call from the marrow registry, how upset he was at first, the walk to the Narrows, his gradual change of heart.

Sarah watched blankly as the words tumbled from her husband's mouth. "I don't understand, Joseph. The people from the registry made it clear that you couldn't get tested if you had the flu. But you went ahead anyway?"

"I didn't get tested at the temple," he explained. "It was at the second drive Father Lazzaro and Imam Hussein organized, when I was feeling better."

"So you cleared it with the registry?"

"No, I didn't think—"

"And what about Dr. Sokel? You have a medical condition. Did you clear it with Dr. Sokel?"

"I would hardly call my heart murmur a medical condition." Joseph should have known Sarah would be upset, more perhaps for not consulting with her than with Dr. Sokel.

"Even though it can lead to blood clots? Isn't that why you have to take the blood thinner?"

"I can always stop the medicine for a few days."

After a long silence, she looked at him sternly and said, "Then there's nothing more to say." Sarah turned away and continued clearing the weeds around her tomato plants.

Joseph was taken aback. "Nothing more to say?" he repeated. "What do you mean?"

"That you can't agree to it until I get assurance from Dr. Sokel that nothing bad would happen to you," she said, running the small rake through the soil.

"I'll call him right now," he suggested.

"I prefer we see him together. In person."

Joseph paced up and down the yard. "Sarah, you're not making any sense. Are you upset because I didn't tell you about getting tested at Fort Hamilton? I just assumed you knew and didn't think it would be a problem."

Sarah didn't respond.

"Or is it because the marrow wouldn't go to Emily? Initially, I had the same reaction. I was upset, angry even, until I realized that as sorry as I felt for the Nussbaums, there was another family out there suffering just like them."

"Another Jewish family?"

The rabbi's head jerked backward. "Is that what this is about—that we should only sacrifice for a fellow Jew?"

Sarah went on pruning her garden without answering. When she finished, she stood up and removed her gloves. "I know you mean well, Joseph, but you're not thinking things through. You were at the drive when they went over all the risks involved in being a transplant donor, general anesthesia and infection. Those risks are much higher for people with heart conditions. You have a family to think about. Your wife. Your son."

"Sarah, listen to me." He took her hand, looked her in the eye, and tried to explain why he wanted to do this, why he needed to do this. Especially at this moment in his life, when he was feeling down about all the horrible things happening in the world—though he was afraid to reveal the extent of his downward spiral. Moreover, he explained, being a bone marrow donor would dovetail with his work with Father Lazzaro and Imam Hussein. This kind of sharing was precisely what their fractured and divisive world needed.

"There's no point in talking," said Sarah, shaking her head, "until we speak to Dr. Sokel."

7

Giovanni's head thrummed with noise, especially in the dark hours of the night. He couldn't close his eyes without hearing and seeing terrible things. He got out of bed, and having promised Letizia he would not go outside so late, he walked the house, from one room to the other and back again.

Pop, pop, pop. Shots firing in the cold night.

He shuddered with each remembered report. Back then, he could muffle the sounds and sights with others, more soothing and promising. The murmurs from a swaddled blanket, the look on Letizia's face when he returned home with their new baby.

He holds the folded piece of paper in his hand. What was the man thinking, on a cold, gusty night, entrusting a flimsy piece of paper with his son's identity and the address of the Swiss safehouse they were headed to? And just like that, the paper flies from his hand, hangs in the air, then drops in the snow, bleeding ink into the whiteness.

But that's not how it happened. No—he opened his hand and let the paper fly out. He did it on purpose.

He sees it now, rolling in the snow, hears the wind howling, now, but not back then. Back then, he could block the sounds and sights with others, more soothing and promising. Now, he hears the shots echoing through the woods, making him shudder, so loud he's afraid his eardrums might pop.

He had to keep on moving, one bedroom to the next, then down to the kitchen and back up again.

If only he could go back and retrieve the paper from the snow before the ink runs and makes the words unintelligible. A name. An address. A clue that might save Luca.

Giovanni slammed his hand against the refrigerator door. Impossible! In fact, he did go back, the very next day. The whole town was on edge after the massacre in the forest, everyone except the two of them in their bubble, Letizia absorbed in her new baby and he relieved that he no longer had to worry about the parents returning for their child. Yes, he felt relieved, it shamed him to say, even secretly happy. But he had to make sure no one would find the piece of paper and somehow link it to him and his new baby, so he went back, scoured the area where he had dropped it until he was sure it was gone. Until he was sure no one would ever know.

Except now he wanted to know, needed to know, for Luca's sake. *Idiot,* he railed at the man in the tattered coat for being so careless. *Idiot,* he railed at himself for letting the paper fly out of his hand.

Then came the shots, Lambertini and his gang of Fascist thugs. *Pop, pop, pop.*

They were sitting ducks out there in the woods. How did Lambertini find them so fast? Had he seen Giovanni take the bundle from the man in the tattered coat? Had he seen him talking to the priest near the abandoned mill earlier in the day? Was that why he gave him a strange look when Giovanni ran into him in the piazza later that morning and said he was on his way to the convent in Genoa. "Sure, Giovanni, but I'm warning you," said Lambertini, "you better let me know if you see or hear anything suspicious."

The shots ring in the air. Snow turning black, turning red.

Red. Red. Red.

The images and sounds are everywhere, surrounding him, pummeling him, drowning him.

His leg throbbing, Giovanni collapsed onto the kitchen floor, desperate to turn his mind elsewhere.

Letizia cradles the baby in her arms. She believes Giovanni's story, that the convent had notified him of a baby up for adoption, and without a moment's pause, he rushed off to Genoa to claim it. How could she not? For so long, she's been praying for this, and finally the Blessed Mother has answered. How will she ever thank her? By raising the child to be a Christian boy, that's how, a boy no different from the other boys in the village, who plays soccer, eats his pasta, becomes an altar boy at San Stefano. A good Italian boy. Their good Italian boy.

There was no one to cast doubt. Dr. Ruggiero might have suspected Giovanni was lying, but he never made any trouble. And sleazy Pietro Lambertini—the only person who could possibly connect him to events in the forest that night—had been killed by the partisans in retribution three days after the massacre. He'd vanished in the snow, along with the folded piece of paper and dead bodies.

They had adopted an orphan from the Sisters of the Sacred Heart. He would embrace the lie with all his soul—until the trouble started, first with Paolo's death and later Luca's sickness, and then he could no longer muffle the sounds and images. They were pummeling him, crushing him, drowning him.

Ruggiero was right: he had no choice but to come clean. He must go to the authorities and tell them what happened. The folded piece of paper was gone, but maybe there were people, organizations that could put two and two together and figure out where the baby had come from, who the parents were, and if there were any relatives left in the world, relatives who might have the same genes and be able to help the son of that baby, his grandson, his precious Luca.

"Now is the time to come clean, Giovanni," Ruggiero had said. No matter how hard it would be or what the consequences.

The doctor was right. It didn't matter if they called Giovanni a criminal or took him to jail, if Letizia found out what he'd done and could never look him in the eye again. His life would be over.

It didn't matter. The only thing that mattered was Luca.

He would go to the mayor and confess.

8

A week later, Sarah stood at the door to Joseph's office, with her hands on her hips and a stern look on her face.

"What's wrong?" he asked. They had been walking on eggshells the past few days since their visit to Dr. Sokel. Sarah brought the registry brochure that listed cardiac conditions as a risk factor for being a bone marrow transplant donor. "What if he goes off the blood thinner," she had asked, "and then develops a blood clot or a stroke? This is my husband," said Sarah, "and your rabbi." Dr. Sokel had said he understood that very well and promised to speak to the surgeon and the anesthesiologist. In the meantime, they should mull it over themselves. Which was precisely what they had been doing since the visit. While Sarah typically prevailed in their disagreements, Joseph was unusually persistent this time and believed that Sarah was on the verge of giving in. But seeing his wife in the doorway with that look on her face, he began to have doubts.

"I just talked to a woman at the marrow registry," said Sarah. "She told me you were going ahead with it. I don't understand. We never agreed."

"That's not true," he explained. "I only filled out some of the preliminary paperwork."

"It's not right, Joseph," she said, her voice faltering. "Our son is out of control. He barely says anything to us, and half of what he does say is lies. And now you're going behind my back too?"

"Please," he said when he saw how upset she was. He took her hand and led her to his chair. "I wouldn't do anything without your blessing, I promise."

She took a tissue from her bag to wipe her eyes. She glanced down at the floor, up at the ceiling, anywhere except her husband's face.

"What is it, Sarah?"

"You can't do it," she said finally.

"But you heard what Dr. Sokel said. As long as they monitor—"

"It's not your heart, Joseph," she said, shaking her head.

"Then what?"

"I found out something about your match. Something that makes it impossible."

What? he wondered, considering that marrow donation was a confidential process.

"The patient is from Italy, Joseph."

The rabbi was confused. "How could you possibly know that?"

"The woman from the registry told me."

"I don't understand. She wouldn't tell me anything. She said it wasn't allowed. So why did she tell you?"

"Because I insisted. I told her if she wouldn't give me any information about the patient, then she'd have to take your name off the registry. She thought I was joking at first. But when she realized I was dead serious, that there was no way you would risk your life for something without my permission, she said she would make an exception."

Joseph couldn't believe his ears. Sarah had always been headstrong, but this was going too far, even for her.

"She wouldn't give me a name or an age, whether it was a man or woman, Jew or gentile. Only that the patient was from Italy."

He looked up but didn't say anything.

"Did you hear me, Joseph?"

He nodded hesitantly.

"You know how I feel about that country."

He knew very well. As much as he wished otherwise, Sarah had never been able to let go of her longstanding grudge against Italy. She vowed never to set foot in the country, eat at an Italian restaurant, or buy any Italian products. She bore the same kind of repulsion toward Italy that many concentration camp survivors and their children felt toward Germany.

"Of course I know. It brings back bad memories, for your father especially. But why bring all that up now? It was such a long time ago and has nothing—"

"Really?" she said, her voice growing louder, her eyes narrowing into slits. "*All that* was my grandparents, whom I never got to meet. And my father, who spent a year in a filthy Italian detention camp being treated like an animal; who watched his parents being beaten for hiding bread, then get shipped off to Auschwitz to die. He still has nightmares. For him, the Italians were worse than the Germans."

"Sarah, we've been over this a million times. It's not fair to judge—"

"Not fair, you say. Mussolini was Hitler's ally during the war. He signed racial laws no different from the Germans' and was just as eager to round up the Jews and send them to concentration camps—both Italian Jews and the refugees that came from other countries in Europe, like my father and grandparents. *I'm* not being fair?"

"You can't blame the entire country because of a few bad people."

"You know the stories—there were more than a few bad people involved."

Yes, he knew. Sarah's father was a reserved man who preferred not to rehash the past, particularly the painful parts. But a few years back, they convinced him to tell his story for a documentary film that was being made by the Holocaust museum in Lower Manhattan. "We left Hungary before the mass deportations started in 1944," he'd told the interviewer in a calm, almost detached voice. He wore the old woolen flat cap he never left the house without, no matter what time of year, summer or winter. "My father had a plan. He heard the Italians were more tolerant than our other European neighbors and the most likely to help us. If we could make it to the port of Genoa, we'd have a good chance of getting to Spain or the United States. But my father was wrong. The minute we crossed the border into Italy, we were harassed and hunted—by the Germans, the Italian police, and the Fascist militias. In a small village outside of Turin, I was thirsty and went to get a drink at the fountain in the main square. A group of boys my age—I was twelve at the time—cursed and spat at me. It was in the same village that a nice old Italian woman gave us some bread and told us where to hide for the night. The next morning, we watched her point us out to the authorities and pocket the reward money."

After seeing the film, Joseph would be forever haunted by the image of the soft-spoken man in his woolen cap, once an innocent boy trying to get a sip of water at the fountain in the village square.

"What your father and grandparents went through," Joseph said slowly, "is horrible. Unforgiveable. But you have to remember, it was fifty years ago, in a very different time. It has nothing to do with my being a marrow donor today. This is about a sick person like Emily Nussbaum, who needs my help."

"No, Joseph, the sick person is not like Emily. He or she is Italian, not American. And Catholic, not Jewish."

"You don't know that."

"Italy is a Catholic country, where the pope's word carries as much weight as the prime minister's. The same pope, mind you, who meets with Arafat, an Arab terrorist, but not Shamir or Rabin."

"It's also a country," he fired back, "with some of the oldest Jewish communities in the world, in Venice and Rome."

"You're not going to change my mind. This is personal for me. I won't let you risk your life for someone who may have sent my grandparents to the gas chambers."

Joseph shook his head. "I can't believe you're saying this. You've seen how much Emily and her parents are suffering. That's all that matters. Not what happened in the past, or what religion the person might be. What if Samuel were sick? Would you want someone who could help asking such questions?"

"I'm sorry, Joseph."

Joseph saw the determination in his wife's eyes. He was not going to convince her. The truth was he'd gone even further in his moral reasoning than he'd let on. It didn't even matter whether the sick person was good or bad. He would give his marrow to Zev Saferstein—the wife beater—if it could save his life.

"I'm sorry," repeated Sarah. "The person from Italy will have to find someone else."

9

Nina entered the hospital that night with her head down. She'd brought a box of arancini, her favorite. Since she'd introduced them to Luca, they were his favorite now too. But what was she thinking? It was late already, well after dinner, and Luca wouldn't be eating anything tonight, considering the shape he was in.

Things were grim. Three weeks had passed since she'd visited the Taviano farm, full of hope after meeting with Dr. Tosti. Yet each avenue seemed to lead nowhere. They'd tested Letizia and Giovanni and almost every employee at Santa Cristina, including Nina, who did it twice just to be sure. No match was found. They contacted Luca's maternal uncle, who laughed when asked if he had any Jewish relatives. Nonetheless, after Letizia's desperate pleas and threats to show up on his doorstep, the Milanese nobleman agreed to get tested. Nothing. Nina even contacted several synagogues in Northern Italy and was able to persuade them to test some of their members. Again, nothing. The international registries, which Tosti claimed held so much promise, came up empty.

"I'm sorry, Nina."

Matteo was standing beside Luca's bed, watching over his sleeping patient, when she arrived on the ward.

"I know you've taken a liking to the boy. We all have, but—"

"But what?" she snapped, reading the dejected expression on his face. "You're giving up, is that what you're telling me?"

Matteo barely moved.

"We'll find a match for him. Someone, somewhere, will turn up, you'll see."

"It's not only that," he said. "The blood cultures came back. The boy has a fungal infection. What we fear most with a compromised immune system and low counts. I doubt he'll be able to survive this."

The news struck her like a punch to the stomach; she gasped for air.

Matteo reached to console her, but she pushed him away. "You're upset, I understand," he said. "But you did your best for the boy. More than I did, I admit. I was angry when you second-guessed me at the conference. When I found out you went to Tosti behind my back, I went crazy. Good thing you weren't around the day he called me to discuss the case."

"What choice did I have?"

"None. The case caught me completely off guard. There was nothing out of the ordinary. All signs pointed to a positive outcome—I would have bet my life on it. Yet for some reason, the boy didn't respond to treatment. I still don't understand."

Something caught at the back of Nina's throat.

"I should have thought of alternative options. I should have called Tosti myself. But I'm a proud man and didn't want to admit defeat. I kept thinking things might turn around. It was stupid. The boy was lucky you were there to take the ball. You made sure he had a chance."

Nina didn't resist when he reached for her hand a second time; she didn't have the strength. Matteo was smiling his gentle smile, without any trace of arrogance. He hadn't shaved in a while and looked tired, almost defeated. "Forgive me, Nina. For everything."

Was this the man she'd once fallen in love with? The kind man, not the slick egotist who cared only for himself? Or both rolled into one?

"Any chance you want to grab a drink?" he asked.

A drink? She could use two, maybe four at the moment. No, she shook her head. "I promised Luca's grandmother I'd stay here tonight. That crazy husband of hers is sick, too, and she's afraid to leave him alone. Why don't you take these arancini from Boninno Jr.'s salumeria? They're just as good as his father's. You remember him, I'm sure."

Matteo nodded.

"One of your many success stories," she noted. "You know his son asks for you every time I go in there."

He smiled. "Thank you for reminding me."

It was bound to be a long, painful night, she thought, watching Matteo leave the ward. She tiptoed around Luca so as not to wake him. Though he was pale and drawn, there was something peaceful about his expression as he slept, despite the gravity of his condition, the deadly fungus circulating in his bloodstream. Was it possible he might not live out the year? This boy who once had so much life inside him?

She felt weak and depleted, as if she, too, didn't have the strength to make it through the year. Nina had been a nurse for a long time. She'd seen many patients die, and it always hurt. But nowhere near how much this would hurt. She had grown close to Luca, bound to him in a way she'd never been to another patient. There would be consequences.

She thought of Letizia's devotion to the image of the Blessed Virgin, the same as her mother's—their convictions, their faith. Nina had always seen those convictions as foolish. Right now, though, she wished she could grab on to something solid, anything.

Luca's hand had slipped from under his blanket and was hanging off the side of the bed. His fingers were so thin, they looked like twigs.

She thought of the row of stones at the edge of Favola. The remnants of what was once a formidable Roman wall, now reduced to rubble. To Luca, the wall was a castle. A castle visited by a hero from overseas named Orlando.

Nina placed Luca's hand back on the bed and covered it with the blanket.

How she wanted to believe in that castle, in Orlando.

To believe in the stories Luca told her at night on the ward.

She couldn't bear the thought that they might end.

PART IV: THE CROSSING

Fall 1992

1

Ever since she was a child, Nina wondered how God could create a world so imperfect, full of suffering and pain and badness. While many Catholics like her mother attributed the paradox to sin—*il segno del diavolo*—Nina came to see it more in the less moralistic terms of *sbagli* or mistakes.

Her port-wine stain was just such a mistake. The congenital malformation occurred during morphogenesis, the development of an embryo into a mature human being. Through faulty coordination between growing cells, a group of blood vessels errantly migrated to the upper layers of skin, remaining cut off from normal signals that direct the vessels to dilate and constrict—hence the purple blotch covering the right side of her face.

Clearly, this was unintentional, an accident of nature. The same could be said of cancer. In Luca Taviano's case, the problem lay in the DNA of a stem cell in his bone marrow, an entangling of chromosomes during cell division where the head of one chromosome somersaulted onto the tail of another. The resulting translocation activated an oncogene that thrust the stem cell into overdrive, continuously producing mutant offspring that crowded out the normal cells in his marrow; unstopped, they would eventually kill him.

Rabbi Joseph Neiman wasn't able to complete morning services at his synagogue in Bay Ridge, likely the early stages of depression taking hold of his mind. Here the problem was thought to stem from a neurotransmitter imbalance—too little serotonin and dopamine—which left him weak and hopeless.

Just as there are *sbagli* that happen inside our bodies and beyond our control, there are others for which we bear some responsibility. Nina's high school history teacher seemed like a nice man, with his thick black glasses and gentle voice. He took her aside after the midterm exam: "Nina," he'd said, "you're too smart to fail this course, but with some extra instruction and effort, we can turn it around." After a series of weekly tutoring sessions, they did just that, and Nina was so grateful when she received her final grade that she didn't say anything when he touched her, then touched her some more—until before she could understand exactly what had happened, she was traveling to the dank basement clinic on Via Cavour, where they inserted a long, thin instrument deep inside her, and from then on would no longer feel at home in her own home.

She should have been more careful afterward. But years later, in the midst of taking a patient's blood pressure at the Ospedale Santa Cristina, soon after starting her nursing career, she saw Matteo Crespi standing in the doorway, with his movie-star looks, and was instantly smitten. It is one of the cardinal rules taught in nursing school: never fall in love with a doctor with whom you work, a married one no less, because it inevitably leads to disaster. For almost a decade, it seemed as if the rule might not apply to her. Then came the nasty letter and her meltdown while taking Luca Taviano's blood.

On the heels of that disaster, Nina would flout another cardinal rule of her profession: never get too close to a patient. The risks were self-evident, and she had seen examples of compromised care because doctors and nurses were blinded by their attachment to patients, letting them leave the hospital before they were ready, giving too much medicine or too little. If the emotional investment went on long enough, there was the risk of burnout and self-destruction. Everyone at Santa Cristina knew the story of Dr. Ricciardi, a surgeon so devoted to his patients that he'd come in on weekends and stay at the hospital all night if there was a complication. The day came when he started acting strangely, talking to himself, forgetting things, weeping in the cafeteria, until one morning he didn't show up for work and his wife found him lying on the bathroom floor, tourniquet wrapped around his arm, a syringe sticking out of his vein.

Nina seemed to be following the same path as Ricciardi in the spring of 1992. She went to the hospital at all hours to be with Luca Taviano, brought him treats and gifts, and soon began traveling around the country on his behalf against the express orders of the hospital administration. She couldn't help herself.

But on the spectrum of human *sbagli*, there was a lot worse than Nina's recklessness. There were husbands who beat their wives, like Zev Saferstein; men who killed other men, like the Mafiosi who murdered the brave judges in Sicily; the old Italian woman who sold out Sarah Neiman's grandparents for a few thousand lira; the Italian Fascists who worked with the Nazis, rounding up Jews and sending them to concentration camps. Nina's mother would invoke evil to explain these more horrific *sbagli*, and here they were in agreement.

How does one live in a world where the *sbagli* accumulate with no end in sight? Letizia and Nina's mother would answer by saying we should place our faith in Jesus Christ, who forgives our sins in this world and prepares us for a better, more perfect life in the next. Nina could never come to terms with that answer. It seemed too easy to give up on this world. There was power in learning to accept your *sbagli* and act in spite of them and in spite of the risks: to condemn the Mafia with Prosecuting Magistrates Falcone and Borsellino; to care deeply for our patients, like Drs. Ruggiero, Crespi, and even Ricciardi. To share our marrows with those who need them.

2

The R train links Bay Ridge to Manhattan and Queens via Manhattan. Rabbi Joseph found a seat in the conductor's car. Across from him sat a teenage boy with headphones on, his lips moving to music Joseph couldn't hear. Above the boy was an advertisement for a Park Avenue dermatologist: "You, too, can have clear, beautiful skin," the advertisement read. "Suck my cock," someone had scrawled under it.

Joseph still couldn't get over Sarah's chutzpah, how she managed to finagle information from the marrow registry and then try to remove his name from the donor list. He called the registry the next day, and sure enough, they had trouble locating his paperwork. It was only a few days ago, insisted Joseph, when he had spoken to a lovely woman there; they had, in fact, spoken at great length. "I'm sorry, Mr. Neiman," replied a man, neither lovely nor helpful. "If you'd like, I can give you the name and number of my supervisor."

The train lurched as it left the Fifty-Ninth Street station, thrusting Joseph into the metal side rail at the end of the row of seats. The teenage boy across from him, Joseph noticed, wasn't affected by the abrupt movement; he sat back and listened to his music as if nothing had happened.

Of course Joseph understood how deep the wounds went for Sarah's family. Her father would tense up whenever anyone mentioned the war. He could never forget nor forgive the people who had spat on him, starved him, and killed his parents. Only he never seemed to get as angry as Sarah—for him, it was more an unbearable sadness that washed over him and left him speechless. Maybe that's what fueled Sarah's anger: someone had to stand up for her father, for the losses he suffered.

Joseph tightened his grip on the side railing as the train picked up speed.

What he didn't understand was why Sarah couldn't see things from his point of view. He was suffering inside too. More and more, he wanted to bury himself in his books and not come out. He felt increasingly helpless, like he was falling into a deep, dark hole. Becoming a marrow donor seemed like a rope being lowered into the hole, a way out. Then suddenly, the rope was snatched away.

The teenager with the headphones exited at DeKalb Avenue. As the train clambered on, Joseph realized he missed the music playing on the boy's moving lips.

Luca woke just after 8:00 p.m. as the night shift came on. The last dose of antifungal medication had so depleted him he'd slept all afternoon. Still groggy, he could make out Nonna sitting in the chair next to him. He felt weak, achy in his arms and legs, and was having difficulty catching his breath. For the first time, he worried he didn't have enough strength to sit up in bed and show Nonna that he was okay. Maybe he really was as sick as Nina let on with her looks. *How sick?* he wondered. *Sick enough to die?* But only old people died. And he wasn't even in high school yet, and there was so much he wanted to do. If only that strong medicine had worked like Dr. Crespi said it would. Should he ask for something stronger?

As he watched his grandmother whispering a prayer, he managed a smile. "I feel better after my nap," he told her.

"I'm glad," said Nonna. "You were talking to your friend in your sleep."

"Orlando and I were discussing the horses at Signore Fabbio's. We agreed the Maremmano with the white streak above his nose would be perfect for me. Tell Nonno."

"I will," she said, caressing his forehead. "You feel hot. I hope the fever isn't back."

"No, it's the room that's hot. I don't have fever," he said. "Believe me, I know when I have fever."

His eyes felt heavy, so heavy it hurt trying to keep them open.

If only Orlando would come with his own Maremmano, the fastest horse in the world, and take him away from here.

Nina took a deep drag of her cigarette. She was glad to be outside the hospital. Another minute watching Luca sleep and Letizia cry, and she might have lost it. She felt jumpy, twitchy, as if her nerves and muscles were firing without any direction. It scared her.

"Nina." Carla had parked her car in the hospital lot and was heading toward her. "Are you okay?" she asked. "You sounded terrible on the phone."

"I fucked up," Nina said, breaking into tears.

"What are you talking about?" Carla took the cigarette from her friend's hand and stamped it out on the ground. "Let's sit down on the bench."

"I told them everything would turn out all right. I promised."

"It's not your fault."

"I gave them hope when there wasn't any to give."

"Calm down, Nina. You're shaking."

"Matteo was right at the oncology meeting. The boy was doomed. What was I thinking?"

Carla grasped Nina's shoulders to steady her. "You were thinking two steps ahead of everyone else, and because of you, the boy had a fighting chance. It's not your fault."

"You're wrong. Everything I touch turns to shit. One mistake after another, I can't help myself. Better keep away from me, Carla," she said, "or you'll go down with the ship too."

"Nonsense. We'll get through this."

Nina shook her head. *No,* she thought. *Not this time.* There had been mistakes in the past from which she'd somehow managed to recover, but this time, she was in way over her head.

For the fifth time that day, Giovanni tried the door to the municipal building in Favola's main square, determined to confess his secrets to the mayor. Still, no answer.

"He isn't in, signore," said Flavia Vitucci. She and her husband, Bartolomeo, owned the bar next door. She had been sweeping out front when she saw Giovanni. "He went to Milan and won't be back until Friday."

Giovanni cursed under his breath.

"How is Luca?" asked Flavia. Like everyone else in town, she was concerned about the boy's welfare. "I pray for him, signore, and hope he gets better. So full of life and energy, that boy. It's so dull around here when he's not chasing his friends through the square."

Giovanni scoffed. Dull, huh? Two years ago, her husband had come to the farm in a huff because Luca had stolen a piece of candy from his shop. What a self-serving ass Bartolomeo Vitucci was, just because he happened to be on the right side after the war, an anti-Fascist who fought with the resistance and remained involved in local politics ever since.

Then again, maybe Vitucci could be of some help. After all, he and his group were the ones who'd found the bodies in the woods that winter night and later took revenge on Lambertini and the other Fascists responsible for the massacre.

"Is your husband around?" he asked.

"No, he went to Turin to see his supplier."

It figures, thought Giovanni, although Vitucci's absence didn't upset him as much as the mayor's. Righteous Bartolomeo Vitucci had always looked down on him for not taking a side during the war, for not taking *his* side. He could only imagine what the man would say if he told him he hadn't gone to the convent in Genoa that Vitucci recommended, that the baby he and Letizia raised belonged to one of the refugees in the woods, a baby whose name had been written on a folded piece of paper that he purposely dropped in the snow.

"Are you all right, signore?" asked Flavia. "You look pale. Maybe you should sit down and rest."

Giovanni waved her off. How was it possible, he wondered, that just when he was ready to divulge the details of an old secret, suppressed and concealed for almost half a century, the mayor and Vitucci happened to be out of town, while Luca grew sicker by the day? How the hell would he find out about Paolo's family, if there were any relatives somewhere on this earth that might be able to help his grandson?

"Is that blood on your pants?" asked Flavia, glancing down at his leg. "*Dio mio*, yes. I'd better call Dr. Ruggiero."

Giovanni felt the warm, wet patch above his left knee. The wound must have opened up, but what did he care? He would take the next train to Milan. There, he would find someone who could help him. He pressed down hard on the leg as he hurried along, happy to extract every drop of pain and indifferent to the blood starting to seep down his pants. If he was unable to find the right person, he would not return to

Favola. There was a fat vessel underneath the muscle at one end of the wound. He would sever it once and for all and let the blood pour out until there was none left in his body.

Letizia watched her grandson sleep. He made a tinny noise when he exhaled. Not very different, she realized in horror, from the sound her mother had made in the days before her death. Giovanni, bless his heart, had put a bed downstairs so his sick mother-in-law wouldn't have to use the stairs. Letizia would sit at her side all day long. On the last day, the noise turned into an awful gargling that made it difficult for Letizia herself to breathe.

But her mother had been in her eighties. How could this happen to a young boy, only nine years old? A good, decent, intelligent boy. How was it possible?

She tightened her grip on the rosary beads. She had been a devout Catholic her entire life, going to church regularly, praying every day. The Blessed Virgin had answered her prayers so many times in the past. Why not now?

Luca shifted his position in bed, turning on his side, away from her.

Was there something she'd done to upset the Blessed Virgin? Dr. Ruggiero had made many strange comments to her in the past about Paolo's and Luca's red hair, about her husband's odd behavior, but she had always attributed them to the doctor's eccentricity. Maybe she was wrong and there was something to them. Why else would the Virgin turn against her?

"Next stop, Times Square," came the announcement on the train's loudspeaker. Joseph took a deep breath. He felt like a sneaky kid who knew he was doing something wrong, like Samuel must have felt when he went to the massage parlor with his friends.

The international bone marrow registry had offices in a building on Forty-Fourth Street next to the Belasco Theater. "I have an appointment with Nancy Wells," he told the receptionist.

Nancy Wells was an older woman with glasses and white hair. From the phone call, he had imagined someone much younger. "I'm glad you came in, Mr. Neiman."

Joseph once again explained that it was all a big mistake and he hadn't changed his mind. His wife was concerned for his safety. "I have a heart murmur."

"I'm sorry to hear that."

"It's not very serious. I had rheumatic fever as a child, but it's never been a problem. Besides, I cleared it with my doctor and have all the paperwork right here to prove it. I'm ready to proceed whenever you are. I ask only that you communicate directly with me from now on. I'm going to give you my number at work."

"Thank you, Mr. Neiman, thank you." Nancy Wells was positively beaming. "You know," she said, "I've been volunteering at the registry for three years and have never had a better job. It gives me such joy to meet people like you."

As he returned the woman's smile, all Joseph could think of was Sarah, how furious she would be with him for going behind her back, for doing something he knew would hurt her. Joseph had never done anything remotely like this in their twenty-five years of marriage, but he had no choice. He needed to give his marrow as much as the sick person in Italy needed to receive it; this transplant would save them both. He just hoped that when it was all over, Sarah would understand and forgive him.

On his way out, Joseph stopped and bought a pretzel from a street vendor. *Wipe off the salt,* he heard Sarah whispering in his ear. *It's bad for you.* Instead, he ran his tongue over the salt and took a big bite. Now that he had started down this path, there was no reason to hold back. In the next day or so, he thought as he chewed, he would sit down with

Samuel and tell him what he planned to do. The boy needed to realize that there were more important things than stealing from the tzedakah box and visiting massage parlors, matters of life and death, in fact. If only he could be made to appreciate that, then surely, he would change his ways.

Joseph polished off the rest of the pretzel, wiped his mouth with a napkin, and descended into the subway station. There was one final thing to do before the procedure: he needed to find Judith Saferstein, make sure her husband never laid another finger on her, urge her to leave him immediately. He couldn't have that on his conscience any longer.

Matteo Crespi had once walked the halls of Santa Cristina with a sureness in his step and head held high. Lately, he was dragging and slumping. Nothing had been going right, at work, at home, with Nina. So he hunkered down and tried to focus solely on his patients. If he could at least achieve some success on that front, it would pick him up.

He peered into the oculus of his microscope to inspect his newest patient's bone marrow smear. The young girl, who was admitted yesterday, bruised easily and complained of being tired, just like the Taviano boy. And just like the Taviano boy, he expected to find the deadly interloper in the magnificent dappled sea of marrow, the large purple blast cell of leukemia. Instead, the marrow looked deserted, with only a smattering of normal-appearing cells. Aplasia, not hyperplasia or neoplasia. A problem of production, not cancer. This was good news for the girl, since it was easier to treat than Luca's cancer.

"Dr. Crespi," said a voice behind him. "Phone call."

"Can you take a message?"

"It's Dr. Tosti from Genoa. He says it's urgent."

He rose from his desk at the back of the blood lab and took the phone from the technician's hand.

"Finally, some luck," said Tosti. "I just got a call from the United States. They found a marrow donor for Luca Taviano."

For a second, Matteo's heart jumped. Then he let out a sigh. "It may be too late. We're treating the boy for a fungal infection."

"Merda," Tosti cursed.

The line went uncomfortably silent.

"Listen," Tosti said finally. "If you can stabilize and transfer him to Genoa, we have a new, experimental antifungal medication. Provided we could get the fever down and make sure there's no organ involvement, I would be prepared to go ahead with the transplant."

Tosti was ten years younger than Matteo—young, enthusiastic, and aggressive, just as Matteo had once been, just as he would like to be again. "I'll do my best," he promised.

3

On September 7, Joseph lay on a gurney outside OR 3 at the Memorial Sloan Kettering Cancer Center. He shivered in the empty, brightly lit hallway, half-naked in the flimsy gown they'd given him to wear. He'd left home at six that morning. Sarah was not up yet, and he tiptoed out of the room so as not to wake her. He didn't even kiss her goodbye. God forgive him.

Samuel heard him on the stairs and ran down after him. "Are you sure about this, Dad?"

Joseph nodded.

"But you shouldn't be alone in the hospital," said Samuel. "I can come. There's nothing important going on at school today."

Joseph was surprised by Samuel's concern. It convinced him he made the right choice confiding in his son. Perhaps he should put himself in harm's way more often. Samuel was finally thinking about others more than himself.

"Don't worry—I'll be fine," said Joseph. "The doctor promised I'd be home before dinner."

"Mom's going to be mad."

She's going to be furious, Joseph thought as he shivered in the empty hospital hallway, wondering what the delay was about. He just hoped her anger wouldn't last too long.

Finally, an orderly appeared at his side, took hold of the gurney, and wheeled him into the operating room.

"Good morning, Mr. Neiman," said the surgeon. "The anesthesiologist is giving you a little something to make you sleep. He knows all about your heart murmur and will be monitoring you every step of the way. So close your eyes and try to relax."

The rabbi's body was covered by a sea of blue, sterile draping, except for an exposed circle around the right buttock. An assistant cleaned the skin with iodine and handed the surgeon a fifty-cubic-centimeter syringe fitted with a long, large-bore needle. The surgeon palpated the hip bone and inserted the needle into the skin. It went through the fat easily, but when it reached bone, the surgeon had to apply considerable pressure to penetrate the marrow cavity.

He hadn't done one of these procedures in a while and forgot how hard it was to extract marrow. *Like drilling for oil,* he thought. *The rabbi is going to have one sore* tuchas *tomorrow.*

The surgeon aspirated as much marrow as he could, filling his syringe and handing it off to a nurse. Then he grabbed a second syringe. He felt for another good spot and plunged the needle back into the patient's hip bone. He repeated this five times on the right side and five times on the left side, collecting approximately five hundred cubic centimeters of marrow, a little over a pint.

That should do it, thought the surgeon, wiping the sweat dripping from his brow with the back of his arm.

While the surgical team worked on Joseph, a technician from the bone marrow registry took the syringes to a laboratory on the second floor. There, the marrow was spun down to remove the fat and bone particles. The remainder—stem cells mixed with red cells, platelets, and white cells—was funneled into a sterile container and placed in a cooler filled with ice.

The transporter turned around to look at the cooler in the back of his van, wondering what he was carrying today—a kidney, a heart, a liver? Just then, the van hit a pothole on the Long Island Expressway and leaned perilously to one side. "This is some serious shit," he muttered to himself, tightening his grip on the steering wheel. "They don't pay us enough!"

The transporter arrived at JFK just in time and delivered his cargo to a representative from Alitalia, who took the cooler through special customs. After receiving clearance, the representative boarded a flight to Milan; passed through the passenger cabins, bearing the cooler in his arms; and dropped it off in the rear galley, where it was stowed at the bottom of the beverage cart. Eight hours later, the Boeing 747 touched down at Linate Airport. A member of the Genoa transplant team waited as the aircraft door opened. The cooler was taken to a car double-parked in front of the international arrivals terminal. A few minutes later, the car was on the Autostrada, speeding toward the cancer institute in Genoa.

Luca sat up in bed with difficulty. His grandparents were next to him, Letizia with one hand on her rosaries and the other caressing Luca's arm; Giovanni mute and dazed but, for the first time in weeks, feeling hopeful again; Nina Vocelli pacing back and forth across the small room. They had passed two major hurdles in the last two weeks: an aggressive fungal infection that would have probably killed Luca had it not been for the experimental medication he received at the cancer institute and a week of the grueling conditioning regimen—three days of high-dose chemotherapy and four days of total-body radiation. The combination had sapped nearly all his remaining strength and energy. Now—the biggest hurdle of all: the transplant.

They were in a special isolation wing. Everyone but Luca wore sterile gowns, masks, and gloves to minimize the risk of infection. On the walls hung photos of Luca's friends Franco and Mario, the Taviano farm, and pictures of horses that Nina had cut out from magazines.

They were relieved when Dr. Tosti finally arrived just after noon. It was hard to recognize anyone covered up in isolation gear except for Tosti because of his brown horn-rimmed glasses. "Here it is," he announced, holding up an IV bag. "Your new marrow."

Nina stared blankly at the bag filled with a yellowish liquid that looked like stracciatella soup. "That's it?" she asked.

"That's it. All the stem cells Luca needs to repopulate his marrow. We inject the cells into his vein, and eventually, they'll find their way to his bone cavities. Until then, we'll give him daily transfusions to maintain the blood counts."

Even Nina was surprised. To her, transplants meant general anesthesia and risky, complicated surgical procedures that involved large, solid organs like kidneys and hearts. In this case, though, it was just a simple, painless infusion of stracciatella soup into a vein.

"Ready, my friend?" the doctor asked his patient.

Luca nodded wearily, glancing over at his grandparents. The last few days had been bad, between the nausea and vomiting and shaking chills. At times, he just wanted to close his eyes and never wake up. Before, he took comfort in the thought that Orlando would come and rescue him, just like he did his best friends and so many other people in Favola. He wasn't so sure anymore.

Tosti walked over to the bed and pulled down Luca's shirt. The central line was just above the left clavicle. The doctor cleaned the middle port with an alcohol swab and inserted the IV line. "Here we go," said Tosti, opening the valve to start the infusion. "Now we wait."

The marrow from Rabbi Joseph entered Luca Taviano's bloodstream less than twenty-four hours after the rabbi was wheeled into the operating room at Sloan Kettering in New York. It contained stem cells—large, purple spheres with thin blue rims that didn't look much different from Luca's malignant lymphoblasts. They would circulate through Luca's veins until they were stopped by specialized cells that lined the blood vessels of his marrow cavities. Markers on the surfaces of Luca's vessel cells and the rabbi's stem cells would recognize each other and embrace, holding the stem cells in place while the rest of the blood flowed by. Chemical signals secreted by the vessel cells would then create an opening in the vessel wall, allowing the stem cells to squeeze through and enter the bone marrow cavity. There, they would find a new home, settle down, and hopefully start producing the red cells, white cells, and platelets needed to keep Luca alive.

In the best of circumstances, a patient had a 50 percent chance of survival. In Luca's case, the odds were worse—first, because his cancer wasn't in remission, and second, because of his recent fungal infection. Probably less than 25 percent. A crapshoot really—but it was his only option.

PART V: LETTERS

1992–1993

1

The noise woke him: voices, beeping, clattering. Rabbi Joseph opened his eyes and struggled to see. The mist again? No, more like a dense fog blocking out the light. He tried to get up, but his body felt heavy. "Where am I?"

"The recovery room," someone answered.

The voice sounded familiar.

"You just came back from surgery. The marrow harvesting. Everything's okay."

Now he remembered. The surgeon looking down at him, the blinding lights, the fluid moving through the IV, into his vein, making him sleepy, sleepy, then out. Through the fog, a figure materialized. "Samuel, is that you?"

"It's me, Dad."

He could see him now, standing beside the bed, his big brown eyes staring at him. "Shouldn't you be in school?" he asked.

"I came after classes ended."

"How did you get here? Does your mother know?"

"I took the subway."

Joseph noticed a tentativeness in Samuel's voice, different from the aggressive tone he usually took with his father. "You were worried about me?"

Samuel shrugged.

Joseph regarded his son. Samuel was almost as tall as he was now, but still had that round baby face, a knapsack strapped around his shoulders: a schoolboy, his boy, his son. The question popped out of his mouth so fast he couldn't stop himself: "Did you take the money?"

Samuel winced, then glanced at the woman standing next to him. Joseph hadn't noticed her before. "I'm sorry, I didn't—"

"That's quite all right, Mr. Neiman," said the nurse, patting Samuel on the back. "The anesthesia can be disorienting when you wake up after surgery. Try to relax. Like your son said, everything went perfectly."

Samuel was blushing.

"You'll be here for an hour or so, and then you can go home. You'll probably be a little tired and feel some pain, especially in the hip area. That's where they took the marrow. But I'm sure you'll be back to full speed in a few days."

He thanked the nurse, and when she left, he reached for Samuel's hand. "I'm glad you came."

"I didn't think you should be alone."

He wasn't alone, Joseph assured his son. Benny was coming to pick him up.

"He's in the waiting area now," said Samuel. "I got here a while ago. You were still sleeping, so I went to see Emily."

"That was thoughtful. When I'm feeling better, we can visit her together."

"She's not on the fifth floor anymore. They moved her to another ward. She's not doing well," Samuel said. "She didn't recognize me at first. Mrs. Nussbaum said she has a bad infection. It spread to her brain."

"I'm sorry."

Samuel nodded. "Mrs. Nussbaum couldn't stop crying. She said Emily was dying."

Joseph squeezed his son's hand. He could see that today's visit to the hospital had shaken him. "Sit down next to me," he said. Joseph wanted to tell Samuel that he understood, that life was full of sadness and suffering, and that his father couldn't always shield him from the sadness and suffering. Instead, he reached up and pushed the hair away from his son's eyes.

"I did it," Samuel said.

"What?"

"I took the money at school, Dad. It was wrong."

"Yes, it was."

2

On September 9, 1992, Luca Taviano lay on his hospital bed, his body emptied of life-sustaining marrow from the chemotherapy and radiation treatments. He was, in essence, dead, unless and until the syringe filled with Rabbi Joseph Neiman's marrow engrafted and started producing red cells, white cells, and platelets.

Thus began the agonizing period of waiting and watching the counts, beginning at zero—a zero white count, not one neutrophil or lymphocyte to fight infection—hoping and willing them to swiftly rise. Letizia and Giovanni rented an apartment across from the hospital. Nina Vocelli stayed with an old classmate from nursing school who worked on the pediatric floor. She had taken a leave of absence from Santa Cristina but would have readily quit if the request weren't granted.

Nina made up a schedule so that someone would be with Luca every minute of the day. They followed the isolation protocol to the smallest detail before entering his room, washing with iodine soap, wearing gowns, gloves, and caps. They took turns giving blood, even though only compatible blood could be administered to Luca, and it turned out that only Nina had the same blood type. Still, all of them were able to give platelets, and it comforted Giovanni and Letizia to know they were doing everything they could to maintain Luca's counts at tolerable levels.

The first complication of the transplant was painful sores that developed in Luca's mouth. Each day, a new sore appeared until his throat was riddled with them and he was no longer able to speak. Several times a day, a nurse would come in and squirt cold water into his mouth to soothe the pain.

While she waited and worried, Letizia clutched her rosary beads and prayed to the Blessed Virgin. Giovanni stood rooted in the corner of Luca's room, silent and still, except when he reached down to scratch his left leg. Nina smoked two packs of cigarettes a day and made friends with the house staff so they would alert her of test results. Thankfully, Dr. Tosti appeared every afternoon with a cheerful expression on his face, regardless of improvement or setback. "Everything according to plan," he would say.

On the fifth day, the white cell count finally rose above the zero line. By the tenth day, the platelet count had stabilized, lowering the risk of bleeding. The donor stem cells had reached their new homes and were dividing and starting to repopulate Luca's empty bone marrow cavities.

By the seventeenth day, the mouth sores had dried up, and Luca was able to talk again, though in a hoarse voice that sounded nothing like him. On the twenty-ninth day, he rode the stationary bike they'd brought in. The fourth week, the second complication arose: a red, flaky rash that the nurse identified as graft-versus-host disease—white cells from the rabbi's marrow were attacking Luca's body. They panicked, fearing the worst. "It's okay," Tosti reassured them, "a little GVHD is beneficial, to kill any of the malignant lymphoblasts that might have survived the chemotherapy. As long as we keep it contained," he said with an exaggerated tilt of his chin. "Right, my friend?" Luca tilted back, smiling. A new medicine was added to his ever-expanding drug regimen.

Little by little, Luca recovered. While he improved physically, though, he grew restless in the confines of his small room. "I don't want to stay here anymore," he cried to Nina on his forty-eighth day in captivity.

"Me neither," said Nina, "but it won't be much longer. How about telling me a story? You never finished the one about Franco's run-in with the wild boar near the Castle, how he managed to leap over the wall at the last minute."

"It's true. Orlando distracted the boar just as it caught up to Franco and was about to bite him on the leg. It was very close."

At the end of the eighth week, Dr. Tosti announced that the critical period was over; he was happy with Luca's progress. "How would you like to go home on Friday?" he asked. "You'll need to be careful of course. You'll have a special diet, and certain things will remain off limits for a while, certain cheeses and undercooked meat. You won't be able to go near the animals for another two months. Maybe sooner," he amended himself when he saw Luca frown. "I know how hard it is to separate a cowboy from his new horse. Right, my friend? You'll follow up once a week with Dr. Crespi at Santa Cristina, and then I'll see you back in Genoa in six weeks. That will be the one-hundred-day mark. Once we pass that, you're golden. Got it?"

Luca nodded, pumping his fist in the air. Letizia went over and smothered her grandson in a hug. Giovanni smiled.

It was the first time Nina had seen Giovanni smile.

3

Rabbi Joseph heard them upstairs when he walked in: Samuel reading from the Torah portion for his bar mitzvah, Sarah coaching him along. "The pitch needs to be higher here," she said. "Then pause before continuing." His son would be sitting at the desk in his bedroom, Sarah behind him, leaning over the chair. They practiced every evening at the same time.

Two months had passed since the marrow harvesting. At first, Sarah was just as angry at Samuel. "You deceived me, both of you," she said. Yet she had forgiven Samuel, not Joseph. She focused all her energy on the upcoming bar mitzvah and would consult with Samuel—not Joseph, never Joseph—on every aspect of planning, from the menu and seating arrangements to the flowers and band options. It drew them closer.

Joseph waited in the kitchen for the coaching session to end. When Sarah came down and saw him sitting at the table, with his winter coat on, she nodded tersely.

"I'm thinking," he started, "that the two of us could go to the Catskills for the weekend, to that nice place by the lake." He had tried to talk to her many times, had written letters of apology, but all his attempts fell on deaf ears. Maybe a change of scenery would help.

"No."

"We can't go on like this. You barely speak to me anymore."

"We speak when it's necessary," she said, wiping down the countertop.

"Sarah, please."

She put down the sponge. "I can't help it. Every time I look at you, I get angry. You did something that you knew would hurt me. What's even worse, you lied about it."

There was no getting around it, no explaining himself. "It's true," he admitted, "but I didn't have a choice. I knew if I told you, you'd try to stop me."

Sarah shook her head and didn't say anything. She sat down across from him and tried to look stern, but Joseph could see she was more upset than angry. "I used to sit at this table with Penny and hear her talk about her husband—the letters he wrote to that other woman, the receipts for the hotels. One second she'd be furious, the next sobbing. She couldn't believe the affair had gone on for so long, that she could be so blind. All the while, I'd think how lucky I was, that nothing like that could ever happen in my house."

"You're right. Arthur was a despicable man. I would never—"

"Oh, but you did, Joseph. You betrayed me. It's not so different really."

"How can you say that?" he asked.

"When Penny confronted Arthur, he denied it. Then he begged her forgiveness. 'For the sake of the children,' he pled. I started to think that maybe she should forgive him. But she couldn't. Because every time she looked at him, she saw him lying to her, and it was a blade across her face. That's how I feel about what you did."

Joseph closed his eyes and breathed in deeply as he did during prayer at shul. In his head, he replayed the night he came home from the hospital. Sarah opened the front door and turned white when she saw him, Benny supporting him on one side, Samuel on the other. He was still woozy from the anesthesia, his buttocks burned with pain, and he dreaded how Sarah would react. "My God, what happened?" she cried. They walked him upstairs to the bedroom and laid him in bed. Benny excused himself and left Samuel to explain the day's events. Sarah was beside herself, not with fury as he'd imagined, but worry. "His lips are blue," she whispered. "Something's wrong. Maybe it's his heart."

"I'm fine," he kept telling her, but she didn't believe him. Nor did she believe Samuel, who was at the hospital when the doctor discharged his father and told them there was nothing to worry about. Sarah called Dr. Sokel and insisted he come immediately.

She was so worked up she didn't stop sighing or pacing. She brought her husband a glass of water, took an extra blanket from the closet, laid a wet towel over his forehead. It wasn't until Sokel arrived, listened to her husband's heart, and assured her everything was fine that she could breathe easily again. "Thank God," she said.

He remembered saying the same thing under his breath. Sarah wasn't mad at him. Her concern for his well-being overshadowed her anger. She would forgive him. *Thank God.*

The next morning, he awoke to find her packing clothes in a valise. "What are you doing?" he asked.

"Leaving."

"Leaving?"

"You lied to me," she said. "You and Samuel both."

"But, Sarah, that's not true. I never—"

"I'm sorry, Joseph, but I can't be in this house right now."

Sarah stayed at Penny's house for an entire week. When she returned, she kept their interactions to a minimum.

Joseph opened his eyes and looked at his wife. "Do you remember the day in shul when I couldn't finish morning services?" he asked. "I told you I was sick with the flu. It's true, I had all the symptoms of flu—the headaches, dizziness, lack of energy—but they didn't come from a virus. It was my mind that was sick, so dark and hopeless. That morning in shul, I felt like someone was holding me underwater and I couldn't breathe. I didn't have the strength to go on."

He waited to see whether his words had any effect.

"I was depressed, Sarah," he said. "But I was afraid to tell you. I was ashamed."

She looked at him without expression.

"Sharing my marrow with someone who desperately needed it seemed like a way out of the darkness. It would help me, give me hope again."

He reached out for Sarah's hand, but she held it back.

4

There was a chill in the air when Nina stepped out of her apartment building just past dawn. It tickled the inside of her nose, a clean, bracing blast of cold air. Winter was approaching, and that was just fine with her.

Passing the salumeria at the end of the block with its familiar smell of cured meats and sharp cheeses, Nina waved to Boninno Jr. as he set up shop. She turned right on Via Mazzini and entered the café, where she and Carla met before work. As soon as Lorenzo saw her, he filled a portafilter basket with ground coffee, leveled it, and turned on his machine.

"Big day today?" he asked, handing her a steaming cup of espresso.

Nina nodded. "The one-hundred-day mark. A milestone in a transplant. Most bad things happen during the first three months. What a relief that's over." She tipped the cup in Lorenzo's direction and downed it.

Lorenzo clenched his fists like he did when Juventus scored a goal. The barista had been following the story of the young boy from Favola ever since he was admitted to the hospital last spring. Time and again, he had seen the dejected expression on Nina's and Carla's faces and had been afraid to ask what happened. Finally, some good news.

"Here," he said, taking out a set of keys from the cash register. "The car is parked across the street."

She slid into the front seat of Carla's old Cinquecento, turned on the ignition, and headed to Favola.

A milestone, thought Nina, but the danger was not over by any means. They still had the graft-versus-host disease to manage, and Luca's immune system would be weak for a long time to come. Plus, there was the chance that some of the leukemic cells could return.

One step at a time, Nina told herself as she passed the hospital. Tosti was an excellent doctor and had been right on target up to this point. He would get them past the next milestone and the one after that.

She beeped the horn as she pulled up to the Taviano farm. Luca opened the front door, bundled up in a jacket and scarf and wearing a surgical mask. His grandparents stood behind him. Letizia held out a wrapped bundle of bread and pastries. "In case you're hungry on the way."

Giovanni patted his grandson on the head. "Don't be too long," he said. "We have work to do in the fields."

Nina assured them they would be back before noon. She buckled Luca's seat belt, and off they went.

"Your grandfather looks so much better," said Nina.

Luca nodded. "He doesn't need the cane anymore."

"I'm glad. And you? How are you doing?"

"Good," he replied, gazing out the side window.

Nina could tell he didn't really mean it. "Don't be upset. You don't feel normal yet, I understand, having to wear the mask and not being able to care for the animals. But we have to focus on the positives. You just passed the one-hundred-day mark. That's big!"

"Yeah."

From everything Nina read about the transplant process, this period was often the toughest. After weeks in an isolation room, weeks of waiting for the counts to rise and worrying about complications, patients were sick of being sick. They also expected that they'd be a lot further along. What they weren't told was how deconditioned they would be; it could take months to regain their strength. Nina would have to be more encouraging.

"Listen, we're over halfway there. Another couple of months and there'll be no restrictions. When are they bringing over the horse?"

"On my birthday. March 11."

"Perfect. By then, the weather will be better, and you'll be ready to ride like a real cowboy."

"Dr. Tosti said no riding until my immune system recovers."

"Are you kidding? You just got a supercharged bone marrow infusion. I'm not worried."

He smiled for the first time that day, then removed a cornetto from Nonna's bundle and carefully picked off the chocolate topping. "Want one?"

"No, thanks," she said. "Hey, cowboy, isn't that the Castle over there?"

They were passing the ridge on the outskirts of Favola, where the old Roman wall stood. A stray cat was perched atop one of the crumbling stones, next to the Italian flag Mario had planted.

"I'm sure of it now," said Luca.

"Sure of what?"

"For a while I thought he'd deserted me. But now I know Orlando was there the whole time. He was behind it."

She glanced over at him.

"The bone marrow transplant, I mean. Orlando was behind it."

Nina had to smile. Still, he had a point. The marrow did, in fact, come from overseas, just like Orlando. They didn't know the donor's name, or even if it was a he, or how old he or she was. Only that the donor lived in the United States and would remain anonymous after the transplant, unless he or she agreed to reveal more information.

"I wish I could thank the donor," said Luca. "He saved my life."

Nina paused. For the past three months, they'd been so intent on the minute details of the transplant—monitoring the fever charts and blood counts, watching for signs of infection—that they hadn't considered the person who made it all possible. They hadn't, but Luca had.

"He's inside me now, Nina. I can feel it."

"You can?" Again, Nina was struck by the boy's words. Yet the more she thought about it, the more they didn't seem so far-fetched. Luca was no longer only Luca. He was—what did Tosti call it?—a chimera, a mixture or hybrid, like the creatures in Greek myths. There was, in a sense, another person inside him—someone else's living stem cells that had traveled over mountains and across oceans to enter his body. She wondered if all transplant recipients felt this way or just the more imaginative ones. "Let's talk to Dr. Tosti. Maybe at some point you can contact your donor and thank him—or her—in person."

Since there was little traffic on the Autostrada, they made good time. They had just passed Vercelli, the spot where Nina had pulled over four months ago on the way to Genoa for the first time, Luca's chart and blood sample on the passenger seat, the cow staring at her blankly from the field as she cried over Matteo.

Lately, she had been so busy that she hardly thought about him. Her anger had mostly subsided. The truth was, Matteo had been supportive these last few months. More than supportive. He lied to the chief of medicine when Romano threatened to fire Nina, said it was he who first contacted Tosti and sent over the records, not Nina. He worked tirelessly to halt the progression of Luca's fungal infection and prepare him for transfer to Genoa. After the transplant, he came to visit Luca in the hospital and donated blood.

"Hey, you know that you have some of my cells inside you too, right? My red cells and platelets."

"I know. I can feel them," he said, patting his belly.

After eating every last bit of chocolate topping, he handed her the cornetto. "You have the rest. Nonna will be upset if you don't try one."

She was happy to share the pastry with Luca, just as she was once happy to share her blood.

Those were the scariest days of the transplant, when the only thing keeping Luca alive were the daily transfusions. Carla drove to Genoa every week, occasionally with her husband, once with her oldest boy, Fabrizio. One afternoon, the two of them were sitting in the blood-drawing room, an IV in each of their arms, when Carla started crying. She said it reminded her of the time Fabrizio had meningitis as a child, confined to a crib that looked like a cage, IVs attached to his tiny arms, the doctors unsure whether he would survive or not. She had cursed, cried, and could barely breathe at times, as if her own life depended on the survival of her child. "That's when I realized," Carla told Nina, "the bond I had with Fabrizio was different. It went deeper than anything I ever had with my parents or even my husband. I could kill for Fabrizio. Or be killed. There was nothing I wouldn't do for him."

"I understand," Nina said.

"You do?"

"I feel the same about Luca. I know it sounds strange—he's not even my child."

"Not really," said Carla. "I always knew you would make a good mother. The way you took care of me in nursing school. The way you are with patients at the hospital. It doesn't surprise me at all."

Nina looked over at Luca sitting in the passenger seat. His hands were back inside Nonna's bundle, peeling the chocolate off another cornetto, passing it under his mask into his mouth. It was good to see that his appetite had returned.

"I'm glad you and I can hang out with each other," she said to him, "even if it's only going to the doctor. I promise, when you get better, we'll do more fun things."

"Maybe you could come and live with us at the farm. There's a spare room. Nonna said she'd fix it up for you."

Nina smiled and stroked his head. "I'm not so sure that's a good idea, even if your grandfather is feeling better. But don't worry, you'll be seeing a lot of me. I'm thinking of getting my own horse. You could teach me how to ride. What do you say, cowboy?"

5

Rabbi Joseph sat back in his chair on the podium. He had been on edge since the day started, but now that Samuel had finished reading from the Torah—beautifully, without a single mistake—and was taking out his notes for the speech, Joseph could relax. He tried to get Sarah's attention. She was sitting in the front row, beaming.

They'd almost had to cancel the bar mitzvah because of a blizzard the day before. A record twenty-six inches of snow fell in New York, prompting a citywide shutdown. Fortunately, the nor'easter moved up the coast and out of the city by midnight, and Benny Levin was able to hire a team of young boys to shovel the sidewalk and front steps early that morning. There was barely any seating left, a testament to the congregation's feelings for their rabbi and his family.

"Thank you for coming despite the weather," Samuel began his speech.

His son, mused Joseph, his only child. Maybe if they had had others, it would have been easier. Instead, they'd invested all their hopes and dreams in Samuel. When he didn't live up to their expectations, they took it personally. But recently, things had taken a turn for the better. While he still argued with some of his teachers and butted heads with other boys in his class, Samuel seemed to be taking school more seriously and had studied diligently for his bar mitzvah.

You see, Sarah, he wanted to leap down from the podium and whisper in her ear, *our boy is going to be okay.*

Samuel began by explaining the day's reading. Terumah told the story of God telling Moses how to construct the tabernacle "so that he can dwell among his people." It was a heavily detailed and, arguably, boring section of Exodus that Samuel tried to make sound exciting by raising and lowering the pitch of his voice as if he were acting in a school play.

"'Two and a half cubits long, a cubit and a half wide, and a cubit and a half high . . . ,'" he intoned dramatically.

This enthusiasm for detail was all Sarah. His wife remembered everyone's name and birthday, likes and dislikes, slights and generosities. The details were critical, and there was no room for error. She approached morality in the same fashion: there was a right and a wrong. No in-between.

"'The wood of the tabernacle should be acacia, covered with gold on all sides, then adorned with bowls, ladles, jars, jugs . . .'"

While the rabbi didn't always agree with his wife's black-and-white views about the world, he was beginning to think that her approach might be better for Samuel, at least for now. There would be time for his son to daven over nuance. At this point in his life, he needed clear directions.

"'The dwelling place should be enclosed by ten curtains of fine twisted linen in blue, purple, and scarlet . . .'"

Emily's illness had had a profound effect on Samuel. He was shaken by her collapse onstage and the months following as she struggled with cancer. He visited her in the hospital often and saw how she and her family suffered. When she died, he went up to his room and cried through the night. "It isn't fair," he'd complained to his father afterward. "She was the best person I knew."

"Where in the desert," Samuel asked the congregation, "would the Jews find such precious materials to build this exquisite tabernacle?"

Emily's death had shaken all of them. Sarah had refused Joseph's offer to spend the weekend in the Catskills and remained unmoved by his admission that he'd been on the brink of depression. But the day of Emily's funeral, as they watched the casket being lowered into the ground, she took his hand and held it tight. It was the first time in a long while that he felt connected to her, connected to her grief as their son leaned against his father's chest and wept.

"God said to the Hebrews," continued Samuel, glancing up from his notes, "let everyone who is *nediv lev*, generous in their hearts, come and bring materials."

Joseph and Sarah's efforts on behalf of Judith Saferstein also drew them closer. After Joseph convinced the board to sever ties with her abusive husband and Judith to sue for divorce, they helped Judith find an apartment far away from Zev Saferstein. "It belongs to a friend who lives in Israel," said Joseph. "He assured me you could stay as long as you wish." They visited her frequently to make sure she was okay. Sarah prepared meals for her and brought challah from Levitsky's bakery. "You'll get through this," she assured Judith.

"The building of the *mishkan* was an actual event," said Samuel. "But the story can also be taken metaphorically. In order for God to dwell on earth, to dwell among his believers, a structure of great beauty must be created, one that depends on those that are *nediv lev*, generous in their hearts."

Samuel was nearing the conclusion of his speech. Joseph had hoped to help his son put the Torah passage in a broader perspective, but Samuel insisted on doing it by himself.

"There are many such people here in temple today. My mother, who organized the bone marrow drive for Emily Nussbaum last summer, who went to the hospital week after week to spend time with Emily and her family, to donate blood. It is through generous acts like these that we draw closer to God and God to us. Emily lost her battle with leukemia last month," he said, his voice starting to crack, "but I'm sure she appreciated the generosity of my mother and all of you sitting here today who supported her during her illness."

You see, Sarah, Joseph wanted to shout from the podium, *what a good boy we've raised.*

"My father, too, is a *nediv lev* and a hero to me. His blood type turned out to be a match for someone in Italy with cancer, someone who needed a bone marrow transplant. In September, he donated part of his marrow to that patient—a complete stranger. It's a painful procedure that comes with risks. Recently, he learned that the patient survived the transplant and is alive today."

Joseph swelled with emotion.

"The Babylonian Talmud says, 'Whoever destroys a single life is as guilty as if he had destroyed the entire world; and whoever rescues a single life earns as much merit as though he had rescued the entire world.' I hope that one day I will be like my mother and my father, so generous in my heart as to draw God down from the heights to dwell among us."

Joseph brushed tears from his eyes. Sarah was doing the same. You could generally count on Joseph and Samuel to cry, but not Sarah—she was the stoic in the family. She looked up and embraced her husband with her gaze, and in that moment, Joseph felt a surge of longing pass between them. Was Sarah finally ready to forgive him?

Samuel folded his notes, went over to his father, and hugged him.

Today Samuel became a man, and in his first act as a man, he, too, performed a most generous act: helping heal the wounds that had threatened to tear his home apart. "Come," said Joseph, "it's time to celebrate."

6

They went to Santa Cristina early to visit Dr. Ruggiero before Luca's appointment with Dr. Crespi. The old man had tripped over one of his cats and had broken his hip. Letizia hoped that a freshly baked cake and a visit with Luca would raise his spirits.

Strange to find a doctor lying in a hospital ward, thought Giovanni when they arrived at his bed. Ruggiero looked out of character in a worn, rumpled gown.

"Ah, the Tavianos," he said, raising himself up on his pillow, "one of my favorite families in Favola. But who is this with you? I don't recognize the boy."

Letizia smiled, her hand on Luca's head. "We hardly recognize him either, now that he doesn't need a mask anymore and has gotten so strong."

"Come closer so I can see you, boy. My eyes are not very good anymore."

Luca stood his ground, not wanting to get any nearer to the old man with his rotten banana teeth. "I'm not *boy*," he said defiantly. "My name is Luca."

"Luca!" gasped Letizia.

"That's quite all right, signora. The boy is his old salty self again. A good sign," he said with a smile. "A very good sign."

"It's been over one hundred days since the transplant," Letizia said with pride.

"Excellent news," he said, taking the cake from Letizia's hands. "How I love a little sweet now and then. Ah, do I smell a little *fragoline di bosco* under that delicate crust?"

Letizia nodded. "Luca's favorite."

"Yes, now I recognize the boy. Who could forget that beautiful red hair? Not many boys like him in these parts, hey, Giovanni?"

Giovanni pretended not to hear as he ran his hand through Luca's thick curls, his hair now almost fully grown in.

"Delicious as always," said Ruggiero, breaking off another piece of cake. "I can't tell you how happy I am that the transplant went so well. I hear the donor is from abroad. Very interesting," he said, glancing at Giovanni. "Maybe it's not just a matter of chance. Do you ever wonder if the donor is related in some way?"

Giovanni abruptly removed his hand from Luca's head. "Like I told you a million times, Paolo was—"

"Yes, yes, I know all about your son, Paolo," said Ruggiero.

"Come, Luca," Giovanni urged, "we're going to be late for your appointment."

Luca was halfway out of the ward before his grandparents turned to go. Ruggiero reached out and grabbed Giovanni's hand. "Stay a bit more, my friend. Your company makes me feel better."

"Of course, Giovan, you stay," said Letizia. "We'll meet you downstairs."

"How's the leg?" asked Ruggiero.

Giovanni muttered under his breath. He had woken up in a good mood, as he had for weeks now. After all the bad luck raining down, things had taken a turn for the better, for the miraculous. Giovanni once again dared to believe that the curse might be over. He began praying before bed and going to church again.

Ruggiero's needling was putting a damper on his mood, as did the reminder of his leg. He hadn't visited his old friend in months; by then, the wound had turned into a hardened, gnarled white scar.

"Funny," went on Ruggiero, "how we have that in common. First your leg causing so much trouble and now mine. Well, I'm glad to see you don't require the cane anymore."

Giovanni began inching away from the bed.

"But I'm warning you, my friend, the leg won't remain silent forever. One of the most important skills in my profession is prognosis, the prediction of what will happen to a patient going forward. From everything I've observed, I expect the wound will open up again, sooner or later."

Giovanni glared at Ruggiero.

"It doesn't give me pleasure to say this, Giovanni, and there's a chance I won't be around to help if it does act up again. My own prognosis is not so good either. I'm an old man, not much longer for this world."

Giovanni was growing increasingly restless.

"Listen to me, not as your doctor but as your friend. The results of the genetic testing are bound to come up again. Your grandson is a smart boy, just like Paolo once was. One day, he'll start asking questions. He'll want to know more about his father, where he came from. What will you tell him?"

Giovanni shook his head. Why would it come up again? There was no reason to search for relatives anymore—the transplant was over. Nor was there any chance that the broken bits of the past could be pieced together. The Fascist killer Pietro Lambertini was long dead, the man in the tattered coat too. They were all dead. *Pop, pop, pop.*

Later that night, Letizia came over and sat down next to him in the living room. The TV was on, one of the popular new game shows featuring the dancing girls in bikinis, but Giovanni wasn't paying attention.

"You seemed distracted today, Giovan, especially after our visit with Dr. Ruggiero."

"The man is a troublemaker," he said. "He should worry about his own problems and leave us alone."

Letizia sighed. "Believe me, I don't want any trouble either. The Blessed Mother has been good to us. You heard Dr. Crespi today. He couldn't be happier. Luca's counts are normal; he's gaining weight; they're stopping the medication for the graft-versus-host disease; Luca might be able to return to school next month. Why would I want to ask questions now?"

Exactly, thought Giovanni.

"But what if Dr. Ruggiero is right? Nina told us that the best chance of finding a bone marrow match was from a relative, someone who shares his blood. Is it possible the donor might be related to Luca?"

"No," he snapped.

"How do you know? It's true we adopted Paolo from the sisters. But where was he born, who were his parents? They must have some record, no?"

Giovanni didn't answer.

"That day I found you at the train station, Giovan, after I got the call from Dr. Crespi that they secured a donor for Luca. Signora Vitucci told me where to look. She was worried about you, remember?"

He didn't want to remember that day, when he went to the mayor's office to confess and the mayor wasn't there.

"You never told me where you were going. The convent maybe, to try to find out more about Paolo, to see if you could help Luca?"

Letizia gripped Giovanni's hand tighter, but he wouldn't look her directly in the eye.

"Not that it mattered in the end—our prayers were answered, a donor was found. Still, maybe we should talk to the sisters anyway. We can go together. All of us, even Luca. Maybe it's time to tell him about his father, that he wasn't our natural child but a gift from the sisters. I've always wanted to thank them."

He shook his head and withdrew his hand. Shivering, he recalled the bitter cold of that long-ago night, the folded piece of paper, the ink running in the snow.

The boy will want to know more about his father, Giovanni. What will you tell him?

7

The letter was waiting for Rabbi Joseph the first week of April. It was written in Italian, and he could only make out a few words. Enclosed was a picture of a young boy with red hair, standing beside a horse. "He's adorable, but nothing like I expected," said Sarah when he showed it to her. "He looks like the Rosenbaum boy in Samuel's Hebrew school class."

The next day, Joseph took the letter to Father Lazzaro so he could translate it. They sat in the front pew of Saint Peter's. The priest put on his glasses and began to read:

March 25, 1993

Dear Donor,
My name is Luca Taviano, and I live with my grand-
mother and grandfather in Favola, in the province of
Piedmont. It is over six months since my transplant, and
I'm almost back to normal now, thanks to you and Dr.
Tosti. Grandpa gave me the horse you see in the picture
two weeks ago for my tenth birthday so that I can learn
how to herd cattle like a cowboy. One day I hope to thank
you in person and give you a ride on my horse. I send also
love from my grandmother and grandfather, my nurse

Nina, and my best friends Mario and Franco. We pray for you every Sunday at San Stefano, the church in Favola.
Love,
Luca

PS: I have a friend named Orlando who looks out for me and other people when they're in trouble. We meet at the Castle outside Favola. Well, not exactly face-to-face. Mostly in my thoughts, though I've never told Nina or Grandma that because I'm afraid they won't believe he's real. Do you happen to know Orlando, or if not, do you have any friends like him?

"My, my, Rabbi," declared Father Lazzaro when he finished reading the letter. "Orlando, hmm? I wonder if he's heard of Ariosto. *Orlando Furioso* was his masterpiece, the story of one of Charlemagne's knights, who defended the faith against the infidels and fell in love with the beautiful Angelica. Is it possible that you know this fascinating character?"

Rabbi Joseph laughed. "No, I'm not familiar with the knight in question, but would certainly like to know this fascinating boy."

Father Lazzaro nodded. "From what you told me, the genetics of the matching process are very specific. Do you think it's possible the child is somehow related to you?"

Joseph had asked himself the same question, especially after seeing the picture of the boy. But in his letter, Luca said that he went to church every Sunday. "I don't see how," said Rabbi Joseph. "Both sides of my family came to the United States from Hungary before the First World War. There was never mention of anyone marrying outside the faith or of any relatives settling in Italy."

It was late afternoon, and the church was empty, its narrow, high-ceilinged aisles dark and dank with a faint smell of incense in the air, very different from the more open, brightly lit synagogue. Breathing in the heavy church air, he began to wonder whether he was thinking about this all wrong. Even if he weren't directly related to Luca Taviano—or if the relatedness went too far back to track or even if there was never one at all and the genetic similarities happened by pure chance—they were still related. The Catholic boy in Favola and the Jewish rabbi in Brooklyn shared important genes, and now they shared the same blood. They might not be members of the same tribe as defined by today's sectarian standards, but they were members of the same tribe on a more fundamental level. Here was the perfect example of the blurring of boundaries that separated people: we are all connected.

Joseph shared the insight with his friend.

"You're right," said Father Lazzaro. "What a shame we need the extraordinary circumstance of a bone marrow transplant to see this."

"I wish my wife felt that way," said Rabbi Joseph. "She can't let go of her bitterness toward Italy. And from the postage on the letter, the Tavianos live in the North, the very same area where Sarah's father and grandparents were captured during the war."

Father Lazzaro hadn't forgotten the stories Rabbi Joseph told him about the internment camp at Fossoli and the later deportation of Sarah's grandparents to Auschwitz. "As an Italian, it makes me ashamed."

"Yet I'm indebted to you for showing me that there was another side to the story. The book you lent me by the professor at Columbia in particular. I hadn't realized it was better to be a Jew in Italy than anywhere else in Europe, that the majority of the Italian Jewish population survived the war. I've pointed this out to Sarah, but it's still hard for her to accept."

"I understand."

"But here," he said, holding up the letter in his hand, "is the perfect opportunity to heal old wounds. Maybe we could visit Italy one day. It would be good for Sarah to see the internment camp with her own eyes. Samuel too. At the same time, we could visit some of the places where Jews were protected from the Germans."

Father Lazzaro thought it was an excellent idea. "I will introduce you to Professor Benedetti. Perhaps the two of us could join you. We could consider it an expansion of our bridge-building efforts. The war was a difficult time in Italy that most people, including many of my relatives still living there, would rather forget. But remembering that period, in its totality—the good and the bad—will not only be important for your family, but for Christians and Jews alike. We can hold you and the Taviano boy as an example of our connectedness."

Joseph could hardly contain his excitement. How different from just a few months ago, when he'd felt burdened and overwhelmed by all the bad things happening at home and in the world. Ever since he'd shared his marrow with the boy from Favola, life had become better. His son was growing up, Sarah and he were getting along again, and his quest to bring together different religions was about to receive a second wind.

8

It was May again in Favola, a year since Luca's visit to Ruggiero's haunted house. The market in the central piazza was filled with stands displaying fresh *carciofi* and *asparagi*, *limoni* and *arance*. And of course *fragoline di bosco*. By then, Tosti had lifted all eating restrictions for Luca. He no longer had to wear a mask and was able rejoin his class at school. In a few months, he would receive his vaccines and be completely back to normal.

On Saturday morning, he woke to a surprise. Nina had dropped off a letter for him from Brooklyn, New York. She had hoped to be there when he opened it, since she had spent a great deal of effort pressing the Italian marrow registry to allow communication between the recipient and donor, but she had to get back to the hospital.

"Should I read it to you?" asked Nonna.

Luca shot up from bed. At last, word from overseas. Luca could barely sit still, yet he held up his hand and shook his head. "No, Nonna, it's best I take it to the Castle and read it there. I promise to tell you everything when I return."

Luca called Franco and Mario and told them to get dressed and meet him as quickly as possible. He grabbed his bike from the shed and rode along the eastern road leading out of Favola to the old Roman wall. On the near end, the wall rose gradually with the land. At its highest point, the three friends had carved out a circular area in the ground where they would sit and look out over the wall, scanning the countryside for marauders. On one side of the circle, Mario attached the Italian flag, and on the other, Franco put up the Juventus team flag. Luca nestled into his usual spot, in the middle of the circle, where he would sit between his two friends. *What is taking them so long?*

Overcome by curiosity, he opened the letter and began reading. Since it was written in a formal style, he had to read it a second time before he understood what it said.

"Hey, you were supposed to wait for us," Franco called out, ditching his bike by the side of the road. He raced up the hill, the chubbier Mario trailing behind. "So?" they asked, sliding into their spots within the circle.

Luca was still digesting the words he'd just read. "I don't think he knows Orlando."

"No? But he must be connected to him in some way. Is he a cowboy at least?"

Luca shook his head. "He's a rabbi."

"A what?"

Luca had wondered the same thing when he read the letter. Fortunately, his donor, whose name was Joseph Neiman, explained it for him. A rabbi was like a priest for Jewish people. He worked in a synagogue, not very different from a church. His good friend Father Lazzaro was a priest at the nearby Saint Peter's Church. The priest translated the rabbi's words into Italian because he didn't speak the language.

"Jewish?" said Mario. "I don't know any Jewish people. Do you?"

No, he didn't. The man from overseas who gave him marrow neither knew Orlando nor was a cowboy. He was a priest for Jewish people.

"That's really weird," said Franco.

"But listen to this." Luca began reading from the rabbi's letter: "'In my experience, everyone wants to believe in someone like Orlando, although people may have different names for him. We all need to put

169

our hope and trust in someone strong and good who helps us in times of need.'"

Franco seemed confused. "Huh?"

Mario said, "Sounds like this Jewish priest is talking about God. But Orlando isn't God. No way."

"We were also wrong about where my donor lives," said Luca. "Not London, Franco. And not Brazil, Mario. He's from America. Brooklyn, New York."

Mario and Franco both thought that was pretty cool. They knew America mostly from the music of Michael Jackson and Madonna and movies like *E.T.* and *Star Wars*. And of course the popular place for hamburgers in Milan that they'd heard about from Gianvito, the one with the yellow arches on the sign.

"The rabbi has never been to Italy, but says that he's always had an *affinità* for the country and its culture. *Affinità*, what do you suppose it means?" asked Luca.

Neither boy had any idea.

"He says he loves opera and Renaissance painting."

Franco pinched his nose, and Mario made a face.

"He's also interested in the old Jewish communities of Venice and Rome," Luca continued. "His favorite restaurant in Brooklyn is called Il Bucatino. He always orders the eggplant parmesan. Wait till I tell Nina! Besides arancini, that's her favorite dish. Her nickname was *melanzana* in school."

"That's a good one for her," said Franco.

"He's fifty-three years old."

Mario was surprised. "That's old. How can that be good, having old-man marrow in you?"

Luca looked over the Castle walls to the pine-covered hills beyond the road, the bell tower of San Stefano in the distance. Joseph Neiman had promised to send a picture of himself in his next letter. What would he look like? One thing Luca was certain about, no matter how old or different he might be, it didn't feel weird to have Joseph Neiman's marrow inside him, even when Luca lived on one side of the world and this man on the other. Even when he was Catholic and this man Jewish, a priest of the Jews who had never received the sacrament or communion.

"So what do we do now?" asked Franco.

"We need to find out more about these Jewish people," said Luca decisively. "We should go to a synagogue and see what a rabbi looks like."

"Good plan," said Mario. "But where can we find one?"

"Ask your parents. I'll talk to Nonna and Nonno. They'll know. Nina will help."

"Then what?"

Luca shrugged. "We'll figure it out."

9

I Rampicanti was named for the creeping vines that covered the two-story house in the hills outside Ticino. The informal restaurant was run by Signore Silvatti, an antique restorer who put a few tables out on his back porch so the locals could buy his wife's delicious agnolotti stuffed with baby squash, rather than giving it away as she used to do. Early in his career, Matteo Crespi had cured the owner's father of bladder cancer, and ever since, he was treated like royalty whenever he came for dinner.

"We haven't been here in a while," said Nina, gazing through the vines down into the valley below, where a tributary of the Po zigzagged over the land. Silvatti's house may have been old—the porch wood was already beginning to soften—but the view was spectacular. "I miss it."

"Me too," said Matteo.

She laughed. "I bet you've taken lots of women here over the years."

"Not true. And regardless, this is our place now."

It was after 8:00 p.m. and dark outside, the only light issuing from a candle that stood in the middle of the table. Nina could just make out the features of the man across from her. Matteo was still dark and handsome, albeit not the flawless Apollo she fell in love with almost a decade ago. His hair was thinning on top, and the skin below his eyes and along the jawline had begun to sag. How had she not noticed this before?

"On the other hand, I hear *you've* been dating up a storm," he said. She wasn't going to deny it.

"My source tells me that your friend Carla is quite the matchmaker."

Carla had indeed been fixing her up. There was the jeweler who wore his glasses on the tip of his nose; the dentist with perfect white teeth; and a friend of Lorenzo, the barista who served them their morning coffee at the coffee bar. But none had interested her. One talked constantly about money, another barely said a word, and the third, while very handsome, was much too young. "The truth is, I've never liked anyone but you, Matteo," she said.

"You can't imagine how happy that makes me, Ninetta. I thought I'd lost you, that—"

"But not like before."

He struck the table with his fist. "I'll do whatever you want. One more year and Francesca will be off to university. Then we can move in together. Maria, I'm sure, would like nothing more; she's dying to get me out of the house. Hey," he said, fixing her with his gaze, "you once talked about having a child. I'm willing, if it would make you happy."

"I'm happy the way it is right now, Matteo. To have you as a colleague and a friend." She patted his hand and smiled. "A very good friend."

Signore Silvatti noticed their plates were empty and came over to clear them. "I see you didn't like my wife's agnolotti," he quipped. "I'll tell her to try harder on the *secondi*."

"I don't understand," said Matteo when Silvatti left.

"Everything's changed," she told him.

Matteo downed his glass of wine. "I know you've been preoccupied with the Taviano boy and his family, but now that he's better, life will go on for them in Favola, as will your life in Rondello. You'll see."

Nina knew that wasn't possible. She would never forget what Luca said—that after the transplant, he felt like his marrow donor was living inside him, that all his blood donors were living inside him, that *she* was living inside him. The truth was Nina felt the same way about Luca, that he was now part of her. "For so long," she said, "I've been wrapped up in my own little world, thinking only of myself and my silly concerns. There are so many other things to consider, so many more important things. I haven't told you, but I've been in contact with Luca's donor."

Matteo was surprised. "I didn't know that was allowed."

Nina explained that the marrow registry usually requires donors and recipients to remain anonymous, but she and Tosti had persuaded them to bend the rules in this case. "Luca has been writing letters to his donor for a while now. His name is Joseph Neiman. A rabbi who lives in Brooklyn, New York."

"A rabbi," repeated Matteo. "Incredible! Then again, given Luca's genetic profile, it's not so far-fetched."

"It gets better," Nina continued. "The rabbi has also been writing to me because he didn't want to share certain sensitive issues with a ten-year-old boy. It turns out that his wife's family were Jewish refugees in Italy during the war. They were heading to the port in Genoa when an old Italian woman betrayed them to the authorities. They were sent to the detention center in Fossoli and then Auschwitz."

"My God!"

"The rabbi believes this coincidence is an opportunity for his family. They still don't know everything that happened to his wife's father and grandparents from the fall of 1943 to the winter of 1944 and would like to find out more, especially since Sarah remains resentful toward Italy. She was initially opposed to her husband's becoming a donor."

Matteo tapped the side of his nose with his finger. "What about the rabbi's family? Where were they during the war?"

Nina realized what he was thinking and shook her head. "Both of the rabbi's parents were born in America. As far as he knows, he has no family in Italy. Still, I can't help but wonder. The Tavianos were never told about Paolo's background. I plan to do some digging myself, first with the pediatrician in Favola, Dr. Ruggiero, and then the orphanage in Genoa."

Matteo nodded.

"All of this has made me curious about Italian history during the war," said Nina. "I've already discovered some interesting things. I bet you didn't know that Santa Cristina provided sanctuary for a number of refugees, including many Jews. There's a place in the cellar near the X-ray room where they hid refugees during German raids. They also had a fake ward for highly contagious patients that the Germans were afraid to enter. The chief of medicine was one of the main organizers—he was a big anti-Fascist back then."

Matteo had no idea.

"Yes, the same chief that wanted to fire me—a hero."

"But he didn't fire you in the end, right?" observed Matteo. "Bravo, Chief—on both counts!"

"Also," Nina continued, "not far from Fossoli, there was an abandoned estate used to house Jewish children. Villa Emma in Nonantola. The whole town pitched in to help: ordinary citizens preparing food, doctors treating the kids when they were sick, printers preparing fake documents. Even the police were involved in the cover-up."

Matteo was impressed—by the efforts of the townspeople, as well as Nina's efforts in uncovering them.

"See, Matteo, this is exactly what I mean about my life being small and petty when you consider what some people had to go through. There's something I never told you, something I never told anyone," said Nina, fingering her wineglass and forcing herself to look Matteo in the eye. "I was pregnant in high school and had to have an abortion."

"I'm sorry, Nina."

"It was a mess, as you can imagine. But there was a young nurse at the clinic who did more for me in a few hours than my parents did in seventeen years. You realize how risky it must have been to work at a place like that. Abortion was illegal back then, and that nurse could have gone to jail for what she did. Well, I'd like to be more like her. I'd like to help people in trouble even if there are risks—the way the chief at Santa Cristina did and the townspeople of Nonantola."

Matteo smiled. "I for one am glad we weren't around during those screwed-up times, but I have no doubt you would have acted just as courageously."

"We may not be in the middle of a war right now," said Nina, "but Italy is still a pretty screwed-up place. Think of how many governments we've had in the last fifty years. The corruption of our politicians who care more about getting bribes than following the law. The crime bosses who don't think twice before gunning down anyone who stands in their way. But this country has plenty of good too: the nurse who helped me at the clinic and the prosecutors in Sicily, Falcone and Borsellino, who never backed down despite constant threats from the Mafia—they're the real heroes in my mind."

"I'll drink to that," said Matteo, clinking his glass against hers. "This conversation is getting a bit heavy. Any chance we can switch to a lighter topic?"

"Sure." Nina nodded. "How about some tiramisu for dessert?"

"You definitely have changed, Ninetta. I just hope there's still some of the old you left. Any chance we can go back to your place after dinner?"

"Maybe." She smiled. "But if I decide to spend more time with you again, it's going to be on my terms from now on. You hear me?"

"Loud and clear."

10

Joseph received another letter from Italy that afternoon. Benny usually brought the mail to Joseph's office right after services, airmail envelopes atop the pile. There had been a steady stream of letters over the last two months, and Benny knew how much the rabbi looked forward to them. This letter was from Nina Vocelli, informing him of the big celebration the village of Favola was planning in his honor at the end of the summer. At last he would have a chance to meet Luca Taviano in person.

Nina had become an important part of Luca's life since the transplant, a mother figure, Joseph gathered, after learning the boy's parents had died when Luca was a baby and he'd been living with his grandparents ever since. Nina wrote in English and had also started translating Luca's letters so that Joseph no longer needed to take them to Father Lazzaro.

Favola, she explained, was a typical, small town in Italy where everyone knew everything about each other. Luca was doted upon, both because of his family's tragic circumstances and his endearing personality. The villagers had followed his illness every step of the way and were overwhelmed when they learned that a stranger from another country was willing to share his marrow with Luca. They'd prayed at home and in church that the transplant would be successful. When their prayers were answered, they decided something had to be done for

Luca's benefactor, something grand, and all agreed to pitch in and bring him to Favola. Plane tickets were being purchased, the rabbi's family was to be housed at the mayor's home, and a big celebration would be held in the main piazza on the night of his arrival. Everyone in town was excited to meet the hero from Brooklyn!

"What's wrong?" asked Benny.

Emotion crashed over Joseph like a wave. "It seems the village of Favola," he said, "wants to throw me a party."

The table was set for Friday night: challah from Levitsky's bakery, candles in her mother's silver holders, the kiddush cup filled with red wine. Just before sunset, Sarah covered her eyes and recited the prayer. "Shabbat shalom," she concluded.

It was just the two of them. Samuel was sleeping at his friend's house, his chair at the table empty. As Joseph opened his mouth to speak, Sarah stopped him. "Maybe we should check on Samuel."

Joseph promised to call after dinner.

"Do you know what he told me yesterday?" asked Sarah. "That he's thinking of becoming a doctor. Can you imagine? He plans to take Dr. Sokel up on his offer to shadow him in the office."

"Good for him," Joseph said. "You must have noticed the books he's been taking out of the library. Ever since I went in for the marrow harvesting, he's become obsessed with the science of transplantation and the immune system—the difficulties of introducing foreign material into the body without the body rejecting it. 'Fascinating stuff, Dad, don't you think?' he asked when I went in to say good night the other day."

Sarah smiled. "It's hard to believe this is the same boy who . . . No, I don't even want to think about it. Let's just hope he stays this way."

Joseph lifted his glass and recited the blessing for the wine. "I believe he will," he said confidently. "In the meantime, we received a special invitation today. The town of Favola wants to fly us to Italy to celebrate Luca's recovery. We would stay as guests in the mayor's house and receive a grand tour of Favola and the surrounding countryside. Doesn't that sound wonderful?"

Sarah sat back in her chair. "I don't know what to say," she began hesitantly. "Believe me when I tell you that I'm happy for you, happy that you had this opportunity. I was wrong about the transplant at first, very wrong, and never should have interfered. You were right. I see that now. Your son sees that. We're both proud of you. But I can't go to Italy. Just hearing about those places from my father gives me nightmares."

Joseph reached across the table and took her hand. "That's precisely why you must go. I've been thinking about it for a while and realize it won't be easy. But this is your history, our history, and the most important lesson we've learned about the Shoah is that we must never forget, painful as it is. I gave your father's and grandparents' names to Nina Vocelli, as well as the time period they were interned at the deportation camp, and she promised to find out as much as she could. I want to see these places with my own eyes. I want Samuel to see them too. These are exactly the kinds of experiences he needs right now."

Sarah turned away.

"Father Lazzaro put me in touch with a history professor at Columbia. Professor Benedetti wrote a book about the Jews in Italy during the war. She's a lovely woman, Sarah. You would like her. Italian but not Jewish, also from Brooklyn. She says the subject has been terribly neglected, and she has been working hard to correct that."

Sarah sighed.

"Do you remember how I told you that the majority of the fifty thousand or so Jews in Italy survived the war, despite Mussolini's racial laws and the German occupation? Eighty-five percent. Of course, it still means that many didn't. According to Benedetti, about eight thousand Jews died, your grandparents included. There were some bad people cooperating with the Nazis, people in the government, the military, even the clergy. The professor wants to identify those people and publicize their crimes. She's working with several agencies urging the pope to make a formal apology about the church's complicity."

"That doesn't help my grandparents."

"But just as important to the professor's research is understanding how so many Jews survived—how forty-two thousand Jews in a country allied with Hitler were able to evade the Nazis. And here's what excites me the most," said Joseph. "Nina Vocelli discovered one of these Good Samaritans living in Favola. The owner of a bar, a man named Bartolomeo Vitucci. He worked with a partisan group that fought against the Fascists and Germans. The group also helped hide Jews among the local people, in churches and convents, and arranged for their safe passage to other countries. I want to meet this man and shake his hand. Don't you?"

She didn't answer.

"That's not all. The nurse believes there's a chance that Luca Taviano could be part Jewish. His father was an orphan adopted during the war from a convent in Genoa. It's possible he was the child of Jewish refugees. The nurse plans to visit the convent to see what she can find out."

Sarah turned toward him.

"The fact is, the boy and I share certain genes that are found predominantly in Ashkenazi Jews. It could be purely coincidental, but maybe not. First, I hoped he might be related to me, but I checked and rechecked, and there's no way. It's much more likely that Luca's father came from a refugee family like yours."

"Is that really possible?" she asked.

"Yes. Professor Benedetti was so intrigued when I told her about the adoption she promised to give us the names of her contacts in Italy and make some calls herself. We have to go. Please tell me you'll reconsider."

"Let me think about it," said Sarah.

11

Matteo Crespi had three patients to see before he left the hospital, but was having difficulty concentrating. He couldn't stop thinking about Nina. He tried to hide his distraction as he gave the first patient her biopsy results, reassured the next that his last bone scan was clean, and explained to the third that he would need another cycle of chemotherapy.

How am I going to regain Nina's trust and love again? Matteo asked himself, bounding down the front steps of the hospital. He found his car in the parking lot and drove to their usual meeting spot, across from the train station.

Nina had changed so much this past year. He'd always been impressed by her skills and intelligence. She was by far the best nurse at Santa Cristina; she routinely knew what to do without his having to ask and was able to smooth things over with patients when no one else could. But she was also a cautious person, hesitant to break the rules and overstep boundaries, at least until recently. In their relationship, Matteo took the lead and Nina followed, whether it was a matter of where to eat dinner or how they would make love. Lately, though, the tables had turned. Nina was launching out in all sorts of surprising directions, and Matteo was having a hard time keeping up. She was corresponding with a rabbi in Brooklyn, visiting synagogues in Genoa with Luca, and studying Italy's history during the war, its role in the Holocaust.

"Sorry I'm late," said Nina, hopping into the passenger seat. "They're short-staffed on the pediatric ward. I may have to go back."

"No problem," he said. "Where are we off to today?"

"Favola. To see Bartolomeo Vitucci, the man organizing the celebration to honor Luca's donor. He owns the bar in the central piazza."

"Must we go all the way to Favola for a drink?" he asked, smiling, though he didn't mind at all since it meant spending more time with her.

"Signore Vitucci fought for the resistance during the war. He was also involved in smuggling Jewish refugees through occupied areas."

"You changed your hairstyle," he observed. "I like it short."

She turned toward him and frowned. "Are you listening to me? We're talking about Vitucci. He might know something about Luca's father."

"You've become consumed by all this, Nina. The war. Jews. Now that I think of it, I don't know any Jews. Do you?"

"Wrong," Nina corrected him. "Leonardo Franconi in your department is Jewish."

"Seriously?"

"Yes. You wouldn't know unless you were close friends and celebrated the holidays with them. Most of the Jews around here blend in. They consider themselves Italians first."

Bartolomeo Vitucci was standing outside his bar when they arrived. A short, squat, balding man in his seventies, he stood with his arms crossed as he surveyed the piazza in front of him. It was market day, and the square was packed with covered stalls, fresh foods from the local farms. Vitucci watched people milling about, conversations on every corner, sellers cajoling, buyers haggling, a lively Babel that he'd enjoyed ever since he was a young boy.

"You must be Signora Vocelli." He bowed before Nina. "Like I assured you on the phone, I'm doing everything I can to make the party a big success. In fact, we just purchased fireworks for the occasion."

"That makes me happy, but it's not why I'm here." She explained that she wanted to find out more about Favola during the war. "The rabbi's wife's family were Jewish refugees back then. They left Hungary in 1943 and ended up in Northern Italy, trying to reach the port of Genoa. Unfortunately, they were captured and interned at Fossoli."

Vitucci threw up his hands. "Ugly times. We did what we could, but there were many bad people. People that would sell their own mothers for a price. The going rate for a Jew was five thousand lira a head."

"That's exactly what happened to the rabbi's in-laws," said Nina. "But there were also many people who protected Jews, like yourself and the people of Nonantola."

"You're thinking of Villa Emma, about twenty kilometers south of here. A small town, a little bigger than Favola. DELASEM, the main Jewish organization in Italy, rented the empty mansion before the occupation to house young children. When the Germans came, they had to find other places for them to hide until they could arrange for transport to Switzerland. About two hundred kids in all. My group helped them get through this region, then handed them off to the next group on their way to the border. But that's just one example. There were many places—convents, schools, even hospitals like Santa Cristina—that volunteered to hide refugees. There were many bad people in those days, but also many good people like your colleagues at Santa Cristina, Dr. Romano and Dr. Franconi. They were both part of our group."

Matteo was surprised to learn about Franconi's exploits during the war. Now in his seventies, Franconi was frail and hunched over and seemed so cautious in his approach to treating cancer. He couldn't imagine him flouting the law and taking such risks.

"Signore Vitucci," asked Matteo, "are you Jewish?"

Vitucci turned out his hands and chuckled. "Me?"

"Then why?"

Vitucci didn't understand.

"Why did you do it?"

"Because I hated the Germans and the filthy Italians who backed them. And because these were innocent people who'd done nothing wrong. Someone had to stand up for them."

"You're absolutely right," said Nina, her respect for the man evident in her expression.

How lovely she looked to Matteo, her passion radiating off the surface of her port-wine stain. Most people were turned off by the mark, but not him. The magenta-colored mistake of nature made her even more attractive and alive in his eyes. He wanted to show her that he felt the same way she did about Vitucci and his heroics, that they were simpatico on this and everything else. "It's wrong," he said with conviction, "that we remember so little of those times. My parents lived not far from here during the war, and of course they hated the Germans. But while they talked about the resistance, they never mentioned the Jews. Nor did we learn much about them in school."

Nina nodded approvingly. "Exactly, Matteo, and it needs to be corrected. Signore Vitucci," she asked, "how well do you know Luca's grandfather?"

Vitucci explained that he and Giovanni had grown up together in Favola. They went to the same school. "I can't say we were best friends. He kept to himself mostly, not like Letizia, who was more sociable. But Giovanni had a rough life, especially after Paolo died."

"Do you remember when he brought Paolo home as a baby?"

"Of course. I was the one who told them about the Sisters of the Sacred Heart, the convent in Genoa that arranged for adoptions back then. They were having problems conceiving a child, and everyone in Favola knew how much this upset Letizia. I was happy it worked out."

Nina glanced sideways at Crespi, then turned to Vitucci. "Signore, he didn't get the baby from the convent."

"What?"

"I checked with the sisters myself, as did Dr. Ruggiero years ago. There's no record of this adoption."

"There must be some mistake."

Nina shook her head. "Do you know any other way Giovanni could have obtained a baby at that time?"

Vitucci's eyes narrowed.

"You realize," continued Nina, "that Luca's bone marrow donor is a Jewish man of Eastern European heritage. That suggests the rabbi and Luca have similar backgrounds. We believe Luca inherited the Jewish genes from his father. Dr. Ruggiero suspected that might be the case when he first saw Paolo, even though the boy wasn't circumcised."

Vitucci looked stunned. "Ruggiero and I are close friends. He never said a word about this to me."

"Well, I can assure you he contacted the convent. But when he confronted Giovanni about it, Giovanni kept to his story, and Ruggiero decided to go along. He figured everyone benefitted—the baby had a home, the Tavianos a child—so what did it matter how it came to be, and why should he risk spoiling what seemed like a good thing? We were hoping you might know something more."

Vitucci was clearly agitated as he tried to make sense of Nina's words. He sat down at one of the tables outside the bar, his gaze shifting from one direction to another as he pinched his lower lip between his fingers.

"What's wrong?" asked Nina.

"There was a family . . . ," he began, then abruptly stopped. "No, no, I must talk to Giovanni before I say anything else. I'm sorry," he said, rising from his seat and hurrying across the piazza.

12

Luca sat on the horse with his back straight, hands firmly gripping the reins. Every so often, he glanced over to make sure Nonno was watching. He had made good progress these past few weeks with Signore Fabbio's stableman. At first, he had to be led around the training circle, but in time, Luca learned to trot by himself, then canter, then gallop.

Giovanni was proud of his grandson. Not only because of Luca's newly acquired riding skills, but also because of the great strides he had made in his health. It was almost a year since the transplant and those terrible months of shrinking, when Luca became so weak and frail. Now he was back to his old weight, there was a healthy glow to his cheeks, and his thick red curls had returned, spilling out from under his cowboy hat.

Giovanni wanted so much to be happy. His boy was well again, happily riding a horse in a corral he'd built just for him, in front of the barn he'd built to house the horse just for him. Letizia was in the kitchen, likely watching the scene from the window above the sink, happily preparing some of her special cakes to serve to the rabbi from Brooklyn at the upcoming party.

But as always, it was a tease. There had never been a real chance for happiness, never, going back as far as his childhood. He was the youngest of six, and his parents were always busy and rarely had time for him.

He swore he would be different with his children when it was his time, but his time never came, and when it did, it kept getting cut short.

He turned toward the house, the kitchen window. Letizia was the guiding star of his life, from when they first met in high school. Why such a lively girl would choose a loner like him, he could never fathom. Yet she stuck by him, choosing him again and again through the years. She was too good for him, and now he would disappoint her, disappoint her in a terrible way.

Life kept on taunting him, making him think that there might be happiness when there never was any, when he didn't deserve it. First Letizia, then Paolo, then Luca.

The skin over his face felt taut, like a sheet of glass.

Fabbio's stableman opened the corral gate. They were ready for the next stage, riding in open terrain. Luca waved as he passed, a proud smile spread across his cheeks, then trotted off toward the wheat fields on the northern edge of the farm.

As the horse went by, the whooshing noise sucked the air out of Giovanni's lungs. He stood alone now, in a space getting smaller and smaller, boxing him in, suffocating him: his grandson riding off on a horse, writing letters to the rabbi from Brooklyn, visiting synagogues in Genoa, asking questions about Jewish people, about the war. The rabbi coming soon to Favola for the big party, surely with a million questions of his own.

And then Vitucci.

The bar owner had come to the farm yesterday after talking to Nina Vocelli. "I don't understand, Giovanni," he'd said. "The nurse claims you never went to the convent in Genoa, that the Sisters of the Sacred Heart have no record of giving Paolo up for adoption. Is this true?"

Giovanni had made no answer.

"She also said that Dr. Ruggiero knew and never said anything."

Giovanni threw up his hands. "She's lying."

Vitucci didn't believe him. They were in the shed, Giovanni feeding the chickens while Vitucci paced back and forth, deep in thought. "There was a family," he finally said. "I think they were Polish, living in Italy since the beginning of the war. They traveled here with other refugees from Assisi in the winter of '43, disguised as pilgrims. We planned on hiding them in the abandoned mill on the outskirts of Favola and eventually transporting them to safety across the Swiss border. But they were exposed before we had the chance, gunned down in the forest, not far from your property. I'm sure you remember."

Giovanni watched the bar owner spit onto the ground.

"Pietro Lambertini was responsible for the massacre, that Fascist pig, getting rich by turning in resistance fighters and refugees," Vitucci said. "We took care of the pig."

Giovanni had been present when they found Lambertini's body in the forest three days later. No one in the town gave a damn about Lambertini, least of all him, and the corpse would have stayed there to rot had not his mother come to bury him herself.

"We found a folded piece of paper in his pocket," said Vitucci.

Giovanni wheeled around. "What?"

"It was wet, and the ink had run. We believe it had the name of one of the refugees, but couldn't make it out. It also had the address of the safehouse in Switzerland they were headed to, which we *were* able to read. The safehouse was raided by the Germans the day after the massacre, and three of our people were killed. We never figured out how Lambertini got that piece of paper, but we suspected foul play. Someone must have sold out the refugees."

Giovanni felt the pail of chicken feed slip from his hands and drop onto the floor with a thud.

"It was just after Christmas in 1943, one of the coldest winters we ever had. You remember? The same winter you got Paolo from the Sisters of the Sacred Heart. At least that's what you told everybody."

Giovanni said nothing.

Vitucci, who had been digging a small hole in the dirt with his foot, suddenly looked up and glared at Giovanni. "The Fascists and their German friends gunned those refugees down in the forest," he said. "But we never found the baby. Yes, there was supposed to be a baby traveling with them. I was warned ahead of time that the group might need more assistance because of it. We recovered the bodies of all eight adults, but not the baby. We just assumed something happened to the baby before they got to Favola."

Giovanni had begun to shake.

"Do you know anything about this baby, Giovanni? Was Paolo—"

"Get out!" he'd screamed, chasing Vitucci from the shed with a shovel.

Giovanni had collapsed on the ground. It was suddenly winter cold in the shed, the coldest, bitterest of winters, when the trees were naked and the ground blanketed white, no sound of birds or other life. It had always been so, even in the spring when the sun fueled the seeds and roots with hope—hope for everyone but him, never for him.

Giovanni grabbed the corral gate with both hands to steady himself. Luca was long gone by now, riding with Signore Fabbio's stableman along the outer edges of the farm. The glass over Giovanni's face cracked and shattered. The walls were closing in on him. He reached down to his leg, an old friend who had provided comfort in the past. No. He gritted his teeth. He wouldn't give Ruggiero the pleasure. The wound had healed long ago, an ugly, gnarled scar that he'd refrained from opening in the few months of hopeful spring as Luca recovered from the transplant.

Pop, pop, pop. He hears the guns echoing in the forest.

Besides, the wound was a tease too. Messy and painful, but never leading anywhere. *No, Doctor, you're wrong. The leg is fine and won't be acting up again.*

This time something more definitive was needed.

PART VI: A SECOND CROSSING

1993

The Mafia wars continued to unsettle Italy during the last years of the twentieth century. Soon after the assassination of Prosecuting Magistrates Falcone and Borsellino, former Prime Minister Giulio Andreotti was put on trial for his connection to the mob bosses that ordered the hit. In the fall of 1993, another shocking event occurred: a priest was murdered outside his church in Palermo. Like the government, the church rarely took a stand against the Mafia. Many priests actually cozied up to crime bosses, just as Andreotti had supposedly done with the *capo di tutti capi*, Totò Riina. Father Puglisi, on the other hand, condemned the Mafia openly and had paid the ultimate price for it.

Outrage spread all the way up the peninsula into the tiny northern town of Favola, where a service was held in the church. Afterward, the townspeople wondered what would become of their beloved country. But a few days later, despite the tragic news and intense August heat, they were able to put aside their sadness. In a few days, they would be welcoming the man who had saved Luca Taviano's life.

The idea for the celebration initially came from Bartolomeo Vitucci and Dr. Ruggiero, but was swiftly taken up by the rest of the town. It was nothing short of a miracle, seeing a healthy Luca scampering down the narrow cobblestone streets again. The two town elders decided to mark the occasion. The festivities would start in the central piazza and follow with a formal dinner in the town hall.

Everyone pitched in. Funds were collected at the church. The hospital in Rondello promised to contribute, as did the synagogue in Genoa that Nina and Luca had visited. Tents, tables, chairs were rented. Elaborate signs and banners were created, and fireworks purchased.

On Friday night, less than twenty-four hours before the rabbi's arrival, a group of women assembled in the town hall to finalize the dinner preparations. They set the long rustic wooden tables with colorful majolica plates. Vases of sunflowers surrounded by candles were placed at regular intervals down the center of the tables. Additional lighting came from old lanterns that hung from the walls. *It looks beautiful,* thought Letizia Taviano as she took out her notebook and began reading from her list: *prosciutto e formaggi,* Isabella Panucci; *agnolotti alla piemontese,* Nunca Treviso; and *parmigiana di melanzane,* the rabbi's favorite dish, as they'd learned from his letters to Luca, Elizabetta Silva.

"Signore Vitucci," she said to the others, "promised to take care of the champagne and wine. And for me, the *dolci* of course." She looked with satisfaction over the room, ordinarily so spare, now beflowered and bedecked. "I think we're ready."

The Neiman family had ascended to a flying altitude of forty thousand feet above the Atlantic Ocean. It was after midnight, and the Alitalia cabin was dark, most of the passengers fast asleep. Rabbi Joseph, however, could not keep his eyes shut for long, even in such large, plush seats. Much to his surprise, they had been bumped to first class at check-in. "Ah, the famous rabbi from Brooklyn," said the lady at the counter, with a welcoming smile. "We've arranged special seats for you this evening. The pilot himself has asked to meet you."

Special, indeed. Joseph had never traveled first class before, and the pilot gave Samuel a tour of the cockpit. Now his son and wife were sleeping peacefully in their seats while a thousand disturbing thoughts raced through his head. When they'd told Sarah's father about their upcoming trip to Italy, he didn't say anything at first. Then he pointed across the room as if there were someone standing in the empty doorway: "That woman, can't you see her?" he had asked. "With the red scarf wrapped around her head and her kind, old, wrinkly face?"

"Who, Papa?" asked Sarah.

"You tell her," he demanded, "what happened to my parents because of her kindness."

The old Italian lady would be long dead by now, thought Joseph at the time, though he didn't say that to Sarah's father. He had shown him the picture of Luca, told him about his caring nurse and the owner of the bar in Favola who'd helped smuggle Jews to Switzerland. But all his father-in-law could see was the treacherous woman from fifty years ago. The point of their trip to Italy was to celebrate the recovery and health of a young boy, he wanted to say, a happy occasion, not to rehash bad memories. Even Sarah had come around. She was as excited as he and Samuel were now, although she was careful not to show it around her father.

Joseph watched Samuel shift in his sleep. His mind traveled back to the bar mitzvah, when his son stood at the bimah, giving his speech, weaving the symbolic nature of *nediv lev* and his father's gift of marrow into the dry, architectural passage from Exodus.

Things are always such a muddle, he mused. True, Jews were wronged by the Italians, but they were also aided. He looked forward to visiting Villa Emma with Luca's nurse. One of the main organizers was still alive, and though he wasn't well, Nina had arranged for Joseph to meet him. A man who wasn't even Jewish, he explained to Sarah's father on several occasions, yet he risked his life for Jewish children.

Even more remarkable and unexpected was the possibility that Luca's father, Paolo, adopted by the Tavianos during the war, might have been Jewish. In that case, the Tavianos themselves were examples of the good Italians, taking in an orphan whose parents might have perished in a camp like Sarah's grandparents. Years later, Joseph would be able to return the favor by giving the family some of his marrow. How wonderful if this turned out to be the case!

"Have you ever been on a plane before?" Luca asked Nina as they pulled onto the Autostrada, heading for the airport in Milan. This time Nina had borrowed the hospital van; Carla's Cinquecento wouldn't be able to fit the rabbi's family and their luggage.

"Never. But I say we take a trip one of these days and visit Brooklyn. I don't know about you, but I'm curious about Coney Island and the Verrazzano Bridge, and the rabbi's favorite Italian restaurant with its *parmigiana di melanzane.*"

"Me too," said Luca, nodding.

From the way he kept moving his hands and looking one way and the other, Nina could tell Luca was nervous. "What if they don't like me?" he asked.

"Are you kidding? That's not possible."

"But we're so different."

"You're thinking about the synagogue in Genoa. Those people were very religious. Rabbi Joseph explained that he's not like that."

"Samuel could ride on my horse if he wants," said Luca. "And I'll take him to the Castle and tell him about Orlando. But maybe he'll think that's stupid. He's four years older than me."

She reached over and patted his head. "There's no way they won't like you."

"The book we bought for them should help too, right?"

"Absolutely! An old Italian Haggadah is right up the rabbi's alley. I told you, he's very interested in the history of Jews in Italy."

Luca hoped so.

"We both learned a lot these last few months," said Nina. "I knew almost nothing about Jewish people before. When we studied the Holocaust in school, I never realized that Italy played a large role. What happened with the rabbi's wife's family was horrible, and it's still hard for me to accept that people in this country were responsible. One of these days, you'll read Primo Levi's book about the time he spent in a Nazi concentration camp. Levi grew up in Turin, a normal Italian boy just like you, except for the fact that he was Jewish."

"People do bad things," agreed Luca. "Like the mafioso who killed the priest in Palermo."

"Yes, but we can't be afraid. We have to stand up for what we believe in, even if there are risks. Not many priests would have spoken out like Father Puglisi. I'm glad the Vatican treated him like a hero."

"The boys and I talked about it at the Castle the other night," said Luca, "and don't want anything like that to happen to Father Bertolini at San Stefano. So we made a plan. From now on, Mario will sit on the right side of church during Mass, Franco on the left side, and me at the very back—to keep a lookout for anyone suspicious."

"Sounds like a good plan."

"And Orlando will do the same in Sicily. He'll protect the priests and judges so they can keep doing their jobs. He won't stop until all the bad guys are sent to jail and there's no more Mafia left."

Nina smiled.

"Look," said Luca, pointing to the sign for the airport up ahead. "We're almost there."

"You know," said Nina, "I keep thinking of your friend Orlando, traveling over mountains and across seas, with his furry beard—"

"And bags of gold."

"Yes. There are so many similarities and coincidences between your story and real life: the rabbi and his beard, his golden marrow, Jews in Italy, the war."

"I asked the rabbi about Orlando," said Luca. "He said he believed in people like Orlando, that almost everyone did. So maybe it's not just my story, Nina. Maybe it's not a story at all."

Letizia had never been very fashion conscious. She had four dresses, all with floral prints and bright colors, which she wore over and over. But tonight was different. She wanted to look her best for their special guests from New York, to show her appreciation, which she worried might not happen if she was her usual, frumpy self.

She picked up the dress that lay on her bed and ran her hand over the soft new material. Giuseppina Friolo, the mayor's wife, had made it for her. It was a sleeveless dress in red linen—simple yet elegant, and she had new white leather sandals to go along with it.

Suddenly, she was nervous. How would she act in front of the rabbi? Of course she wanted to thank him for what he did, but she was afraid that she'd get carried away and start hugging him or crying. He'd think she was a crazy person. She vowed to remain as calm as possible.

Where was Giovan? The clock on the night table showed it was half past four. Nina and Luca would be on their way back from the airport with the Neimans, and the celebration was due to start in less than two hours. Her husband was never one for parties and socializing, but this was different—the entire town had rallied to honor Luca and his donor. It would be a great day, perhaps the most memorable day in their lives.

Giovan had been in a bad mood these last few months. Once again, it came on so quickly and unexpectedly. After the transplant, he was the happiest man in the world, cheerful and talkative as she'd never seen him before. One day he'd even thanked Nina for taking care of Luca with a kiss on her forehead. Then without any warning whatsoever, the blackness rose up again, the long walks and muttering. It all seemed to revolve around Paolo and his ancestry. But Giovan swore he'd made every effort to find out what he could. Why couldn't he just let it rest when everything was going so well and they were about to celebrate the miracle of Luca's recovery? They should thank the Blessed Virgin for their good fortune.

Letizia would talk to him when he got back. It would be terrible if he looked depressed at the party. She should have thought of it sooner. Dr. Ruggiero could have prescribed something to make him feel better, but now it was too late. She would tell him to be happy, if only for Luca, and only for a few days.

Luca and Nina waited at the gate as passengers passed through customs on their way out of the airport. They recognized the Neiman family instantly from the pictures—the rabbi tall and on the portly side with big brown eyes and a bushy beard; Sarah Neiman a diminutive brunette with angular features; and Samuel, who looked more like his father, but with the sharp expressiveness of his mother.

Rabbi Joseph made a beeline for Luca. He grasped his shoulders and studied his face. "It's good to meet you, Luca," he said. "Sarah, Samuel, look how handsome our young friend is."

Luca smiled, even though he didn't understand the rabbi. He turned to Nina and said something to her in Italian.

"Luca says you look exactly as he'd imagined. Only we expected you to arrive by horse," she joked, "not airplane."

This made Rabbi Joseph laugh. Then for some reason, an image of Emily Nussbaum flashed before his mind—the child who hadn't survived as opposed to the child before him who had—and without warning, tears pricked his eyes.

They were huddled at the gate, blocking traffic, and people stared at them. Samuel, embarrassed, poked at his father's side, while Sarah explained that her husband tended to be very emotional at times.

"You could say the same about us Italians," Nina replied, in between fielding questions from curious bystanders.

Suddenly, people around them began to cheer and clap. They were deeply moved by the meeting of the young boy and his bone marrow donor from America.

"See what I mean?" said Nina.

The trip back from the airport went by quickly; everyone had something to say, and Nina was busy translating from English into Italian and back again. Rabbi Joseph asked about Luca's grandparents. Sarah wanted to know how far they were from Venice and Lake Como. Luca chimed in about the synagogue in Casale Monferrato that they planned to visit, one of the oldest synagogues in all of Italy. Samuel wanted to know where Luca kept his horse and when they could take it out for a ride. They talked freely and easily, as if it weren't the first time they were meeting.

"Here we are," Nina said as they entered the town limits of Favola. She parked the van a block from the central piazza in front of the mayor's house, a two-story gray stone building with clusters of lemon and bergamot trees flanking the entrance. The mayor was staying at his sister's, she explained, and had graciously offered his home to the Neimans. "We'll take your bags to the room so you have a chance to freshen up before the party."

But the entire town had assembled in the piazza an hour early. When they spotted the van, they began filing down the street to greet their guests, eager for the celebration to start. A light breeze carried the smell of tomato sauce and braised veal from the town hall. Floodlights illuminated the fountain in the middle of the square, and fireworks unfolded in the evening sky. A band played the triumphal march from Verdi's *Aida*.

Luca saw Nonna crossing the street in her new red dress and waved her over so she could meet his new friends.

"Where's Nonno?" he asked.

The clearing was less than a mile from the Taviano farm, up the hill and beyond the meandering stream that Luca and his friends would swing across on a rope they had tied to a tree. Giovanni sat against a slender pine at the western edge and gazed at the space that had consumed his nights these last fifty years. Now covered in green grass, the trees in the forest beyond the clearing were flush with leaves, the ground below warm and moist. He could taste the soft summer earth on his lips.

He was surprisingly calm. There was no other choice. But how would he explain himself to Letizia? He was always so bad with words.

He had lied to her, plain and simple. There was never a trip to the Sisters of the Sacred Heart in Genoa. It was here in Favola, fifty years ago, in the dead of winter, where he'd received the baby. The baby whose name was not Paolo, although what it was he couldn't say, because the folded piece of paper had fallen into the snow and disappeared. Because he'd *let* the paper fall into the snow and disappear.

Only it hadn't disappeared. It was worse than he'd imagined. Bartolomeo Vitucci's words reverberated in his head, making him sick to his stomach. And the strange look Lambertini gave Giovanni when he saw him in the piazza that day. The bastard must have been nearby when he accepted the bundle and piece of paper from the man in the tattered coat. He must have picked up the paper after it had fallen into the snow. For soon after, he would give the ambush signal to his men hiding in the forest and then later, pass on the address of the Swiss safehouse to the Germans.

But Letizia mustn't believe that Giovanni ever meant for anyone to get hurt. No, he'd swear over his mother's dead body. How many times had Lambertini approached him, offering him good money for information? The Fascists knew about the corridor used by the resistance that ran just north of his property. Lambertini had begged him as a friend and patriotic Italian to alert him when the traitors and whatever scum they dragged along with them were passing through. But Giovanni despised the man and had always refused, just as he'd refused to help Vitucci and his group of partisans. As usual, he kept to himself and minded his own business.

He heard the baby's cries when he was out in the fields that morning and tracked the sound to the abandoned mill just below the clearing. There, he found a small group of nuns and monks. But they weren't nuns and monks, merely dressed to appear like them, under their heavy winter coats and hats. They weren't even Italian, except for the priest who approached him as soon as he realized Giovanni wasn't a threat. "I'm Father Nunzio from San Ignazio in Assisi," he'd said. "Escorting this group of pilgrims to a sanctuary outside of Milan. Please get word to Signore Vitucci that we've arrived, as soon as possible."

Giovanni warned the priest that he could hear the cries a mile away. If they didn't quiet the baby, it wouldn't be Vitucci who came, but Lambertini and his Fascist thugs. The priest was equally worried and had been pleading with the parents to leave the baby in a safe place and then come back for him when the war was over. Did Giovanni know anyone that would take care of the baby for a while? "It would be a great act of charity," said the priest.

Of course he knew someone, he answered instantly. Letizia had wanted a baby for as long he could remember and had finally agreed to adopt one from the Sisters of the Sacred Heart. Of course they would take care of the baby, for as long as necessary.

The priest thanked Giovanni and told him to return after the sun went down, giving him time to convince the parents. They would provide Giovanni with the baby's name and the address of their destination in Switzerland. If for some reason the parents never made it back to Favola, he should bring the child there, and if they'd moved on, he should do whatever he could to find them. Of course, said Giovanni. And no matter what happened, he promised the priest, he and his wife would always care for the baby as if it were their own.

But Letizia mustn't think that's what he was thinking at the time, or wanting or planning. He was doing a good deed, a great act of charity as the priest said, stepping in when he usually kept his distance. It was only when he let the paper slip from his hand and heard the shots fired that everything fell sideways.

Pop, pop, pop.

Lambertini had seen right through him. He obviously never believed Giovanni was on the way to the convent in Genoa and must have decided to keep a close eye on him. Nor had Giovanni bothered to alert Vitucci and his men that the refugees were waiting at the mill. He thought only of himself and his new family. And then everyone was dead—the man in the tattered coat, the priest, the entire group.

It was all his fault. He knew this the minute he heard the shots. That's why he went back for the piece of paper the following day, to cover his tracks; why he was relieved when he couldn't find it; why he was even more relieved when they killed Lambertini.

So he stuck hard to the story he told Letizia. That had been the plan anyway when Bartolomeo Vitucci told them there were babies at the convent in Genoa that needed a home. Letizia had assumed their child would come from that convent, and so Giovanni said it had. It was a lie he'd kept hidden in the depths of his bones for fifty years.

He'd wanted to say something to Letizia at breakfast, but the words kept getting trapped at the back of his mouth. Meanwhile, she went on and on about the rabbi's arrival and how much work was still left to do, talking a mile a minute, barely even looking at him. Then she was off to Giuseppina Friolo's to pick up her new dress. It wasn't the way he hoped to say goodbye.

He wrote her a letter, explaining as best he could. He apologized for not telling the truth, begged her to forgive him. He had loved her from the first day and only wanted to make her as happy as she made him. At least she must believe that. And when the time came, he hoped she would make sure that Luca understood how proud he was of him, how much he loved him.

As hard as Giovanni tried, he wasn't satisfied; he was always bad with words. They would have to do.

Giovanni was calm as he rested against the pine tree at the edge of the clearing. He had killed those people in the forest that cold winter night fifty years ago and then dared to smile after the massacre, when he realized the baby would be theirs forever.

He reached down and scooped up a handful of soil—the same soil that had nourished his wheat and grapes and corn for so many years, that might still contain traces of ink from the piece of paper with the name of the baby, the baby they would rename Paolo and who would later father a son named Luca. He placed a handful of soil on his tongue, tasting its bitter earthiness, forcing himself to swallow. In the distance, he heard the sound of fireworks—pop, pop, pop—exploding over the piazza. It must be full of people now celebrating the heroes of the day, the rabbi and his grandson, Luca. *Pop, pop, pop.* They were probably wondering where he was, but it was better this way.

Giovanni would have liked to thank the rabbi, but there was no way he could face him. Not the rabbi, not Letizia, not Luca. It was better this way. He was an old man, not long for this world anyway, just like old Ruggiero. A slight breeze made the hair at the back of his neck stand on end.

He took the gun from his pocket, cocked the trigger, and squeezed.

PART VII: HOMING

1994–2001

1

It was Samuel Neiman who first told him the truth, a year after Nonno's death. The rabbi had invited Luca to spend the summer with his family in New York—three weeks at their home in Bay Ridge and three weeks at Samuel's camp in the Adirondacks. Luca was eleven years old at the time, Samuel fifteen. They were paddling in a canoe on Lake Tatum when his new friend asked, "Are you mad at him?"

"Who?"

"Your grandfather."

"Why should I be mad?"

Samuel was sitting at the head of the boat. He took his oar out of the water and turned around. "You mean you really don't know?"

"Know what?"

Samuel hesitated. "Maybe I better not—"

"No, please, you must to tell," Luca blurted out. He'd been determined to master English since his letter-writing to the rabbi began, but whenever he became excited or upset, the words got mangled.

And so, far away from home, on a small lake in Upstate New York, Luca would learn that his grandfather's death was a suicide and that Nonno wasn't Luca's father's real father.

"Adopted?" Luca wasn't familiar with that English word.

"It means agreeing to care for a baby that doesn't have a family," Samuel explained to Luca. "But that's not what happened."

Luca shivered, despite the wave of heat rising off the surface of the lake.

"Your grandfather took your dad from a refugee family during the war—a couple from Eastern Europe that was trying to escape from the Germans, just like my mother's grandparents. A Jewish couple. That's why it was difficult to find a match for your bone marrow transplant—you inherited genes from them, your real grandparents."

The world went still and silent, muffling the shouts of other campers in their canoes.

"My father said your grandmother didn't know, that your grandfather kept it from her too. She was probably waiting until you were older to tell you—that your father was adopted, that is—even though he really wasn't."

Luca revered the boy sitting in front of him in the canoe; Samuel was older, smarter, from the big city. He hadn't spent that much time with him, a few days in Italy the year before, a few weeks in New York this summer. Yet this boy, this stranger, knew more about him than he knew himself.

Who the hell was this boy?

Who the hell was *he*? The son of Paolo who was not the son of Giovanni and Letizia, but of some other people whom he didn't know. People who went to a synagogue, not a church, who spoke a language other than Italian, who may or may not be alive at the moment.

"You okay?" asked Samuel.

He could feel himself rocking with the canoe. It all sounded so unbelievable. Yet maybe not. For as long as he could remember, he'd felt different from the other kids in Favola. Luca was *rosso*, like Nina with her beauty mark.

Something at the back of his throat made it hard for him to swallow.

"Time to head back in," called one of the counselors from a nearby canoe.

When the shock subsided, Luca grew angry. Was he the last to know Nonno's secret? Why didn't Nonna or Nina say anything after Nonno died? As he dragged the canoe up the shore, Luca scraped his hand against the side of the boat. A scab formed just below the wrist. At night, lying in his bunk, unable to sleep, he picked the scab off and watched blood trickle from the wound. He would continue to pick the wound for the eight remaining nights before his flight back to Italy.

2

Seven years later, Nina poked her head through the crack in Luca's bedroom door, the tenth time that morning. "Don't forget warm socks. The winters are cold over there."

He smiled. "I'm not going to the North Pole, Nina."

It might as well be the North Pole. Luca was leaving, for good this time, not just for summers with the rabbi and his family. He was almost a man now, with a whole new life apart from her—dating girls, working at the coffee bar down the street, and writing short stories, one of which had just been published in the local paper. In a few days, he would board a plane for New York and start college at Columbia University. Already, she missed him.

"You'll be back in December, before Christmas, right?"

"Mannaggia," he said, his hand in the air. "How can I get anything done with you interrupting me every two seconds?"

"Sorry, sorry," she said, backing out of the doorway.

It wasn't just to remind him not to forget this or that article of clothing that prompted the intrusions, or getting his schedule straight in her mind. She wanted to see him, keep his image fixed in her mind and not let it slip away. Reluctantly, she withdrew to the kitchen for another coffee.

He had grown into such a handsome young man. She could scarcely remember the wild boy with the mop of curly red hair hiding behind his grandmother at the hospital almost nine years ago. Now that Luca was eighteen and over six feet tall, she had to reach up to kiss him. There were no more tantrums; his behavior had mellowed with age. He was conscious of the way he dressed and used gel in his hair like Matteo. But there was none of the ego that typically accompanied good-looking Italian men. From early on, Luca seemed wise beyond his years. If only Letizia and Giovanni were around to see him now.

Nina poured what remained in the stovetop espresso machine into her cup, grabbed an ashtray, and sat down at the kitchen table. She had almost quit, but the last few weeks had so frayed her nerves, she was back to where she had started. Only one cigarette left in the pack she'd bought yesterday.

Luca would be fine in New York, she told herself. The rabbi and his family were there, as was the rabbi's friend at Columbia, Professor Benedetti, who had been a big help with the application process. Besides, Luca didn't need anyone to look out for him. He could take care of himself.

Nina took a long puff. Through the window, she could see little Tino Battaglia playing his violin in the apartment across the street. There was a time, not so long ago, when she was worried sick about Luca, though not in the aftermath of his grandparents' deaths as she might have expected. They told Luca that Giovanni's heart gave out; they said the same thing when Letizia died a few months later, although in her case, it was actually true. Letizia was so shaken over her husband's death, the knowledge of how Paolo came into their life, Giovanni's lies, and her blindness that her heart literally began to stutter and seize until one day it stopped beating altogether. Luca was distraught, even more so than when he was sick and fighting for his life; the only parents he ever knew were gone. But the entire town pitched in to distract the restless child and keep him in motion: Signore Fabbio's stableman came every day for riding lessons, Mario and Franco helped him secure the Castle from marauders, and Nina moved in with him.

Little Tino saw her watching him through the window and waved his violin bow. She waved back.

Luca's troubles had started a year later, after the first summer he spent with the rabbi's family in Brooklyn.

"What happened to your wrist?" Nina noticed the bandage as soon as he emerged from the arrivals gate at the airport in Milan.

"None of your business," he said coldly.

From that point on, Luca wanted nothing to do with her. He cursed at her for no apparent reason. He refused to play with Mario and Franco, or anyone else in Favola. Whenever she mentioned his horse, he scoffed. One day, he flung his cowboy hat at her in a rage. She became alarmed at the behavior and cried over dinner with Matteo.

"Do you think Luca is depressed?" she asked him.

"No," he reassured her, "it's normal for a kid his age. I've been through it before with my daughter."

"Maybe he needs help," she said, "someone to talk to."

"Let me try," said Matteo.

As he grew older, Luca looked up to Matteo, no longer making fun of his habits. He actually adopted a few for himself, including tapping the side of his nose with his finger. He talked of becoming a doctor, an oncologist, too, though primarily for children, because he'd always had a special way with children.

Nina sucked on the coffee left in her cup and stared at the empty cigarette box on the kitchen table. "I'm going out for a second," she called to Luca in his room.

It lasted almost a year, his cycling back and forth from anger to indifference to occasional near normalcy, while Nina consoled herself with wine and cigarettes and convinced him to move into her apartment in Rondello. The first sign that things were improving happened after the second summer with the rabbi's family. Luca greeted her at the arrivals gate with a big hug. For days after, he didn't stop talking about what he saw and did in New York City: the World Trade Center, Central Park, Times Square, Coney Island. He seemed calmer, more grounded and mature.

Matteo was right; it had been a phase all kids go through. Luca must have also needed a break from the people and places that had caused him so much pain. What that poor boy had to endure. Thank God he turned out all right.

Luca was sitting at the kitchen table, eating leftover tortellini from the night before, when she returned with her cigarettes.

"I thought you were quitting," he said.

"I am—just not right this moment."

"New York, not the North Pole," Luca reminded her again. "It's not that far."

Her boy was grown up and leaving home. Yes, that's how she thought of him—*her boy*. She always hoped he would call her Mama, and every so often, he did. Then it was right back to Nina again.

"I'll write and call like I did in the summers, Nina."

She nodded, trying to hold back the tears. *Over mountains and valleys, across seas and oceans.* Why couldn't he just stay at home and study in Milan like his father had done?

3

Luca's suitcase was already full, and there were still clothes left on the bed. Should he start another suitcase or just stuff the rest into his knapsack? He already had a stack of things to put in the knapsack: Primo Levi's book about his experience in Auschwitz, his camera and lenses, maps of New York City and the subway lines, his Walkman and favorite cassettes—Green Day, Smashing Pumpkins, Pearl Jam.

Nina had given him the Walkman for his thirteenth birthday. They went to celebrate at I Rampicanti. "Matteo's not coming?" he had asked.

"No, I wanted it to be just you and me tonight," she answered.

Nina was unusually silent on the way. When she pulled over in front of the restaurant, she took the keys out of the ignition and remained in her seat without moving.

"What's wrong?" he asked.

"It's time you knew the truth," she said.

"Nina, please," he said, almost as embarrassed as she was at the moment.

She took a deep breath before she began speaking: "Your grandfather didn't die of a heart attack, Luca."

"Really?" he said in mock disbelief. "You don't think I knew that?"

She stared at him blankly.

"I'm not stupid," he said. "I saw the way people looked at me, Dr. Ruggiero and Signore Vitucci, the way they whispered behind my back. Then Samuel filled in the details."

"Oh," she said, clearly surprised. "Why didn't you say anything?"

He shrugged his shoulders, swallowed hard.

"I'm sorry."

"It's okay," he said, seeing how upset she was. "I'm not mad."

The Walkman sat on his desk next to the knapsack. It was the Sports version with the yellow casing and fat black buttons. He was ecstatic when Nina gave it to him that night. He took it everywhere he went, walking to school, riding his bicycle, even skiing with Matteo.

There was a time, however, when Luca *was* mad at Nina, very mad; she was the only one left to blame for keeping him in the dark for so long. Only not the night they celebrated his thirteenth birthday. By then, he had made peace with the secrets that had been kept from him.

Luca picked up the Walkman on his desk and ran his hand over the plastic casing. There was a dent on one side. He had dropped it on the street the day after Nina gave it to him when his bicycle jumped the curb.

What changed then, he asked himself, *allowing things to return to normal with Nina?* It was hard to say exactly, but what stood out in his mind was the day his new school in Rondello played a football game with his old school in Favola. Luca scored the winning goal in the final seconds of the game, a hook shot into the upper corner of the net, a perfectly placed ball. The entire team raced out and jumped on top of him. Signore Vitucci had been on the sidelines, watching, and for the first time looked him in the eye without wavering. "Bravo," he said, smiling. "You take after your father. Paolo was the best player Favola ever had. Your grandparents and I loved to watch him play. The next Baggio, we predicted."

"Do you ever wonder about those people in the woods, your father's real parents?" Nina asked him that night in the car outside the restaurant.

"No," he snapped. "Why should I? They're dead, and we don't know anything about them—not their names, where they were from, what they even looked like. Nor will we ever."

Besides, he remembered thinking back then, *I know who I am.* The football game against Favola had brought all the pieces of his life back in order after Samuel's shattering revelations. After scoring the goal and hearing Vitucci's praise, he knew exactly who he was: the son of Paolo Taviano. From that day on, he'd worked hard to improve his soccer skills and become one of the best players on his team, just like his father. Paolo was the son of Giovanni and Letizia Taviano. Luca was their grandson and the rest a blank that didn't make sense. So he erased it from his mind—the refugee couple in the forest and their Jewish origins—despite the fact that at the very same time, Nina, the rabbi, and Professor Benedetti were working to resurrect Italy's past, its role in the war and the Holocaust, where his father might fit into that past. They never pushed or challenged him during their investigations, so Luca simply blocked it out and moved on.

Glancing at the weathered Walkman on his desk, he thought about Matteo's offer: "That thing looks like it got run over by a truck. Maybe it's time for a replacement. Have you heard about the new gadget Apple is coming out with? It's a quarter of the size and all digital."

Of course he'd heard about it.

"I'll get you one if you want."

As much as he might have liked to possess the latest technology, he loved his old Walkman, dents and all, and was reluctant to part with it. He placed it in his knapsack so he'd have it for the plane, right on top of the Primo Levi book he'd been reading and rereading—he couldn't get the story of the famous Italian Jewish writer out of his mind. Maybe he was wrong that night in the car—wrong about knowing who he was.

4

On the last Wednesday in August, Rabbi Joseph met Samuel for lunch at Amir's Café on Broadway across from the Columbia campus. The owner was an eccentric Egyptian man who wore the traditional long white shirt and caftan of his country and peppered his speech with Yiddish: "Would you like some schmaltz with your falafel?" It was a popular place, and Samuel had been a fan since his freshman year at Columbia.

Over hummus and baba ghanoush, Samuel told his father about the experiments he was working on in the biology lab. They were splicing genes from bacteria, inserting them into fruit flies, and studying the mutant offspring. "Are you following?" his son asked while mapping it out on the table with salt from the shaker.

"Sure," Joseph answered, though it seemed like science fiction to him. "And all this time," he said, "I thought you'd eventually realize the highest truth lay in the Torah and become a rabbi like your old man."

Samuel tilted his head to the side. "Really, Dad?"

"No, not really." He smiled. His son would be a doer, exactly what he hoped for him to be, carrying out research in a lab or caring for sick people in a hospital. He'd like to tell that to the headmaster at Poly.

"You're not disappointed?"

"Of course not," Joseph said.

"Good, because I was never cut out to be a rabbi. That's why I had so many problems at yeshiva. I felt like you and Mom wanted me to be someone I wasn't."

"We never meant that. We just wanted you to know where you came from."

Joseph decided to walk around campus before returning home. In the courtyard of a dormitory on Amsterdam Avenue, he watched people carting things back and forth—luggage, books, a chair. A mother and father were moving their daughter into her new room. Soon they would be doing the same for Luca Taviano. Incredible how things had turned out! Eight years ago, Luca was the anonymous recipient of the rabbi's bone marrow. Now, he was a part of his family.

Joseph couldn't resist a chuckle as he crossed the street. In the end, Sarah's husband had shared his marrow with a boy of Jewish ancestry, not a Catholic boy whose family might have been responsible for the death of her grandparents. Then again, that might not be altogether true. Giovanni Taviano may not have been as innocent as they first thought. Nina told him about the piece of paper found in the pocket of the dead Fascist leader. Bartolomeo Vitucci, the owner of the bar in Favola, believed Giovanni had passed the note to Lambertini after taking the baby and was responsible for what happened in the forest and at the Swiss safehouse, even though Giovanni vehemently denied it, swearing he never had anything to do with that Fascist pig. Nina didn't mention any of this to Luca, nor did Vitucci. Luca loved his grandfather, and they didn't want to tarnish his memory of him, especially since they couldn't be sure exactly what had happened in those chaotic days almost fifty years ago. Everything was always such a muddle.

A muddle like Luca himself. "You are in me," the boy had said to Joseph on the day they first met, while toasting to Luca's health amidst the fireworks and Italian folk music in Favola's main piazza. Such a simple, literal notion, yet how insightful. Luca was indeed a muddle. In him were Joseph's marrow cells, the Jewish genes of Luca's father, and the Catholic genes of his Milanese mother. He was a concrete, living example of the coming together of differences, of the pluralism that Joseph had always dreamt about and worked to achieve with Father Lazzaro and Imam Hussein.

Sarah had wanted to steer Luca to Judaism, to his paternal roots, but Joseph was firmly opposed. "Let him steer himself in whatever direction he chooses," he said. And it was hard to disagree, as Luca seemed to march to his own beat, always laughing and telling stories. To Joseph, Luca was a fortuitous experiment. How would such a muddle turn out?

They couldn't wait for him to arrive each summer. Sarah turned the downstairs guest room into Luca's permanent room. She decorated it with pictures of horses at first, then soccer players when he was no longer interested in horses. She took an Italian class and even started cooking Italian food. As Joseph watched the mother of the new student carrying her daughter's valise into the dormitory, he pictured Sarah doing the same next week on Luca's move-in date.

It was hot and humid outside, a typical August afternoon in New York City. Joseph wiped his brow with the handkerchief he carried in his pocket, then took a seat on the steps of Low Memorial Library in the center of campus. Students and professors crisscrossed the green in front of him, singly and in groups, chatting, debating. Some had settled down to have their lunch, others tossed around a Frisbee, a few napped. Directly opposite was Butler Library, floor upon floor of books. It always excited him, being on a college campus. Yet it also came with a tinge of guilt. Not everyone had the opportunity to spend time at such a place. Samuel was fortunate, Luca Taviano too.

Sarah's father had spent his college years running from the Nazis. On their second visit to Italy, Nina Vocelli took them to the detention camp at Fossoli, preserved now as a museum. They saw the spare wooden cabins fenced in by barbed wire where Sarah's father and grand-parents would have been imprisoned; the three-level, narrow bunkbeds and outhouses; the train station where prisoners were brought in and then shipped out to much worse places. The village outside the camp looked as quaint as any other small town in Northern Italy, and yet its citizens were, at one time, intimately involved with what went on inside the barbed wire. Many had profited by making bread and clothes for prisoners, arranging for their transportation. "Do you think they're ashamed of what happened here?" Samuel had asked his father. Joseph would have liked to answer yes, but how could he be sure that was the case?

The county archives were housed in a nearby town. In the Fossoli prisoner lists, they found the three Kovacs, Sarah's father and his parents. Another document recorded the date they were transported to Auschwitz: September 23, 1944. Nina asked one of the clerks if any inmates at the camp had babies. She must have been wondering how many other refugees had taken the same risks as Luca's grandparents.

Over the years, Joseph, Nina, Professor Benedetti, and Signore Vitucci had spent a great deal of time and effort trying to identify Luca's father and grandparents. Vitucci remembered hearing that the group in the forest was from Poland. He also remembered they were disguised as Catholic pilgrims traveling from Assisi.

From her research, Professor Benedetti knew of a particular church in Assisi, San Ignazio, that worked with the Italian Jewish organization DELASEM. She'd contacted the church several times, but no one was able to provide any information. Then recently, she'd received a call from a nun who had just returned to Assisi after spending several years in South America. The nun remembered a couple from Czechoslovakia, the wife pregnant at the time. In fact, the baby had been delivered while the couple was staying at the cloister attached to the church. A baby boy.

Professor Benedetti had called Joseph last week with the news. It was possible that Vitucci got the country of origin wrong, thereby compromising the initial search. She promised to retrace their steps with this new information, including contacting the Czech government, known to have kept excellent records during the war.

Joseph was excited by the promising turn of events. His first instinct was to tell Luca, but as he thought more about it, he wasn't sure how the boy would react. While Luca had always shown interest in Benedetti's Italian Remembrance Project, it never took on the personal dimension it did for Sarah and Joseph. The refugees killed in the forest, the detainees at Fossoli, the Italian Jews deported to concentration camps—Luca seemed at pains to keep them at a distance, as if he were afraid to acknowledge their connection to him. Yet at the same time, there was no such ambivalence in many of the stories Luca had written and shared with Joseph. He recalled one in particular, about a boy who discovers an old photograph of his father wearing the detested uniform of Mussolini's Blackshirts; from then on, the boy becomes obsessed with learning everything he can about his father's wartime experience and what else he might be hiding.

Let's see what Benedetti comes up with first, thought Joseph as he rose from the steps of Low Library and headed toward the subway.

5

Luca hadn't visited the cemetery in over a year. It wasn't intentional. He was just busy: filling out college applications; dating an older girl who wrote for the local paper; and playing football at school, now the captain of his team. And it wasn't the first time he was leaving the country. Only this time was different. This time, he would not be returning to Italy after the summer. This time, it would be for much longer, maybe even permanent, and he wanted to say goodbye.

"How about some company?" Nina asked as he prepared to leave the house.

He shook his head. He wanted to do this on his own.

"I understand," said Nina.

Luca wasn't so sure. Yet he was hesitant to share his feelings with Nina, and it made him sad. They'd been so close over the years. He told her practically everything, the first time he kissed a girl, the first time he got drunk. But his sense that this chapter of his life was over—and the possibility their intimacy might not continue in the next—would hurt Nina, as it hurt him. He had outgrown Favola and Rondello, the smallness and insularity of Italian village life. Ever since his first taste of New York, he'd wanted more and more of the big city's diversity and grit and anonymity, traveling by train to different boroughs, walking on the big, open boulevards with people from all parts of the world. So many things he wanted to see and do.

"Remember, don't drive too fast," she said, handing him the keys to the car.

"Who, me?" he asked innocently, trying to lighten the mood.

As he approached the outskirts of Favola, Luca spotted the old Roman wall up ahead. Two young boys were playing in the spot that he and his friends had carved out in the ground behind the higher end of the wall: a new garrison manning the Castle, scanning the perimeter for marauders, the Italian and Juventus flags still flying on either side. He hadn't spoken to Mario and Franco in years. They still lived in Favola and would likely live there the rest of their lives.

Nonna and Nonno were buried in a small grassy plot next to San Stefano's, two blocks from the main piazza. His grandparents had buried his father there after the accident and saved two spots for themselves. His mother was buried in a family plot in Milan.

He had no clear memories of his father or mother, only what he saw in pictures, which never made them seem real. But Nonna and Nonno, they were very real, even now, eight years since he'd last seen them. Nonno tall and gangly, with his strong grip that would hoist him up on his shoulders or toss him onto the seat of the tractor next to him, the smell of soil clinging to his clothes. Nonna with her round, ruddy cheeks, always talking and smiling, handing him something to eat, hugging and kissing him. That was a long time ago. Today, they would understand him even less than Nina.

He parked in front of the cemetery. Stepping out of the car, Luca took a deep breath as he regarded his hometown: the church, the main piazza, the orange-brown-colored houses with red-tiled roofs, the farmland and forested hills beyond, the smell of the soil and pine trees and sunflowers. They were outside him, but also inside, deep within the marrow of his bones—his home, the only home he'd ever known. Yet the people and things that bound him to his home were slipping away:

his grandparents, the farm he once lived on and where another family now lived, the Castle manned by new boys, Orlando, even Nina and Matteo.

Father Bertolini stood outside the church on the far edge of the cemetery, talking to a man Luca didn't recognize. When the priest saw Luca, he waved and began walking toward him.

"Luca Taviano, so nice to see you again. You've come to pay your respects, I assume. May I accompany you?"

Father Bertolini was a middle-aged man, tall and thin, with a smile at once kindly and intrusive.

"I've heard many wonderful things about you, your achievements in school and on the playing field. And soon you'll be attending university in New York. You've become very close to the rabbi and his family. I remember them well from their visit here a while back. A lovely family. I'm very happy for you, Luca, but I hope you'll always remember your roots back here in Favola, the church where you were baptized and took communion."

He nodded. How could he forget? Granted, he didn't care much for religion or the church, especially since he'd moved to Rondello with Nina, who cared even less as her involvement in the women's clinic in Monteveduto grew. Nonno, too, had had a rocky relationship with the church. There were long stretches, he remembered, when his grandfather refused to attend services with Nonna and Luca, and when Father Bertolini sternly inquired after him.

They wound their way through the uneven rows of the small cemetery and were now standing in front of the three graves. Three simple headstones with no epitaphs, just names and dates. Giovanni Taviano, Letizia Taviano, and in between, Paolo Taviano.

"Don't worry about your father and grandparents," Father Bertolini said, looking down at the graves. "I'll be watching over them while you are gone. And don't think they can't see you now just as I do, an intelligent young man of whom we're all very proud. Please give my best to Signora Vocelli and tell her she's always welcome here. Goodbye, my son," he said, placing his hand on Luca's shoulder. "Good luck on your journey."

"Father," he said as the priest started to walk away. "There's something I've been wondering about."

Father Bertolini turned around.

"The church has strict rules about burial, right?"

The priest looked at him uneasily.

"Yet you buried my grandfather despite—"

Father Bertolini put up his arm to stop him. "Your grandfather," the priest said, shaking his head, "struggled greatly throughout his life over the choices he made. He needed help and counsel, which I always tried to provide, and yet perhaps I failed him in the end. If he took his life, it was done out of extreme duress and emotional turmoil. He was a good, decent man. I would have never turned my back on him."

Luca thought of Primo Levi, a man who survived the horrors of Auschwitz only to kill himself later in life after the danger had long passed. His suicide created quite a stir when it was reported in the news four years ago. In extreme circumstances like war, Levi wrote, it wasn't always easy to judge right from wrong. Had Levi, like Nonno, felt guilty about some of the choices he made in his life?

In any case, Father Bertolini was wiser than Luca had imagined. Nonno *was* a good man; he would have never hurt anyone intentionally. Maybe not a hero like Bartolomeo Vitucci or the doctors at Santa Cristina who hid Jewish refugees on their wards during the war, but a good man nonetheless. Luca was grateful the priest understood that. This is where his grandfather belonged, next to his wife and their son.

"And my father?"

The priest looked at him quizzically.

"He was Jewish," Luca said.

The priest nodded. "True, but we didn't know that at the time of his death. Besides, Paolo was baptized and took communion here. He came to church every Sunday with your grandparents."

Yes, Luca thought as he said goodbye to the priest. *A good Catholic boy just like me.* But it wasn't true. Paolo Taviano had no idea who he really was, or where he came from, when he died. Nor did Luca until very recently. How could that not matter?

Before returning to his car, Luca took one last look at Favola and the surrounding countryside. He breathed in the smell of soil and pine trees in the air, a smell he would never forget. Then he recalled what Rabbi Joseph once told him, that Luca reminded him of a line in a famous Walt Whitman poem: "I am large, I contain multitudes."

Favola was certainly a part of him, but maybe only one part. Home, but maybe not the only home. Perhaps there would be others, across mountains and valleys, seas and oceans, in New York and elsewhere.

6

Rabbi Joseph was on the podium, reciting the Amidah, when the beadle barged through the doors at the back of the synagogue. Usually calm and reserved, Benny Levin motioned wildly with his arms. *What is so important,* Joseph wondered, *that he needs to make a scene in the middle of morning services?* Rabbi Joseph decided Benny would have to wait. He closed his eyes and continued the prayer.

A minute later, he felt someone tugging at his right arm. He turned to find Benny whispering loudly into his ear, "There was a terrorist attack in Manhattan. They flew planes right into the World Trade Center."

What? Had Benny lost his mind? Only a few years ago, terrorists targeted the same site, a bomb exploding in an underground garage. Had they returned to finish the job?

"You have to come right now, Rabbi," said Benny. "Sarah is waiting in your office."

So it really was true. Joseph's knees buckled. What about Samuel? He was at school in New York. All the way uptown at Columbia, but he spent plenty of time downtown too. Was there a chance he could be near the World Trade Center?

"It's okay, Rabbi," Benny reassured him. "Sarah spoke to Samuel. He's in his dorm room. He's fine."

Thank God. "And Luca?"

"They're trying to locate him now."

Joseph shook his head. "Is there anyone else we know who might be down there?"

"Marty Cohen's firm has an office in one of the towers. And Zev Saferstein likes to meet clients for breakfast at the restaurant on the top floor."

The rabbi turned to his congregation, and in as firm a voice as he could muster, relayed the shocking news. He said a quick prayer and told them to return home and make sure their families were safe.

He found Sarah sitting at the desk in his office, the phone pressed to her ear. When she saw him, she put up her finger so he wouldn't interrupt. A small TV had been placed at one end of the desk. Benny must have brought it in. The news was reporting on the attack. The south tower had been reduced to a pile of rubble. The north tower was in flames. There were images of people jumping from windows on the highest floors, reports of other planes headed for other targets. Joseph, glued to the TV, watched in horror.

"Oh, thank God," Sarah said, hanging up the phone. She had been speaking to Samuel, who told her that Luca was at a preschool near Columbia during the attack. "He volunteers there on Tuesdays, reading stories to the children. But he's back on campus now."

Joseph breathed a sigh of relief. Then it dawned on him: that's just what President Bush had been doing. The TV kept replaying the scene when the president's chief of staff interrupted Bush, reading to a group of second graders in Sarasota, the distressed look on his face when he received the news. "We should be with our children now," he said to Sarah.

"Not possible," said Benny. "They closed the tunnels and bridges. No one can enter or leave the city."

"As long as we know they're safe," said Sarah.

Joseph sat down sideways on his red lounge chair. The world had gone mad. In the past, when something terrible happened, he felt overwhelmed by sadness, a great wall of sadness pressing down upon him, making it difficult to breathe. On this day, however, he experienced more of a strange numbness, as if he couldn't quite believe or make sense of what he was witnessing. That dreamlike quality would persist over the coming hours and days: when the wind suddenly shifted and blew the smoke southwards into Brooklyn, with its bitter, acrid smell; when he heard that Marty Cohen's firm was on the twenty-sixth floor of the south tower and that there was little chance that anyone survived the attack; when he went to Cohen's house to comfort his wife and listened to Marty's last message saved on her cell phone; when he received the call from Imam Hussein, who expressed his disgust at the horrific act committed by men of his own faith, and then had to hang up abruptly because the police had arrived and were demanding to search his mosque.

7

Six weeks later, Luca was sitting outside Benedetti's office when the professor turned the corner, balancing a stack of books in her hands as she hurried down the hallway. "I'm sorry," she apologized, "my class ran late."

Professor Benedetti was always composed, even when out of breath. She dressed impeccably, her white hair perfectly coiffed and a brightly colored scarf looped around her neck.

"Come, Luca," she said, smiling as she opened the door to her cramped, dark office on the fifth floor of Hamilton Hall. She put her books on the desk and took a seat across from him. "We're midway through the first semester. How's everything going so far?"

"Okay," he said, turning out his hands.

"It was a rough start to the year," she acknowledged. "But things have settled down, and at least life on campus has returned to normal. I saw your adviser last week, and he had only positive things to say about you. I was also happy to learn the literary magazine accepted one of your short stories. Bravo."

Yes, it has been a rough start, he thought, arriving in New York the week before the attacks on the World Trade Center. It was difficult enough meeting new people without everyone being on edge, jumping at the slightest noise. Then came the professor's message that she had uncovered some new information about his father's family. She'd probably thought the news would make him happy, but strangely, it had the opposite effect, unsettling him even more.

For so long he had decided that the little he knew about his father would be all there was to know. Paolo was the man in the photographs, the stories his grandparents and other Favolans told about him. He was *not* one of the Jewish people Luca met at the synagogue in Genoa or one of the refugees from Eastern Europe that he'd read about in the professor's book. Since he couldn't square the two vastly different worlds, he would choose just one, the more familiar one.

Primo Levi's story had already begun to upset the delicate order in his mind. Levi had grown up not far from Favola, in an Italian household not very different from his own. Yet Levi was also Jewish, bullied at school for it, imprisoned at Fossoli, and eventually deported to Auschwitz. He proved that a person could straddle both worlds. Luca's father had been clueless about his Jewish roots. And while that was no longer the case with Luca, he always assumed that he himself would never know more than a few meager and unsatisfying details about that part of him.

What if Benedetti were able to provide him with a more complete story? The idea scared Luca. Yet he couldn't stop thinking about it, and over the following days and weeks, he would call and stop by the professor's office to see if she had learned anything new.

"You should be happy, Luca. It's an honor for a freshman to have a story published in the literary magazine."

That was the thing: he wasn't sure. Not about the story being accepted or school in general, but about his father. On the one hand, he wanted to know more; on the other, he worried that it would somehow change the way he thought of himself, the way he thought of his grandparents, Nina, Italy.

"Are you feeling homesick? It happens to many foreign students at the beginning of school. They're not as used to being away from home as Americans. But it doesn't last long."

"It's not that. I can't stop thinking about my father."

She leaned forward in her chair and looked at him intently. "Ah, now I understand," she said. "You've been waiting for news. Well then, I'm glad I called you in." The professor cleared the center of her desk to make room for the folder she withdrew from her bag. "Today, if you'll permit, we'll reverse the roles. Instead of you being the storyteller, today it will be my turn. *Va bene?*"

He nodded.

"There is a small church in Assisi named San Ignazio," she said, beginning her story with a smile. "During the war, the clergy at San Ignazio decided they couldn't stand idly by while innocent people were being imprisoned and killed by the Germans and their collaborators. They risked their lives to help those people."

"Like the church in Turin we visited with Rabbi Joseph and his family," said Luca.

"Santa Chiara. Yes, they were doing the same kind of work there."

An old priest had given them a tour of Santa Chiara two years before on the rabbi's second visit to Italy. Father Montaldo explained how they would dress Jewish refugees in the habits of monks and nuns, pretending they were part of the church and convent next door. Most of them didn't speak a word of Italian and so were instructed to keep silent when confronted by the Italian police or Gestapo. During raids, the refugees were hidden in the cellar of the cloister, a dark, dank chamber of underground vaults. The rabbi told the priest he wished Sarah's grandparents had found such a place to hide. Then they might have made it out of Italy alive.

A nun at San Ignazio named Sister Nunziata, Benedetti continued, remembered a young couple from Prague, Jacob and Sabina Havel.

The husband, a doctor, was a great help to the other refugees and staff. In fact, he made a special concoction for Sister Nunziata to relieve her migraines. The couple had left Prague soon after the Germans invaded the city in 1939, after one of the doctor's patients, a government official, had warned them that the Germans were getting ready to round up the Jews. They made their way to Yugoslavia, to a small town forty miles from Zagreb not yet affected by the war. There, they lived in peace for a year until the Ustaša, a Croatian paramilitary group, began hunting down anti-Fascists, Jews, and Gypsies.

Luca had read about the Ustaša and their atrocities. "But Italy controlled Yugoslavia at the time, right?"

"They did," answered Benedetti, "and it was a good thing for the Havels because the Italians routinely defied the Germans and Croatians. They provided safe passage for many refugees into Italy. The Havels eventually ended up in the Jewish ghetto in Rome. Despite Mussolini's strict racial laws, they were able to live freely there, until the fall of '43, when German tanks rolled into the city. Dr. Havel himself happened to be in the old synagogue when the Gestapo entered, demanding the famous ransom of fifty grams of gold in exchange for the community's safety. He realized immediately that it was a trick."

"Dr. Havel was a smart man," said Luca, though he was beginning to wonder why the professor was going on and on about this man. *What could he possibly have to do with me?*

"Dr. Havel," she continued, "was also shrewd in making connections. He arranged to meet the DELASEM official in Rome who was organizing a network of churches and monasteries throughout Italy that would provide food, shelter, fake documents, and medical care for native-born and foreign Jews. Dr. Havel offered his services in exchange for protection. He and his wife were assigned to San Ignazio in Assisi. The plan was to eventually smuggle them to Northern Italy with the help of local resistance groups and then over the border into neutral Switzerland."

"But you've spoken only of the two Havels," observed Luca. "If they didn't have a child, they can't be related to me, right?"

"Actually, when the Havels arrived in Assisi that November," the professor continued, "Sabina Havel was eight months pregnant."

"Oh," said Luca, his heart beginning to pound in his chest. So this wasn't just one of the many stories Benedetti had compiled for her research. It was *his* story.

"Sister Nunziata had never encountered a pregnant refugee before and wondered how the young mother would be able to travel in her state. As it happened, the baby came early, delivered in the nearby convent by Dr. Havel himself, which only made things worse in the sister's mind. Surely they wouldn't survive on the road with a crying infant. She begged the Havels to leave the baby with her. She would care for the child until the couple could return and retrieve him. But Sabina refused to part with her boy."

The professor was quiet for a moment, watching him.

"Her boy?" Luca said at last.

"Yes. His name was Daniel," said the professor. "Daniel Havel."

Luca sat back in his chair, trying to catch his breath.

"Are you okay?"

Suddenly he was back in Santa Chiara, the dank, cold cellar of the cloister where they hid refugees, refugees like Daniel Havel and his parents. It made him shiver. Everything had become real with the utterance of that name. His father had been someone else before he was Paolo Taviano. Someone else entirely.

"The Havels left Assisi with their baby," said the professor, "and it was Daniel's cries that your grandfather heard when the group of refugees crossed the woods near his farm. The Fascists could have heard the cries too. That might be how they discovered where the refugees were hiding."

Luca recalled how strangely Nonno had acted over the years, the outbursts and disappearances, the wound on his leg. He had to ask: "Are you sure my grandfather didn't have anything to do with it?"

No, Benedetti was not sure, but unlike Bartolomeo Vitucci, she wasn't convinced that Giovanni was to blame. "We'll never know exactly what happened that day in the forest," she said. "How the Fascists found the refugees before the partisans, what arrangements your grandfather made with Dr. Havel, how the piece of paper ended up in Lambertini's pocket. The only thing we know for sure is that if it hadn't been for Giovanni, Daniel Havel would have ended up dead too."

Luca studied her face, trying to decide if she was holding anything back or shading the truth for his benefit. His grandfather who wasn't his grandfather.

"Ever since I learned of Jacob and Sabina Havel," said the professor, "I've been in contact with the Czech government and several Jewish organizations to see what we could find out about the rest of their families. The bad news is that there are no more Havels from this family left. Every one of Jacob's relatives, eighteen in all, had been killed in German concentration camps. The same seemed to be true for Sabina's family, the Novaks."

So he had no relatives left on his father's side.

The professor shook her head, smiling. "I said, *seemed* to be true. Your grandmother, we now know, had a cousin who survived the war."

Luca leaned forward, the hair on his arms tingling.

"We are trying to locate her now," she said.

Luca left the professor's office in a daze. What did all this new information mean? Would he be able to integrate the story of the Havel and Novak families from Czechoslovakia—a country he'd never been to and knew almost nothing about—into his own story? He needed to talk it through with someone, someone who might understand.

"That's great news," said Samuel. Luca found him studying at his favorite cubicle in Low Library. "You may have a relative out there that you never knew existed. A blood relative. Aren't you excited?"

Luca wasn't sure.

"My father is right," Samuel continued. "There are so many different strands in you. You're a muddle or a multitude or whatever it is he likes to say. The Ashkenazi gene you share with him and your father, the Italian genes from your mother. And I bet if we studied your chromosomes, we'd find a lot more strands. Did you know that each of us carries about one hundred thousand pieces of DNA from viruses—viruses, not apes or chimpanzees? That's over five percent of our genome."

"Well, I don't feel much like a virus. Or a multitude. I'm a foreign student at Columbia who feels most at home at the Casa Italiana, speaking Italian with people from my country."

"I get it. It's the same for everyone, me included. We're most comfortable sticking with the tribe we're born into. But you have a chance to be more. The genes inside us are what make us who we are. How can you ignore them?"

I can't, Luca realized.

"Besides, you've always been curious, eager to explore new areas of the city, meet new people. Don't you want to know more about your real grandparents from Czechoslovakia and this cousin of your grandmother?"

Samuel was right. He could no longer resist his natural curiosity. Nonno kept getting in the way all these years, but now he had to push him aside. It was wrong of Nonno not to tell his father, not to tell Luca. His father died without ever knowing his history. Luca, too, would have never known had he not gotten sick and needed a bone marrow transplant. It was time to bring the Ashkenazi genes to the surface, as Samuel said, to find the other home that had always been part of him, that had in fact saved his life.

8

Nina arrived at the women's clinic in Monteveduto early on Thursday morning, just as the sun rose. She hadn't slept well the night before. Actually, she hadn't slept well since Luca left for New York four months ago. It was one thing after another: protests outside the clinic in September; a nursing strike at Santa Cristina in October; and, most recently, Luca's feverish calls and emails at all hours of the day and night. After Professor Benedetti had informed him that he had a distant cousin in Czechoslovakia, Luca could think of nothing else. He began studying Czech history and reading Czech literature. He was immediately drawn to Kafka, Schulz, and Kundera. "Do you think my stories have a Kafkaesque quality?" he asked Nina on the phone one night. Soon after, he told her he wanted to take up Czech and enroll in a study-abroad program in Prague. "It would give me a chance to get to know Peter—my grandmother's cousin's son," he said. "He doesn't live far from the city."

Nina was glad she had moved in with Matteo during this stressful period. For so long, she had resisted, believing she would be better off alone. But Luca had left a big hole in her life. It was nice to have someone next to her in bed, someone to console her after she hung up the phone with Luca. "He doesn't want to come home for Christmas," she complained to Matteo one night in early December.

"That's not true," said Crespi. "He's just excited to see Peter Novak."

"But not me?"

"Nina, the boy never knew his parents. He never had a real family."

"What is that supposed to mean?"

"Just that it's understandable," he said, pulling her closer to him. "This cousin in the Czech Republic, however distant, is the only link he has to his parents besides that crazy uncle in Milan."

Understandable, she thought, *but that doesn't make it any easier.*

"It will be okay," Matteo reassured her, pushing the hair away from her face, away from her birthmark. "You'll see."

To prevent herself from constantly thinking about Luca, she made sure she was busy, filling almost every second of her already full schedule. She worked four days at Santa Cristina instead of the usual three. She volunteered for Professor Benedetti's Italian Remembrance Project—last week, she'd spoken at two high schools in Turin and handed out flyers at a concert in Genoa. And she spent at least two mornings every week at the women's clinic.

The clinic was located on the first floor of a nondescript building with no signs or displays, just outside the center of Monteveduto, a sleepy town twenty kilometers from Rondello. As Nina fiddled with the lock on the front door, she spotted the baker standing outside his shop with arms folded across his chest, glaring at her. The baker was one of many townspeople who fiercely objected to what she—and the rest of the clinic staff—was doing there.

Nina turned on the lights and computers in the office. Soon, the staff would start trickling in, baker and candlestick maker notwithstanding. Nina was proud of the work they did. Last year alone, they saw over one thousand patients. The trial supported by the AIED, the major family planning association in Italy, was clearly a success. Most of their northern centers were in the three big cities, Milan, Turin, and Genoa, where the need was greatest. But what about women in the countryside who were less educated and informed or had no money to pay for such services?

A little over four years ago, a seventeen-year-old girl was admitted to Santa Cristina, her blood pressure barely detectable. A week before, she had inserted a knitting needle into her vagina to terminate her pregnancy and wound up in septic shock. Fortunately, they were able to administer the right antibiotic before it was too late. During the girl's recovery, Nina visited her often, to comfort her and also to understand what had happened. The girl explained that she was afraid to tell her parents, even her boyfriend, and, as a last resort, sought advice from a local prostitute. The advice nearly killed her. Nina saw herself in that girl, in her terror, in her desperation. *Why did it have to come to that?*

"It doesn't," said Matteo when she spoke the question aloud. He had found her under the tall oak tree outside the hospital, smoking a cigarette. "Remember the nurse in Naples you told me about," he asked, "the one who once helped you, changed your life? Maybe it's your turn now. To do something important for the women around here."

He was right. This was no time for wallowing, yet that's exactly what she had been doing. Was it just too personal for her, the ugly past coming back to haunt her? Or the taboo nature of women's rights in a deeply Catholic and conservative country, her mother and the baker giving her the evil eye? But she was no longer the young girl crying on the shoulder of the nurse in Naples. She'd grown stronger, more vocal, able to acknowledge her *sbagli* and determined to do the right thing in spite of them, as she once had for Luca at Santa Cristina and was doing now in her work for Professor Benedetti.

"I can help," offered Matteo. "I have some money saved up. There are also a few doctors I know who might be willing to lend a hand."

Was he saying that to make her feel better? No, he meant it. That was the thing about Matteo Crespi—he always surprised you when you least expected it.

So Nina traveled to Rome and met with Maria Louisa de Marchi of the AIED. She told her about herself and the young girl she'd taken care of at Santa Cristina and of her desire to open a clinic in a rural area. De Marchi agreed to support her, though she warned Nina that it wouldn't be easy, that there would be backlash from the local government and church. The agency would donate a small sum for the trial project, and Nina would have to find funding for the rest.

As she watered the plants in the waiting room, the head nurse at the clinic walked through the front door. "You're here early again."

"It makes me happy," said Nina. Besides, what else could she do at five in the morning when she couldn't get back to sleep?

"You may not be happy for long. There's another protest scheduled for this afternoon. That lousy priest again from the church around the corner."

Nina shook her head. The first people she went to for funding were contacts of Benedetti from the Remembrance Project, members of the clergy who went against the grain in rescuing Jewish refugees during the war. Surely, they would recognize the suffering of young women like the girl who'd almost died at Santa Cristina. Yet not only did they not recognize it, but they actively sought to prevent *her* from helping. It didn't make sense. "A serious muddle," as the rabbi liked to say about the church in Italy.

"Then we better make sure they have enough energy to hold up their signs. I'll buy some cookies from the baker down the block," she said with a smile. "If he'll sell them to me."

9

Luca and Nina's room was on the top floor of the Tepisplatz Hotel in the Old Town. It had a dormer window with a thin shade that allowed light from the full moon to stream in. The mattress was hard on his back, and every so often, a swishing sound could be heard behind the walls, the running of a sink or a toilet flushing. But even if Luca were in his own bed, he would have had trouble sleeping. In a few hours, he would meet Peter Novak. Peter planned to drive in from his hometown of Kladno and take Luca and Nina to the Pinkas Synagogue, where they would see the names of his grandparents engraved on the walls of the Holocaust memorial. Afterward, he would show them around Prague and then drive back to Kladno with them for the night.

"Is it time to wake up?" asked Nina groggily, lifting her cheek from the pillow on the bed next to his.

Luca shook his head. He told Nina he was jetlagged and wanted to take a walk. "Go back to sleep," he said. "I'll come get you before breakfast."

Outside, it was pitch dark up to the height of the smaller three- and four-story buildings. The upper half of the world, lit by the moon, was a mottled, bluish gray. The narrow, winding cobblestone streets were deserted. Luca zippered his coat to block the cold, damp winter air from seeping in. He passed medieval buildings and baroque churches, the famous astronomical clock in the main square. On the Charles Bridge, he crossed the Vltava River as it wound its way through the city. High above, in the hills, stood the famous Hradcany Castle. Like Kafka's castle, it was enchanting and also unsettling.

It had been almost two months since Professor Benedetti had told him about his grandmother's cousin, Malvina Novak. Like the rest of the Prague Jews, her name appeared on one of the synagogue lists that fell into the hands of the Germans. After the roundup in August 1941, she was deported to Theresienstadt, then a year later to Auschwitz. Her skills as a seamstress had saved her from the fate of the rest of the family, sewing buttons on the coats of German officers and repairing their uniforms. Primo Levi had been similarly fortunate because of his chemistry background; he worked in a rubber factory rather than having to do hard labor outside in the freezing cold; of the 650 people on Levi's transport from Fossoli, he was one of only 20 to survive Auschwitz.

Malvina Novak had returned to Czechoslovakia after the Russians liberated her camp in '45. Unfortunately, she'd passed away a few years ago. But her son, Peter Novak, still lived in his mother's house in Kladno. "He's your cousin too," the professor had said. "To be precise, your second cousin once removed."

A garbage truck rumbled up the block ahead of him. Two men jumped down from the back and started hauling trash into the compactor. There was a grinding noise as the metallic boom descended on the garbage underneath. Luca stepped up his pace. A small coffee shop was just opening. He could use an espresso but decided not to stop, taking the high road up the hill toward the castle. In the four months he had been at Columbia, he was determined to walk every square inch of New York City. He walked in the morning, the afternoon, the night, to get away from school and sort things out in his mind. Just like his grandfather used to do in Favola. "Where's Nonno off to now?" he'd constantly asked his grandmother. Nonno had been restless too, with the secrets he was carrying.

Trudging up the steep incline to upper Prague, passing the immense Gothic church with its ribbed, pointed spires, Luca thought he was done worrying about those secrets, after the jolt he had received on the lake with Samuel and then the anger he felt toward Nonno, then Nonna, then Nina. He had made peace with all of them because the secrets had no connection to the life he was living. It was a past that was essentially unrecoverable and dead.

As he rounded the corner, the street opened to a hillside where the grass was still green and the maple and linden trees still had most of their leaves. Turning back, he could see lower Prague in the morning mist, the red-tiled roofs and green copper domes of churches, as the sun began to rise above the horizon. It was the view captured in the postcards sold in the hotel lobby.

Then the professor had breathed new life into that buried past. There was a living relative out there, a real person, a link to his father beyond football and faded photographs. A link to others before and after him, parts of whom were inside of him, woven into the fabric of his body, the DNA of his genes. That was when it dawned on him—he was on one of his long walks, passing the Guggenheim Museum, with its spiral tower that seemed to echo the helical structure of the DNA molecule—that there was something missing in his life. Something he had unconsciously been yearning for on the football field, the reason he never felt quite right in Favola and Rondello, why he traveled to the States and enrolled in an American college, across mountains and valleys, oceans and seas. A missing piece to the puzzle that if found, would make everything fall into place.

Luca reached for that missing piece, hardly able to think of anything else in the last few weeks of his first semester at Columbia. He almost failed his world history final and handed in an English essay riddled with grammatical mistakes. It didn't matter. All he cared about was getting to Prague and meeting Peter Novak at the start of winter break. Nina begged him to come to Italy first so they could spend

Christmas with Carla's family as they did every year. They flew to Prague together, the day after Christmas.

The birds were now awake and singing in the trees. Luca checked his watch—it was almost 7:00 a.m. He should return to the hotel. The rising sun had dried the morning frost, and the sky was now a bright blue. Even Kafka's castle looked harmless in the distance. The day was full of promise.

10

Nina couldn't go back to sleep after Luca left. She, too, was restless about what the day would bring. After showering and dressing, she sat in the chair beneath the dormer window with an unlit cigarette in her mouth. This time, she was quitting for good.

Luca's knapsack lay on the floor next to the bed. She'd always resisted the urge to go through his belongings. Yet with nothing to do but wait and worry and suck on her cigarette, she reached for the knapsack and examined its contents: chewing gum, Walkman, map of Prague, a book on the history of Jews in Czechoslovakia, the Columbia Magazine. Attached to the periodical by a paper clip was a handwritten note from Samuel: *Check out the article on Weinstein, the guy I'm doing research for. I thought you'd find his new project interesting. Good luck in Prague and call if anything crazy happens.*

The Columbia scientist was studying a process known as stem cell homing: how cells injected into the blood find their way home—that is, to the place in the body where they belong. Nina remembered wondering about that very journey nine years ago when Dr. Tosti entered Luca's hospital room with an IV bag filled with the rabbi's bone marrow. Professor Weinstein had recently discovered a specific protein that sat on the outer membrane of stem cells and acted like a key. The protein fit into a groove or lock located on blood vessel cells outside the bone marrow. Stem cells circulated in the blood until the key recognized and opened the lock, which then opened a channel in the vessel wall through which stem cells could squeeze and gain entry into the marrow, their new home.

The workings of the human body were intricate and lovely. At the moment, though, Nina couldn't help feeling uneasy as she thought about the homing process. It mirrored what was happening right now on the streets of Prague: Luca's quest to find a home, a place where *he* belonged. She quickly put everything back into the knapsack and zipped it shut.

Peter Novak appeared at the hotel after 8:00 a.m. He apologized for being late; there was a lot of traffic entering the city. They were waiting for him in the breakfast area of the hotel, a nook at the rear of the main floor that looked out onto a small trellised garden.

"No problem," said Luca. "We're just happy to see you." He held out his arms and moved forward to embrace his cousin, but Peter only offered his hand. Luca shook it vigorously.

Peter was nothing like Nina had imagined, though exactly what she'd imagined, she couldn't say. He was tall and thin and wore black jeans and a sweatshirt with an Italian football jersey over it. His brown hair was messy and matted, and when he smiled, she could see that most of his teeth were bad. He didn't take his eyes off her birthmark except when he turned around to make sure they saw the name on the back of his jersey.

"Baggio," said Luca. "He's one of my favorite players too!"

Nina wondered what Luca thought of his cousin. They couldn't be more different, and not just in age, Peter being older, around the same age she was. She had watched Luca getting ready this morning, standing in front of the bathroom mirror, applying gel to his hair, adjusting the collar of his shirt, making sure everything was just right. She imagined all the girls at Columbia swooning over the handsome redhead from Italy.

Luca had a million questions for Peter and couldn't resist firing them off as his cousin sat down and took one brioche after another from the basket on the table. Peter answered in broken English while he munched: He worked in construction. He was married once but was now separated. No children. And no, he'd never read Kafka. He wasn't much of a reader actually; he preferred watching football. There was a pub in Kladno where he and his friends went to watch the games. Yes, he was Jewish but hadn't been to a synagogue in years. There weren't too many Jews around these parts, and he didn't like to advertise. And yes, he'd been to the Holocaust memorial at the Pinkas, but it was a long time ago and he hardly remembered it.

Luca nodded politely and asked if Peter had any questions for him.

"No," answered Peter, looking out the window at one of the trellis posts that had come loose. "Right now, I'm not working, so I have lots of time and am glad to have some company. Especially a cousin from Italy. Besides football, I love pizza. There's a place near my house I could take you to that makes great square pizza."

An uncomfortable silence followed while they drank coffee and picked at the bread basket. "Maybe we should get going," suggested Nina.

It was a short walk to the Pinkas Synagogue, past the main square. Just inside the gate was the old Jewish cemetery. It was as cluttered and chaotic as described in their guidebook, tombstones lying on top of each other and pointing in different directions. Luca wanted to find Rabbi Loew's grave. Peter had no idea whom he was talking about. "Legend has it that he created the golem out of clay," explained Luca.

"Oh," said Peter.

The synagogue was small and narrow, but the vaulted ceilings and white walls made it appear more spacious. Peter asked one of the attendants where the memorial was. The man led them to an adjacent room. A black marble panel covered each wall. It was filled with names engraved in white, one after another, with practically no spacing in between. It seemed to go on forever.

"The deceased are listed by community, not alphabetically," said the attendant. "Over seventy-seven thousand names in all. Over seventy-seven thousand people who died in a span of four years. Almost the entire Czech Jewish population. Are you looking for someone in particular?"

"Jacob and Sabina Havel," said Luca. "My grandfather and grandmother. From Prague."

The attendant led them to another wall and scanned the names until he found what he was looking for. "Here we are," he said, pointing to the lower right corner of the panel in front of them. "Jacob and Sabina Havel."

They stared at the names engraved in stone, and all the names around them, before them, in front of them. It was dizzying. Nina had read about what happened in Czechoslovakia during the war before coming to Prague, but standing in front of the massive list of the dead was difficult: men, women, and children. Nina watched Luca step up and touch the names of his grandparents, his real ones. She wondered what they called Nonno and Nonna in Czech. Luca's hand shook as it passed over the engraving.

Terrible things had happened in Italy, too, she thought—to Sarah Neiman's grandparents and so many others. But nothing like this. Sudden roundups took place in all the major Italian cities, but most of the Jews were able to evade the transports. They were aided by their Christian neighbors, policemen, and priests, as Professor Benedetti chronicled in her book. Nina couldn't help but feel at least some pride in the way many of her countrymen had acted.

"The Novaks from Kladno," said Peter, pointing to a panel on the adjacent wall. "My mother's brother and parents. From everything I heard, they weren't religious at all. I don't get it. They could have easily passed for Christians and avoided this mess."

Luca moved from one panel to another, a dazed look on his face.

"You might want to look at the drawings," the attendant suggested to Luca. He was a spindly man with glasses that rested on the tip of his nose, clearly sensitive to the emotional toll the memorial took on many viewers. They followed him into the next room.

"The drawings were made by children," he said. "Prisoners at Theresienstadt."

Luca was riveted by the colorful crayon drawings: a park with a swing set; a girl being pushed high in the air, almost touching the sun; a black birdlike creature with an extended, menacing wing.

Luca drew pictures, too, when he found himself in a similar predicament, only he used words instead of crayons, and strung them together in a hospital ward instead of a concentration camp.

The synagogue suddenly felt cold.

"That's enough for one day," Nina finally said, taking Luca's arm. "We can always come back."

They walked out together in silence.

She tried to divert his attention. A feral cat stood guard at the entrance, purring at them. Up ahead, street clowns performed in front of the police station. Luca wasn't interested. Nina asked Peter if he could start his tour of the city, and off they went: Saint Vitus Cathedral, Hradcany Castle, Charles Bridge, the municipal building. Thankfully, they kept moving at a good pace from one site to the next, except for a brief stop at a small church off the main square, where they listened to a youth group performing music from Bach and Handel. At the end of the day, Peter dropped them off at the hotel. He needed to fill his gas tank and would pick them up in half an hour.

"How are you doing?" Nina asked when they got back to the room. "That was a lot to digest in one day."

Luca didn't answer. He'd barely said a word since their visit to the Pinkas Synagogue. He stood by the dormer window, gazing out at the sky. Then he turned around, and the words came pouring out in a torrent.

"Did you taste the dumplings we had at lunch? Like balls of lead. Disgusting. And the language, it sounds like they're gargling with those dumplings. What was he even saying all day long, Peter, rattling on about God knows what?"

"Well—"

"I don't mean to sound like a jerk," he said, not giving her a chance to answer. "Believe me, I tried; I read everything I could find about Czechoslovakia, the culture and history. And Prague is a beautiful city, the river, bridges, medieval buildings. Really beautiful. But Jacob and Sabina Havel," he said, the muscles in his face tightening. "I have no idea who they were. I don't know what they wanted in life. There isn't even a picture of them to see what they looked like. And Peter Novak—why would I want anything to do with him? We have nothing in common."

Because he's your cousin, Nina thought, *the only blood relative left in the world on your father's side.*

"Not that I don't feel terrible for what happened to them," Luca continued. "It makes me sick. But from a distance, Nina, from a distance. Everything is foreign here. It's not my city. These are not my people. I don't feel them inside me. Can you understand?"

He began to cry.

"I thought I was going to find something in Prague, some answers, the missing piece that would make me whole. What was I thinking?"

"It's okay," she said, rubbing his shoulder.

He pushed her hand away. "No, it's not."

"I know how disappointing this must be for you, but it will be okay—"

"No, it won't. It's never going to be okay. Why the hell did I even come here?" He was shouting now. "It was you, always pushing me in this direction, feeding me all this bullshit about where I came from, my roots."

"Don't say that."

"Why? You deny it?"

Nina could only stutter in her defense.

"All I wanted was to block it out. But you," he said, pointing at her with an accusing finger. "You. You kept giving me books by concentration camp survivors and bringing me to those damn churches and deportation camps."

As she reached forward to calm him, Luca grabbed her arm. "You know best, right? Because you're my mother," he said, tightening his grip, harder and harder. "That's what you want me to call you, right? Mama. But you're not!"

"Stop it," she cried. "You're hurting me."

"You don't understand," he said, finally letting go of her arm. "You never will."

Luca's words hurt Nina more than his hand, and all she wanted was to run off and lock herself in the bathroom. But she couldn't bear seeing him like this. "It's not true," she said. "I do know how you feel. Your parents died when you were a baby, and you never had a chance to experience their love. My parents, on the other hand—they didn't even want me. They made me feel worthless. To them, I was a nobody."

"So now this is all about you?"

"No," she said. "It's all about *you*. Since the day I met you, you're the only thing that's mattered to me. Can't you see that? *Can't you see that?*"

He closed his eyes and shook his clenched fists in the air, then collapsed onto the chair beneath the dormer window. Drops of blood trickled from the corner of his mouth.

Nina knelt down beside him and wiped away the blood. "You must have bitten your lip. Here, let me have a look."

"It's nothing," he said, his anger subsiding. He saw that her arm was red and bruised from where he grabbed her. "I'm sorry, Nina."

"It's okay," she said. "We're all searching for who we are and where we belong in this *pazzo* world, and no matter what we find, it never seems enough. But there's one thing I'm certain about: I will always be here for you."

She took Luca's hand and placed it on the right side of her face, over her birthmark. "You used to like the way it felt, the rush of blood under the skin. Can you feel it now?"

"Yes," he answered, feeling her blood pulse against his hand, feeling its warmth.

"That's me," she said to him. "Inside you."

May 22, 2017
Memorial Sloan Kettering Cancer Center
New York, New York

Almost sixteen years have passed since our trip to Prague when an orderly on the transplant ward directs me down the hall to room 1407. I open the door a notch, and there is Luca, sitting by the bed of a young girl, uttering words I've heard before:

Orlando comes from a faraway land and crosses mountains and valleys, seas and oceans.

Only now Luca is a grown man, not a sick child. It's the young girl in bed who is sick and in need of help. He is the doctor caring for her. The girl is asleep. She must have nodded off at some point in the story, but still he continues in the same spirited manner. I look out the window above his head, almost expecting to find the tall oak tree, but there is only the darkening sky and exhalations of smoke from the smokestack across the East River. We are fourteen floors above ground and far from Italy.

For a second, I feel faint and have to lean against the door—I've been here before, not exactly in this spot but in a similar one, twenty-five years ago, standing by the medicine cart late at night in the pediatric ward at Santa Cristina, watching a young boy, my patient at the time, tell his story to the oak tree outside his window.

I am sixty-four years old now, almost Letizia's age when we first met. Back then, it was only my eyes that sagged; now every part of my body is sagging. It doesn't bother me as much anymore; there are so many more important things to worry about. I remain committed to helping Professor Benedetti promote her Remembrance Project. Last month I attended the Prayer for Peace in Assisi with Rabbi Neiman, Father Lazzaro, and Imam Hussein. Not long ago the Italian legislature passed our initiative allowing women to purchase the morning-after pill without a doctor's prescription.

But satisfied and content as I am with my life, I worry about Luca. On the outside, he seems to have everything: looks, health, respect, means.

"We all love Dr. Taviano," the head nurse on the transplant ward at Sloan Kettering told me during a visit six years ago. "He's not just a great doctor, but you can tell how much he cares about the children, their families, us nurses, even the orderlies. I'm sure you know how some doctors can be real jerks, and believe me, we have our share. He's different."

The nurse didn't have to tell me that. I could see from the way they fawned over Luca, and over me because I am his family from Italy.

"His girlfriend is a lucky woman," the nurse said.

Girlfriend?

The nurse explained that whenever anyone showed interest or wanted to fix up Luca with a friend, he always brought up the girlfriend in Italy.

Who could she possibly be talking about? I wondered.

"Some of us think it's an excuse and that maybe he's, you know, not interested in girls. But I don't believe that."

I had to laugh, considering the number of girlfriends he's had over the years, in Italy and New York. No, Luca wasn't gay. He was just young and not ready to settle down yet.

"Actually, it's not only that," continued the nurse. "He's so committed to his patients, coming in at all hours of the day and night, spending time with them, reading, talking, comforting them. I get the feeling he doesn't have much of a life outside the hospital. That's not always a good thing."

I asked Luca about this girlfriend in Italy later that day. He just laughed and told me yes, it was an excuse. "Why?" I asked him.

"Because I don't want people at work knowing my personal life, Nina—as you yourself once advised, remember, considering the mess it caused you at Santa Cristina."

"Fine, but what about your personal life. *Is* there anyone special?"

"Not yet," he answered, then switched to a different topic.

Afterward, I talked to the rabbi and Sarah. They, too, had their concerns. It wasn't that he didn't date or express interest in women, just that the interest never seemed to last.

A chill ran down my spine as I wondered whether the person who had started out the happiest of all might not turn out that way in the end. Was Luca afraid of commitment? After all, a string of important people hadn't lasted very long in his life. Maybe he feared that he wouldn't last very long either, knowing full well the risk of long-term complications in bone marrow transplant survivors. Maybe he wasn't as strong and confident as he appeared. I thought of our trip to Prague where he'd met Peter Novak, how upset he was that he felt nothing inside. It was the same a month later when he reached out to his mother's arrogant brother in Milan; his uncle had just won a seat in parliament and, as usual, had no time for him. Luca would remain unconnected to the only people in the world that he was supposedly most connected to.

Rabbi Joseph didn't see things as bleakly. Luca was a mixture of different races and cultures—that's why he had no problems getting along in New York and why he could empathize with so many different patients at the hospital. He was a living, breathing example of the pluralism that we should all aspire to. But maybe the muddling had a downside. Sarah had once objected to raising Samuel in a mixed community rather than the Orthodox one she'd grown up in. If everyone's perspective is equally right, she warned her husband, then there is no absolute right, and everything goes. It could leave you without bearings, adrift and lost.

I hardly slept the night after my conversation about Luca with the head nurse on the transplant ward. I was staying in Luca's room at the rabbi's house in Bay Ridge at the time, surrounded by posters of Luca's favorite football stars on the walls. I kept returning to that article in the Columbia Magazine on stem cell homing, how complicated and precarious the process was, the many different points at which it could go awry. What if a stem cell never reached home or ended up at the wrong home or recognized too many homes as home?

I went to the hospital first thing the next morning and begged Luca to come back with me to Italy, to return home. He could work with Dr. Tosti at the cancer institute in Genoa, perhaps set up his own children's wing. I'd help him find a nice apartment in the old city, with a view of the port. He used to love watching the boats passing in and out of the harbor.

"You don't have to worry about me, Nina," he said with a reassuring smile. "I'm fine here."

"But I don't want you to be alone."

He laughed. "I'm not alone. I'll always have you, right? And Rabbi Joseph and Sarah. Samuel. My friends at the hospital."

"That's not enough."

"I also have my patients. You know how much I love the kids. Their innocence inspires me. They're the ones worth fighting for. I remember you once thought that too."

"I did, it's true, but you can't feel like that about all your patients or you won't last long in this field. Believe me, I've seen the effects of burnout. And regardless, you still need someone to share your life with. Get married, have kids of your own. Don't you want that?"

"Don't forget the picket fence and dog," he quipped. "And look who's talking, Ms. Conventionality."

"Matteo and I have had our issues, but we love each other in our own way."

"I'll find someone eventually, you'll see. And then you can plan the wedding."

Six years have passed since then, and I haven't been asked to plan anything. Recently, though, Luca started dating the transplant nurse, the one who asked about the imaginary girlfriend in Italy and started me down the path of worry. She seems sweet and is clearly smitten with him. Luca said he might bring her to Rondello for Christmas this year.

I remain standing in the doorway of room 1407. Luca has just finished his story, and I'm about to call to him when his young patient begins to stir in bed. "So what happens next?" asks the girl, opening her eyes.

"I thought you were asleep."

"No," she says. "I was listening the whole time."

"I'm glad. Then you know that Orlando was listening too. He never stops listening."

"Can you tell me about him again?"

"Of course," he says, covering her with the blanket.

Luca sits back and begins from the beginning, his voice steady and sure.

He comes from a faraway land and crosses mountains and valleys, seas and oceans.

ACKNOWLEDGMENTS

While researching how Jews fared in Italy during World War II, I read the remarkable works of Primo Levi and two superb histories: Alexander Stille's *Benevolence and Betrayal* and Susan Zuccotti's *The Italians and the Holocaust*. I am grateful for their intelligence and insight.

My first novel has been a long time in coming and many friends have helped and encouraged me along the way: Beth Rothenberg, David Rothenberg, Steven Fisch, Allison Schneirov, Matthew Kneale, Shannon Russell, Jillian Kearney, Quang Bao, Ellen Tien, Sandy Gruenwald, Charles Messina, Kenny Brachfeld, Howie Lipson, Neal Merker, Tom Aiello, Donna Maddalena, Jeanne Morris, Giulia Melucci, Eric Hofmann, Howard Altmann, Monica Cohen, Rhonda Pomerantz, Alan Rosenbach, Mert Erogul, Nellie Hermann, Lionel Derriey. *Mille grazie!*

I especially want to thank those who have read and reread my manuscript too many times to count: Matthew, Donna, Jeanne, Sandy, and Ellen.

To my agent, Jennifer Lyons, thank you for sticking with me and being so supportive during the drought years.

To my editors Jodi Warshaw and David Downing and everyone else at Lake Union, thank you for loving this book as much as I do and helping me make it better.

ABOUT THE AUTHOR

Photo © 2019 Donna Maddalena

David Biro graduated from the University of Pennsylvania, Columbia Medical School, and the University of Oxford. He teaches at SUNY Downstate Medical Center and practices dermatology in Bay Ridge, Brooklyn. He is the author of *One Hundred Days: My Unexpected Journey from Doctor to Patient* and *The Language of Pain: Finding Words, Compassion, and Relief.* He has also been published in the *New York Times*, *Slate*, the *Philadelphia Inquirer*, and various medical journals. David lives in New York City with his wife and twin boys. For more information, visit www.davidbiro.com.